A WITCH'S MAGIC

Also by N. E. Conneely

A Witch's Path Series
Witch for Hire (Book 1)
A Witch's Path (Book 2)
A Witch's Trial (Book 3)
A Witch's Concern (Book 4)
A Witch's Rite (Book 5)
A Witch's Demons (Book 6)
A Witch's Magic (Book 7)

Witch's Path World
Handyman for Hire
Oceanside
Fireball
The Golden Egg

Michelle's Case Files

The Earth Born Cycle
Earth Born (Book 1)
Fire Forged (Book 2)
Spirit Formed (Book 3)

Fey Hearted
Fey at Heart (prequel)
Fey Hearted

N. E. CONNEELY

A WITCH'S PATH BOOK SEVEN

A WITCH'S MAGIC

Copyright © 2019 N. E. Conneely

All rights reserved.
No part of this publication may be reproduced or transmitted in any form or by any means, electronic or mechanical, including photocopying, recording, or any information-storage-and-retrieval system, without permission in writing from the publisher or author. Requests for permission to copy part of this work for use in an educational environment may be directed to the author.

This book is a work of fiction. References to historical events, real people, or real locales are made fictitiously. Other names, characters, places, and incidents are the product of the author's imagination, and any resemblance to actual events, locales, or persons, living or dead, is entirely coincidental.

ISBN: 978-1-393-07796-1

To friends old and new, thank you for being here with me. I hope you enjoy this book and are as excited as I am to fall into new adventures.

CHAPTER ONE

I crouched down and held out my hand, palm down, fingers curled to look as harmless as possible, and in the sweetest, and highest pitched voice I could manage, I said, "Here, puppy. Who's a good dog? Who wants to come over here?"

The dog perked its ears, cocked his head to the side, and then his eyes slid from the gently extended hand to the one tucked by my side. The one that happened to be holding a slip leash.

"Yes, you're a good puppy," I repeated.

The dog took one careful step closer and then another. He reached my hand, and his nose just barely brushed against my fingers.

I started to reach forward with the open loop of the leash. The dog whirled around, tail thumping heavily into my legs. I swayed to the side as he scrambled away. The tail lashed again, this time with a phantom tail extended past it, whacking into my legs and sending me toppling to the ground. My shoulder ached from the impact with the concrete. "Narzel take it."

If he wanted to play that way, well, I had magic too.

With a twist my wrist, I summoned my wand and pointed at the dog. "*Sowil*." A small containment field snapped into place around the dog. He wasn't going anywhere until I let him out.

I picked myself up off the floor, wincing as I rolled my shoulder. That was going to leave a bruise. I readjusted my grip on the leash as I caught up with the dog. I shoved my hand through the spell, slipped the leash over his head, and sucked the power back out of the containment spell. The dog looked up at me, tail tucked between his legs.

Glancing around and not seeing any of the other escaped creatures that had turned Happy Paws Rescue into a less than happy place today, I dismissed my wand and held my hand down for the dog to sniff. His nostrils flared, and his tail wagged ever so slightly. "Yes, you're a good boy. You just had some magic get to you, yes you did."

His ears came up, and his tail wagged a little more.

"Who's a good boy?" I continued the high-pitched babble as I led the dog outside to where Cherokee County Animal Control had cages and trucks waiting. "This nice lady is going to take you somewhere safe and remove the magic from you. You were never meant to be magical."

I handed him off to Ryeleigh, a fey animal control officer with ash-green skin, pointed ears, and sage green hair in a ponytail. She got the dog settled in one of their specially crafted cages that could hold this dog and whatever magic had attached itself to him.

I turned back to Happy Paws, the site of my first case back at work, which was shaping up to be a great dinner story and a unique location. The house, a cheerful bungalow, was backed by an attached building that lacked significant character. As far as rescues went, the kennel was exceptionally clean and well-maintained, and the dogs had nice big rooms. They even had an indoor run for foul weather. I hadn't made it over to the cat housing yet, but if the dog section was anything to judge by, it would be equally nice.

I snagged another leash and summoned my wand with a twist of my wrist as I headed back in for more critters. Thanks to a bracelet and some elven crafting I didn't understand, it allowed me to summon and dismiss my wand as I pleased. A vast improvement over the usual wand sheaths.

Inside the dog section of the kennel, I walked quietly and listened. I couldn't hear anything, but that didn't mean another dog wasn't hiding in a corner, ready to bark flames at me the moment I got close.

That exact issue was why the head of Happy Paws was in the hospital. Unfortunately, due to the amount of morphine she'd been given, she couldn't tell us how many critters were currently on premises. The police were trying to find someone else who knew that information, because going through the records hadn't gone well. Apparently, a mix of cats and dogs had gotten into the bungalow. Three animal control officers and a hedge-practitioner were still taming that mess.

Unlike me, who'd been born a witch with magic and a three-hundred-year life expectancy, hedge-practitioners were human. Many hedge-practitioners, including Officer Rodriguez, who'd called me to this scene, were competent and capable, but they didn't have the same power as did a witch. Even one like me who'd had an injury and was rebuilding her abilities.

Claws clacked against the concrete floor. I froze, scanning the aisle and open kennel doors as I tried to locate the source of the sound. The dog kept moving and trotted out from the kennel ahead of me. It stopped, looked at me, and barked.

A shock-wave crashed into me, forcing me back several steps.

I shook my head, trying to clear out the slight ringing in my ears. I'd met some dogs who could bark loudly, but none that carried the concussive waves with their bark. That was new. I dug around my pocket, pulling out a slightly squished liver treat and held it out on a flat hand. "You have such beautiful chocolate fur. And I love your ears."

The dog stretched out his nose and sniffed.

"Are you a lab mix? You look like you might be a Labrador Retriever." I inched closer.

The dog wagged its tail and trotted over, slurping the treat off my hand. I slipped the leash around its neck as it gulped down the treat. I wasn't sure the dog had bothered to chew the treat before swallowing.

The lab walked quietly next to me as I led it out and handed it off to Ryeleigh.

As the leash changed hands, Ryeleigh glanced at the cages behind her. "My colleagues who were in the main house came out with several animals. We filled their truck, and they're headed to our facility. They also found a list of animals. I think we're only missing two cats. There may have been a bunny on premises as well. Rodriguez is looking for them."

"Thanks." I headed for the main house. Hopefully, the bunny could take care of itself, because a day when cats could pass through walls and dogs could bark with concussive force wasn't one when a bunny rabbit needed to be depending on its speed to escape.

The front door opened without a squeak. At one point, this had been an orderly room, with a few chairs and a desk. Now, the chairs were turned over, the magazines were strewn across the floor, and a smelly puddle decorated one corner. Wand in hand, I made my way around the front desk and into a hallway.

"Son of a—" Rodriguez bellowed as he scrambled through a doorway.

I was halfway to the room when I spotted a cat lurking in an office doorway. Not taking any chances, I pointed my wand at it. "*Sowil*."

The containment spell popped into place around the cat, who promptly hissed and scratched at the barrier. It could do that all it wanted, it wasn't going anywhere.

"Get back here, you hellcat!" A cat darted out of a room, barreling down the hall with Rodriguez hot on its heels. Both his hands were streaked with blood, and somehow he had a scratch across his cheek too.

"*Sowil*."

The cat was still running when the shield formed around it. It collided with an interior wall of the spherical containment spell, sending the sphere rolling down the hall with the cat sliding around inside. The containment spell came to a stop against the wall. The cat stood up, shook itself, and stumbled two steps to the side before laying down. I turned to Rodriguez.

He leaned against a doorway, panting heavily, glaring at the cats. Along with the scratches I'd seen earlier, the shirt of his previously pristine uniform was torn. Rounding up cats, it seemed, was more difficult than finding the dogs. "It's good to have you back."

"How did you manage without me?" I kept my tone light, not wanting either of us to relive the last few months.

It turned out burning yourself out as a witch and healing wasn't exactly a picnic. Rebuilding magical powers was hard, and I'd only just gotten to the point where I could use significant amounts of magic in the past few weeks. It would be a long time before I had the power I once commanded so casually, if I ever did again.

For now, I was happy to be back. Michelle Oaks, of Oaks Consulting, providing permanent solutions to magical problems. Even though this was my first day back, business was as good as ever. Every police contract I'd had before losing my powers had renewed. Life didn't get much better than this.

He held up a hand that was still oozing blood. "With difficulty, as you can see."

I grimaced. "I have healing charms in the car, but I think the department would want you to go to the hospital."

"I know." Rodriguez sighed. "Is that everyone?"

"I've heard there might be a missing rabbit."

Rodriguez shook his head. "The rabbit didn't make it."

"I see." I eyed the bloody paw prints crisscrossing the hallway. The rabbit explained that. "Why don't we each grab a cat and we can get out of here."

"That one's mine." He pointed at the cat at the end of the hallway.

"Whatever you want." I scooped up the containment spell holding the remaining cat. It hissed and clawed the inside of the spell for the entire trip. I was all too happy to put it in a cage and remove the spell. Rodriguez looked rather gleeful as he locked up his cat. I removed its containment spell too.

Ryeleigh checked off two more cats from her list. "That's everything but the rabbit."

"The rabbit didn't make it," Rodriguez said.

She made a note. "Where is it? They'll want to send it off for a necropsy and magical evaluation."

"Michelle can do the magical evaluation."

Ryeleigh jerked her head up, eyes darting between Rodriguez and me. I gave my best professional smile, the one that said I was capable and willing to get to work.

"I have orders to send them off to the state lab," she said evenly.

I kept smiling politely as my heart sank. My first day back and people assumed I wasn't up to the job.

Rodriguez locked eyes with Ryeleigh. "I'm not sure what you're implying, but Michelle is trusted by the department, competent, and qualified. As far as magical evidence, I outrank everyone but the top brass. Michelle can examine the rabbit. We will develop and implement the best plan for removing the magic from the building. I will be working beside her and review her performance if there are any doubts."

The animal control officer shrugged. "Fine, but you get to tell command why I didn't send everything to the Georgia Bureau of Investigation."

"Done. They give you any flack, send them to me. I'll inform them of our department's strict policy to do work in-house, especially considering how long it takes to get things back from the GBI." Rather than waiting for Ryeleigh to answer, Rodriguez turned to me and tipped his head towards the building. "I'll show you the rabbit."

I followed him inside, ignoring the sound of Ryeleigh calling her boss. At times like this, it was nice to be a consultant. They might fight over what I did, but I wasn't involved in the fight itself.

Rodriguez guided us through the building, down the hallway decorated by bloody paw prints, and then to a small room near the back of the house. The enclosure for the rabbit took up most of the room, with a pet door leading outside. I suspected a covered run let the rabbit go out and enjoy the great outdoors without risking it getting away or being attacked. No one had expected the danger would come from inside.

In life, the rabbit would've been huge. The biggest one I'd seen, and I'd seen some large bunnies running around North Georgia. Whatever breed of rabbit this was, it wasn't your average wild rabbit. Unfortunately, the cats had had a little too much fun killing it, and what was left looked nothing like the majestic creature it had once been.

I extended a slender strand of magic and probed the rabbit's remains. As sad and gross as it was, I moved the tendril of magic along the skin and across the visible innards. Magic dotted the outside of the rabbit, but the inside only had tiny traces, perhaps transfer from the cats. I probed the floor around and found more magic clinging to something on the ground. Squatting down, I spotted a black hair that was pulsing with magic. Since the rabbit had been brown, it had to belong to one of the cats who killed it.

I probed the rabbit's remains again, including its blood. A more extensive exam matched the results from the first. "The rabbit wasn't affected by the magic, so whatever did this to the rest of the animals is something they use for the cats and dogs but not for the poor rabbit."

"Any idea what that would be?" Rodriguez asked.

"A food or air treatment, maybe a cleaning agent? This isn't my specialty. Do you think our neighborhood animal control officer would be in a mood to help us out?" I turned away from the rabbit, not wanting to think about how it died.

"Maybe. If not, I have a few ideas. Give me a minute to collect the remains."

I waited outside while Rodriguez gathered the rabbit's corpse. Not that I was squeamish, but he didn't need my help.

"Got it," he said as he joined me. "Let's do a quick survey of the rest of the buildings before we talk to her again."

As we walked, I opened my shields, letting myself sense the magic around us. While there were bright flashes of magic in some rooms, the cats' kennel was absolutely coated in it. I turn my focus to the dog's kennel and found it awash with magic too. Whatever had caused this was localized.

"Did you feel that?" Rodriguez asked.

"That the magic only affected the kennels?" I waited for him to nod before continuing. "I did, and the magic feels the same in the two buildings."

"They wouldn't eat the same food." He sighed. "Let's see if we can get a helpful answer."

Outside, the animal control officer was sitting on the bumper of her truck, making notes. She looked up as we exited the building. "Boss said he didn't know you were back, Ms. Oaks. And, um, I'm sorry for arguing with both of you."

"It's been a while since I was working with the police." I shrugged. "Communication issues happen."

"Thanks." She glanced at Rodriguez.

"Rabbit remains, still contaminated with magic." Rodriguez held out the bags.

"Boss said you would know what to do."

"Yup." He stowed them in a cooler in the back of his car.

Ryeleigh shuffled nervously. "Like I said, I'm sorry about before."

I was running out of things to say, so I smiled.

"You can make it up to us." Rodriguez shut the trunk of his car. "We found magic coating both kennels, but not much anywhere else. The rabbit's area was mostly clear of magic."

She tipped her head to the side. "What about the cleaning supplies? Those might be the same for both kennels."

I locked eyes with Rodriguez. "There was enough magic I might not have noticed the chemicals. We'd need to find the stock for both kennels and check."

"Ryeleigh, you're free to go. We'll finish up here," Rodriguez ordered as he headed to the dog's portion of the facility.

"Yes, sir! I'll get these guys to decontamination."

I turned back to the building as Ryeleigh loaded a crate with a hissing cat into the truck. That hiss captured my frustration perfectly.

In a building slathered in magic, I needed to find the extra potent magic. Maybe trying to feel the magic around me had been the wrong way to solve the problem.

I let down the shield that prevented me from seeing magic all the time. Happy Paws lit up like a second sun. Squinting at the building, I adjusted how brightly magic appeared until the glow didn't hurt my eyes. When the spots in my vision faded, I looked over the building again.

Between the even coating over both kennels and the comparative lack of magic in the main office, it was hard to tell where to start. I'd really expected to see a concentration of magic. "I can't find the source."

"I hope it's still here." Rodriguez sighed. "Maybe their chemical storage room is shielded?"

"Worth a try." I really wanted the source to be on sight, not something that could travel from rescue to rescue. One day of wrangling magical cats and dogs was enough.

Inside was both less and more disturbing now that we had removed the animals. Scorch marks on the walls, rusted metal doors, and muddy paw prints on the ceiling were more reminiscent of a horror film than an animal rescue. On the more positive side, the rabbit was the only casualty. The building damage was repairable.

We rounded a corner in the dog kennel. Instead of a storage closet, I spotted a crack running up the wall. Fixable, but expensive. Hopefully, their insurance included a magical damage rider.

"You'd think the supply room would be easier to find," Rodriguez grumbled as we stared into the last kennel in the building.

"We could try the feed room again. Maybe we missed a door or cabinet." I was clutching at straws. A few months ago, I'd have figured out a crafty spell to find the cleaning supplies, but even with all the work I'd put into regaining my powers, I wasn't what I'd been. And power sucking spells, no matter how crafty and useful, would leave me drained for the day. I was no use to anyone that way.

I hadn't always relied so heavily on powerhouse spells. Back when I'd first started Oaks Consulting, brains, not magical brawn, had been my style. Retro was in vogue these days, so it was time to return to my roots and embrace what had built my business—and my power—to begin with.

Too bad I was all out of bright ideas.

The door to the feed room hung unevenly, the hinges having taken the brunt of the damage this morning. Though the rest of the room hadn't escape unscathed. I could picture what it had looked like most days, with tidily labeled barrels of food, stacks of bowls, and a grid on the wall showing what each dog got morning and night. A set of cubbies above a table made it easy to organize medication. Or it had, before the dogs had opened the door, raided the food, chewed through the bottles of a few tasty medications, and had too much fun. The feathers were a nice touch, but exactly what they'd come from was beyond me. Given the lack of blood, my guess was a pillow.

The coating of magic hadn't changed from what was in the rest of the building, but this was the last place the cleaning supplies could be in this kennel. But where? Other than a floor to ceiling poster about workplace policies and procedures and the mess left by dogs, there wasn't much to look at.

"Maybe they store everything in the office."

A metallic glint caught my eyes. There, blending in with the border of the poster, was a doorknob. "Or they're too clever for their own good."

As soon as my fingers touched the metal, a buzz of magic flared against my skin. With the residue in the room, I hadn't been able to separate the spell from everything else. Now that I was touching it, I could feel the pattern and flow of the spell. It had two parts, one that only allowed authorized people into the room, which would keep out most humans, elves, and fey, but not a witch with any skills. With hardly a moment's thought, I twisted the edge of the spell to recognize Rodriguez and myself.

The second spell, though, had been cast to ensure what was in the room stayed in the room. Either by design or accident, the spell didn't differentiate between the magical and physical. It would work equally hard to keep a bucket from rolling out the door as it would to contain any magic within.

If the cleaning supplies were anywhere, this was it. I twisted the knob and pushed open the door.

Bright undulating magic flooded my vision. I threw an

arm up as I frantically damped my sensitivity to magic, but that didn't stop the spots in my eyes.

"Michelle?"

Lowering my arm, I looked at Rodriguez around the spots that were fading from my vision. "Other than being careless, I'm fine. I didn't think it would be so bright." Now that I could see the magic without going blind, I had quite a few thoughts.

"I don't perceive magic as well as you, and I can tell this isn't normal cleaning magic."

That was true. For one, it was far too active, as if the spells hadn't been finished, so they kept changing, trying to close the magic into a single spell.

Once I could see past the mass of energy, it didn't get better. One shelf, separated from the rest by mops and brooms with a red-lettered sign reading Magically Enhanced Cleaners, held four oversized buckets of cleaning solution. One had a pump arching out of it, with a single drop of glittery purple solution clinging to the nozzle.

Even without probing the drop, I could feel and see the spells. It was the same magic that coated the kennel, only a hundred times more concentrated and twisting as it tried to find the missing part of its spell.

"Well, this is new and horrifying." I explained what I'd found to Rodriguez. "I can look at it more closely if you want, but this stuff is trouble in a bottle."

"I don't want it at the office. Once I document it, you can take it and dispose of it." Rodriguez took a slim camera out of his pocket and started taking pictures.

The magic twisted around the bottles of cleaner, reaching toward Rodriguez and myself. While I was usually more than happy to disenchant things, this wasn't worth the risk. "A local place, Regional Disposal Experts, accepts magical waste now. I'll take these there."

"Can they handle this?"

"I think so. They have a crusher and a setup for controlled burns. That should do."

"Great." Rodriguez put the camera back in his pocket. "Help me get these to the car."

I set shields around the buckets before we touched them. What this mess would do if it interacted with my magic was a nightmare I didn't want to consider.

Half an hour later, we'd documented the cleaning solutions from both sets of kennels, and Rodriguez had the samples he needed. Now the buckets of nasty were in my trunk, carefully strapped into place. Short of a car accident, they weren't going anywhere.

Rodriguez shut the trunk of his car and dusted off his hands. "I'm glad you were here. I don't know what I would've done without you."

"This sure made my first day back an exciting one." I kept my voice light, not wanting to get lost in memories that were still too fresh.

"I do what I can." He hesitated. "I, uh, better get back to the office. This report will take hours."

The tightness in my gut eased. "Same, but I'll take these to the Regional Disposal first."

Rodriguez nodded awkwardly and headed to his car.

I settled in the driver's seat and took a deep breath before cranking the engine. He hadn't mentioned the past, the day I'd risked my power and life, and lost both in their own way. Thanks to a crazy old witch and her curse, I had found a way back to my powers. But back didn't mean the same.

Following Rodriguez onto the road, I flipped on the

radio and toggled the presets until a new song with a nice upbeat rhythm filled the car.

All the demons were dead. I had a nice job with the police, and no one wanted to kill me. My powers were still growing. One day, I might be as powerful as I'd been before. Until then, I had enough magic to do my job, and that would have to be enough.

CHAPTER TWO

Regional Disposal Experts, for all that their name made them sound local, hadn't been around very long. The chain-link fence around the property still had the shine, and the grass hadn't fully grown in on the sides of their entry. The facility itself wasn't much to look at, with blocky containers and structures intended for a purpose that had nothing to do with artistry. As tidy as it was, the smell that lingered around every disposal site didn't encourage lingering.

None of that stopped the short man in coveralls and a baseball cap at the gate from smiling at me. "What can I do for you, ma'am?"

"Magical goods disposal. I have four containers of a magical cleaning solution for the incinerator." That was one fire I didn't want to see. Sure, the flames would eat through the magic, but until the energy ran out, it could be exciting.

He pointed at a cinder block building with an overhang. "I'll meet you over then and take care of it."

By the time he walked over, I had the car parked under

the awning and the buckets of poorly magicked chemicals on the scale. A credit card swipe later, and the mess was no longer my responsibility. "You'll want to be careful with those."

He picked up two of the buckets. "They'll go in the burn room now."

"Great. Have a good day." I shoved my wallet in my purse.

Two buckets collided with a thud and sloshed. He muttered a curse.

My eyes went to the scale, but it was too late. While trying to pick up all four buckets, he had pinched the pump, sending a stream of magical cleaning solution onto my pants.

"Son of a—" In his haste to correct the problem, his fingers slipped off the handle.

Oh, no. I wasn't dealing this mess again today. "*Nazid.*"

Without my wand, it took an extra shove of magic, but the spell caught the bucket and held it aloft until he could get a better grip on the handle.

"Thank you, Ma'am." He had the good sense, if rather belated in its arrival, to settle for picking up just two of the buckets at one time. "I best get these to the burn room." He turned and pushed through a door labeled Employees Only. If he'd noticed the splash of solution on my leg, he hadn't mentioned it.

While I didn't see any of the cleaning fluid on the floor, there was an easy way to check. I switched my vision, opened my eyes to a wash of magic covering everything. The floor doubled and then tripled. Snapping my eyes closed, I turned my attention inward.

The strange magic in the cleaning solution had already attacked the shields that separated my magic from the rest of the world. It had gone through, in part by adjusting itself to match my shields and it part by eating through my shields. That probably had something to do with the enhanced cleaning spell on them.

I had to get home before I became as problematic as those poor cats and dogs.

After two tries, I blocked off the magical portion of my vision, and the world returned to normal. Well, except for the magic clawing through my shields. On my way to the car, I added two different shields between the core of my power and the twisted mess of spells attacking me. Those would have to hold.

My hand shook as I slid the key into the ignition. If I couldn't drive home safely, I'd have to call Rodriguez. The last thing I needed on my first day back at work was to be carted into a decontamination room. Besides, my parents were at the lodge. They could help.

The twenty minutes it took to drive home stretched out endlessly. Every red light lasted for hours. Every speed limit was too fast and too slow all at the same time. When I finally turned the car onto a gravel road with a freshly painted wood sign for Landa's Lodge, I let out a shaky breath. Almost there.

My vision doubled for a moment, and I swore.

The gravel road curved around a towering oak. The driveway spilled me into a parking lot in front of a log home that defied the word cabin. Along with apartments for permanent residents like myself, the lodge operated as a bed and breakfast, and lunch and dinner. Perfect for the cooking challenged like me.

I let the car coast into the last spot on this side of the lot. With the car safely parked, there was only one more hurdle: navigating the sprawling building with my vision playing tricks on me. Abandoning my purse, I focused on the ground. First out of the car, then one step.

Narzel, the trickster of legend, had a good laugh at my pitiful navigation of the stairs. Later, when swearing didn't take so much effort, I'd think of an appropriate term for my frustration.

The hallways blended together, but somehow I found my door. The nob turned under my hand, and if I'd been thinking better, I would've wondered why. But the magic had gotten through the barriers, and all I knew was safety lay behind that door.

I stumbled through.

"Michelle, you're early." The voice sounded familiar, but I couldn't place it.

Were there six heads or nine? Blinking did nothing to sort out the confusion. Maybe twelve? But why would twelve people be in my apartment?

"Are you okay?"

No.

"Michelle?"

I hadn't said that out loud? Odd. I'd meant to.

"Get Dr. Stiles."

The heads pitched sideways as if they were standing on a wall. What a pickle. Closing my eyes dealt with that terrifying image nicely. I could almost hear Narzel laughing.

My head throbbed, and the light filtering through my eyelids seemed rather brighter than usual. Neither of which were good signs, considering my last coherent memory was of my normal vision doubling as I parked at the lodge.

Taking a deep breath, I slowly opened my eyes. In a rather pleasant turn of events, I was looking at my bedroom ceiling. Which explained why I was comfortable, other than the dwarves hosting a lively dance in my head. As an added bonus, it was a singular ceiling above me.

Which left one question. Who'd helped me? Because getting into bed hadn't been in my skill set last I remembered.

"How's the head?" A light but purposeful voice came from my left.

Moving was a risk, but I wanted to know who was in the room. Luckily, the dwarven party didn't notice the motion. Unfortunately, they continued their dancing.

The tidy woman with deep creases bracketing her mouth and eyes that seemed to see through my skin sat primly in a chair next to the bed. "I'm sure it hurts."

"Dr. Stiles, it is good to see you."

She snorted. "You didn't seem nearly so excited when confirming our appointment yesterday."

Having a doctor, even one I liked, examine me for what felt like the thousandth time since my injury hadn't sounded fun. But yesterday, my magic hadn't been contaminated with that cleaning goop and all of its problems. "The situation changed."

"Yes, I can see that."

If my head hadn't hurt so badly, I would've rolled my eyes. "So, what's the prognosis, doc?"

Dr. Stiles leaned over and mercilessly shined a penlight in my eyes. "You'll make it. Nancy and I decontaminated your magic, nasty bit of spellwork that, and put you to bed."

I groaned. Of course, Mom had been here. "Who else knows?"

"Your dad, myself, and Susanna. I suppose since Susanna knows, Ethel does too." She settled into her chair and smiled. "Ethel won't be pleased that we had to drain most of your power to fix you, but you'll be healthy enough for the convention."

"You did what? You know my magic hasn't been regenerating like it used to. It'll be days before I'm back to full strength. Ethel was clear—I have to be able to do magic at the convention." Reaching for my magic had the dwarven dance team doubling their tempo, but I had to check. Sure enough, only a handful of magic remained.

A cool finger rested against my temple. "While I'd wanted to leave the headache to remind you to be more careful, it hardly serves when you're panicked over the convention."

The dwarves vanished, for which I'd have been more grateful if I didn't have to explain to Ethel why I wasn't at full power. "I didn't do this to myself. A careless worker at Regional Disposal splashed me with a poorly spelled cleaning solution I was dropping off for disposal."

"That will teach me not to assume." Dr. Stiles sighed. "This could be a good thing. You've had trouble with magic regeneration, and draining yourself was a treatment we talked about."

Of all the ways my magic wasn't what it had been before, the slower magic regeneration was the most frustrating, and the one that had kept me from returning to work for so long. "But not right before the convention."

"It couldn't be helped." She leaned forward. "I had many conversations with Ethel while you were recovering. As premier, she needs you to be at your best. As her heir, you need to be at your best. That said, she's far from heartless, and she's practical. The work you do with the police helps witches and will help you when you're premier and dealing with the politics that come along with the position. Being short on power isn't ideal, but you are a capable and well-liked witch."

"Well-liked might be going too far." Not that everyone hated me, but witches could be an insular group, and my upbringing hadn't been normal. After I had spent my childhood clanless, some witches didn't approve of me. Being a member of both my mother's clan, the Wapiti, and my father's, the Docga, only made those set against me less happy. According to their rules, it was one clan or none. I'd never been good at living by outdated rules made by change-adversed witches stuck in days of yore.

Basically, Ethel believed in me. Having spearheaded the spell that rid the world of demons, even when it had damaged my magical abilities nearly beyond repair, had only strengthened her belief. But the traditionalists didn't like much about me, be it my age, personal history, or newly regained magical abilities. Even having made my mom be an interim premier to smooth the transition between Ethel and myself hadn't won any points from that faction.

After a quick knock, the door swung open. Susanna poked her head into the room, a phone in one hand. As usual, her silver hair was smoothed back into a perfect bun, and her suit was a soft blue, likely an attempt at harmonizing with the vivid shades Ethel loved to wear. "The premier would like an update."

I sighed. It didn't do any good to remind myself that I'd signed up for this. Susanna had been hovering around for days and would continue to do so through the convention. I'd been informed Susanna knew my schedule and would ensure I made it to every event. Plus, she'd smooth over any problems. If I was lucky, I could manage three days without needing that service. Not that luck and I had ever been on the best of terms.

"She can speak to the premier for a moment." Dr. Stiles didn't move from her chair.

Susanna handed me the phone. With a sigh I hoped Ethel couldn't hear, I braced myself for the conversation. "Hello?"

"How are you?"

I filled her in on my condition. "Mostly worried about the convention."

"Do not show weakness," Ethel said sharply. "From the moment you arrive, your every action will be watched. You must appear confident."

"And when I don't have the magic to back up that confidence?"

"You have plenty of magic to hold the office." Ethel sighed. "We have enough time to win them over. I won't die until the transition is secure. I've seen that."

"Yes, premier."

"Rest. We will face the clans together." Ethel hung up.

I handed the phone back to Susanna.

Dr. Stiles ushered Susanna out of the room, then studied me. "It's a convention, Michelle, not war. You'll be fine."

Why was it that war sounded like the less dangerous of the two?

CHAPTER THREE

"Mom, I'm fine," I repeated futilely.

She pressed a hand to my forehead. "The headache is gone, but you're dreadfully short on magic."

"Nancy, that's not a metric for health, and you know it." Dad captured Mom's hand in his.

"I'm a mother. I'm entitled to worry when my child comes home with tainted magic and I end up treating her." The unspoken again hung in the air.

"This one wasn't my fault," I muttered, not that the facts of the situation had mattered so far.

"Nancy." Dad's voice softened. "This isn't like before."

Mom pursed her lips. "No, Greg, it isn't. It's like the time before and the time before that. One magical injury after another."

"I'm right here," I said. Not that it mattered.

"And she's an adult, doing the job she chose." Dad motioned to me.

Mom rolled her eyes. "It's dangerous! How many times do you have to see our child injured before you recognize that?"

"I'm here, right? You can see and hear me?" Even with the little magic I had right now, I'd have felt an invisibility spell. There wasn't one, sadly. That would've been better than having my parents argue over me like I was seven, not twenty-seven.

Dad looked directly at me. "Yes, I know you're here."

"This is between your father and I." Mom hardly glanced in my direction.

"Is it? Well, then I suggest you continue the conversation elsewhere." I yanked open the front door and motioned for them to leave. "I'll see you in the morning and look forward to spending time with you at the convention."

"Sorry," Dad muttered as he walked out the door.

Mom glared at me. "Your job isn't safe. Why, if you hadn't worked with the police—"

"Let me stop you right there. I chose to work with the police. I chose to work on dangerous cases. I chose to fight demons, and I chose to do that spell. Getting my powers back is wonderful, but I'm not going to change my life. This is what I do, and every day I hope I can continue to work with the police when I'm premier."

I clamped my mouth shut before I ruined the moment by saying something I'd regret. Like a better mother wouldn't criticize my job so harshly.

"You nearly died." Her eyes filled with unshed tears.

Well, what kind of monster would I be if that didn't yank at my heartstrings? I gently wrapped my arms around her. "I love you, and I don't plan on fighting any more demons or trying any more spells that court death. Okay?"

She nodded and dabbed at her eyes with her sleeve.

"You can scold me for poor choices after the convention, deal?"

She nodded again and hugged me tightly. "I love you so much."

"I know, Mom. I know." And because of that, and the times she'd put aside her own feelings and done what was best for me, I hugged her back.

Even so, it was a relief when the door closed behind them. One thing I'd learned in the past few months was it didn't do to dwell on past decisions. Which seemed like a great philosophy while I was brewing a cup of tea, but it didn't make it any easier to leave the memories in the past and write the report for Rodriguez.

By the time I finished the report, my stomach was rumbling. "Just a few more minutes."

A knock came from the other door to my apartment. Not the front door, but one next to my dining room table that connected my apartment to the one next door.

The day's excitement faded away. Only one person would be at that door.

"Come in."

Elron stepped through, waist-length silver hair pulled back by three braids on each side of his face that joined in the back to make a six-strand braid. The style left his pointed ears bare and let his blue eyes sparkle. Not many elves would fall in love with a witch, but this one had.

"Aren't you a sight for sore eyes." I went up on my toes to give him a kiss.

Moments later, he leaned back, the sharp angles of his face softened by the happy smile. "What did I do to earn such a lovely greeting?"

"You showed up." I grinned. "While you're here, Susanna won't come back demanding to go over one more detail. Mom and Dad won't come back and fight about my job, and for a few hours, I can forget that I'm terrified to be introduced to the clans as their future premier."

"In that case, what would you say to a sunset dinner with a guard no one will challenge?"

"Well, I'd say the very sexy elf I'm engaged to knows how to show a girl a good time."

Elron returned my smile and led me into the garden.

Landa's landscaping would never dare to be anything but perfect, and the picturesque English garden's pebble paths crunch underfoot. The destination wasn't a surprise. Not much could hide tonight's guard, a thirteen-foot-tall *T. rex* who'd adopted me. He wasn't really a dinosaur, more of a magical construct who looked like one and was immune to most magic.

Ty leaned his big purple and pink head down for cheek scratches, and I obliged. He grunted and thumped an oak tree with his tail.

"We had a chat. He will not let anyone disturb us while we eat." Elron pointed behind Ty, where a table for two was set with covered plates.

I kissed Ty's nose. "Thank you."

He nudged me gently before taking a careful step back, narrowly avoiding trampling a hedge.

I wrapped an arm around Elron's waist and gently squeezed. "Thank you. After days of being hounded by everyone, this is perfect."

"A reminder that when I cannot be with you, I am still here, supporting you." He pulled out my chair. "When you return from the convention, we will have dinner again, just the two of us."

"I can't wait."

Elron smiled as he uncovered strawberry salads and filled the cups with lemon water.

"How was work?" I stabbed a strawberry, wishing it was the man at the disposal company. That was a story about my day I wouldn't enjoy telling.

"The greenhouses are doing well. I settled in a new Helenium today. Lovely orange-red flowers. If you catch it at sunset, you can see a small sun setting into its petals."

"Elron, that sounds lovely, but I haven't a clue what Helenium is." There were a few downsides to being in a relationship with an elf who specialized in rare magical plants.

He studied his plate for a moment. "It is similar to a sunflower. This variety of Helenium looks like a smaller sunflower, but the coloring and the magic are unique."

"It's hard to picture. I'll have to come see it." A simple pleasure to look forward to after the convention.

Elron nodded. "By then, I may have more news. The university is reviewing a plan to expand the department. Two more greenhouses and a show garden. If it is approved, I will need to do more trips searching for specimens."

"That's exciting! Could some of those trips include me? I've been asked to review cases across the country, so we could pair up our work travels." The stack of requests on my desk only grew. There simply weren't enough witches willing to work directly with the police, and magic had a way of causing problems. It was a daily reminder of why someone like me, who believed in witches working with other groups, needed to be the next premier.

Elron arched a brow. "Now that is an idea I can agree with. While you are at the convention, I will make a list."

We lapsed into silence as we ate. As if noticing the lack of conversation, the cicadas increased the volume of their buzzing symphony. This wasn't the first romantic dinner Elron had done over the past few months. Every one of them managed to remind me of the night he proposed, and why he hadn't been willing to set a wedding date.

Now the demon was dead. We still didn't have a

wedding date. In fact, we hadn't spoken of it. The ruby set in a silver band rested heavily against my skin.

Maybe elves were patient enough, with their multi-millennia lives, to be engaged with no hint of when the wedding would come, but I was not. I didn't have Elron's view of time, though I now shared his lifespan. Another bit of magic and twist of destiny we'd hardly spoken of. He still felt guilty for bringing the woman who cast the spell into my life.

To his credit, he'd asked her to heal me when I had no magic of my own. Linking our deaths to his last breath hadn't been part of his plan. Shared life should have made marriage seem like less of a commitment, but if anything, it had made him keep his distance.

"How was work?" he asked.

"Good. Took more magic than I'd like. An entire animal rescue and all the animals in it ended up affected by a poorly spelled cleaning agent. Rodriguez and I got the animals out. The owner will have to get a witch, or several, to come in and remove the magic. It was too big of a job for me while I was on call."

"And the animals?"

"Safely in the hands of animal control. They'll be treated and re-homed." My mind was still on the lack of wedding plans. I hadn't been happy when I discovered my life had been joined to his. He could feel as though pressing the marriage issue would make me feel trapped.

"Michelle?"

"Hum?"

Elron set down his fork. "You have not looked at me for five minutes."

My cheeks heated. "I haven't?"

"No, and I would like to know what is bothering you." The blue eyes that usually seemed so kind drilled into me.

I pushed my plate away and folded my arms on the edge of the table. "I want a wedding date."

He dropped his gaze.

"At first, you wouldn't set one because of the demon. Well, I killed him. I killed all of them. I told you'd I'd move mountains and walk through fire to be at your side, and I meant it. So, can we make some wedding plans? There's an elf I'd like to marry." I held my breath.

He lifted his head. Deep creases ran across his forehead. "You still want to marry me after everything?"

"Yes, I do. Then, and now, my love for you is tougher than dragon hide and as unrelenting as the ocean." I reached across the table, palm up, hoping he would meet me halfway. "In a nice blend of a witch and Elven traditions."

His fingers brushed my palm. "Spring?"

"Spring is a great time for a wedding. Perhaps even in a garden?" I resisted the urge to capture his hand. He had to come to me.

"Rebirth, renewal, hope." His fingers curled around mine. "A good time of year for a wedding."

"So it's settled, spring?" I bit my lip to keep from saying too much. Months of waiting, and here we were.

A slight smile spread to a joyful grin. "We'll marry in the springtime."

"In a garden, with the first blooms around us," I added, not wanting him to wiggle out of the agreement later.

He bowed his head. "As my lady wishes."

I snorted. "Don't go all formal on me now."

He lifted my hand from the table and pressed a kiss to my knuckles. "I would never."

"Right." I couldn't help but smile. "I do want one thing."

"Michelle, I—"

I held up a hand. "Stop. It's not that serious. I don't want to tell anyone we picked a date until after the convention. It'll give me something to look forward to."

"Ah, if that is what you want."

"I do."

I winked, but it was mostly for show. I needed this, something good I could hold on to. Because last night I hadn't found peace praying at my altar in the woods. No matter how many times Ethel, Mom, Dad, Elron, or Susanna told me all would be well, I didn't believe them. The witch community wasn't going to fall in love with me at first sight, not a formerly clanless witch marrying an elf.

Trouble was coming, only I couldn't see from where.

CHAPTER FOUR

"It is my pleasure to introduce to you my chosen successor." Ethel's voice was strong and firm as it rolled across the auditorium. Her gaze kept lingering on the section closest to the stage, where the ministers of every clan of witches in the country were sitting. Well, almost all of them. Both my parents were ministers, and they were in the two seats to my right.

From my seat behind Ethel, I couldn't see her expression, but from the time I'd spent with her, I suspected it was a warning glare followed by a stare that felt like she could see into their souls.

As the premier, Ethel was the head of all the ministers, really of all the clans and witches in the country, but we still needed supporters, especially during a transition of power.

Even without being at the front of the stage, I could see too much of the crowd. In past years, the premier's opening speech probably hadn't drawn this much of a crowd. At least half were frowning, and that didn't bode well for my time as heir apparent, never mind premier.

"She is a witch born with the mark of the Ieldra and has already lived up to the promise of power and ability written into her skin by her clan scar. Many of you know her from the recent great work, where she was the focus point and caster of the spell that rid our world of demons."

Soft gasps and whispers raced through the crowd as the witches who hadn't known who I was started putting the pieces together.

Ethel waited for the audience to quiet before continuing. "The future premier, Michelle Oaks." Clapping, Ethel turned to look at me.

I stood up with a polite smile plastered on my face. My palms were sweating, but with more than ten thousand witches and six cameras focused on me, I didn't dare wipe my hands on my slacks.

The ten feet between my chair and the podium seemed like a mile. Months ago when Ethel Bailey had told me I'd be making this speech, it hadn't seemed nearly so scary. Now, under the hot lights and with everyone watching me, I wished I was back home at the lodge, surrounded by peaceful forest.

Rather than running away, I did exactly as I had been instructed and took careful steps over to the podium. Ethel moved back, her smile encouraging and yet toothy enough to remind me of the stakes. In a few seconds, I would be speaking as the future premier, and all these people would be weighing and measuring my every move.

I rested my hand on the edge of the podium, grateful to feel solid wood under my fingers. I glanced down, and as promised, my speech notes were there. Taking a deep breath, I started the speech I'd rehearsed at least a hundred times.

"Good evening, and welcome to the Fall Convention.

In case you missed the premier's introduction, I'm Michelle Oaks of the Docga and Wapiti clans, the next premier." My notes included a prompt to smile, so I did, and I hoped it was warm and appealing rather than frightened.

"In the few hours I've been here, I've already heard twice as much fiction than fact about me." Ethel's advice—*Smile. Don't look nervous. Check your notes*—kept echoing through my brain, making it difficult to remember what I was supposed to say. "For instance, I haven't yet, nor do I ever intend to, munch on babies or drink their blood. I had a spinach omelet for breakfast."

Chuckles rippled across the audience, and I smiled a little wider. "Like you, I'm a witch." I pushed magic out of me, sending up bright flares of red, white, and blue sparks that fizzled out high above my head. "I want all of us to prosper, live long, healthy, happy lives, and fully integrate into the society in which we live."

My smile faded and I took a deep breath, steeling myself for what I was about to announce. Once I said these words, there was no going back. I wouldn't be able to take them back or wish them away. "I grew up without a clan. While some of you may consider that to be a handicap, I consider it to be an experience that shaped me as an individual and gave me insight into what all of us could have. There are a great many benefits to the clan system, but all of us need to take a good look at the world around us. We cannot continue to hold to the old ways, ignoring everything else."

A heavy silence settled over the audience.

"As premier, I will be working to find a balance between our culture and progress, because I've seen witches abducted to bend them to a clan's will. I have watched my family members be tortured in the name of tradition and clan." I forced my eyes to stay open so I couldn't relive the memory of what had been done to my mother. "And I have watched the laws of this land rendered unenforceable because agreements signed years ago forbade them from interfering in internal matters."

I let my gaze trail over the crowd, doing my best to make sure each of them felt like I had looked them in the eye. "That ends today. We are witches. We will always be witches, but we do not harm one another. We do not use clan ties to hurt other witches. We are not above the laws of this land, but part of it."

The rapt attention and lack of normal shifting or whispering unnerved me. I just needed to get through one more line. "I hope you will join me in building a new way of life, one where tradition and progress can live side by side."

Stepping back, I waved and started back to my seat. Behind me, the light applause slowly grew until it was thunderous, with witches all across the room amplifying the sound of their group. It was more support than I'd expected, and that in and of itself was a win.

My mom and my dad both gave me proud smiles as I settled into my seat. I took a deep breath, feeling like a great weight had been lifted from my shoulders. The speech was over. It had resonated with some, and that was good enough for now. Hopefully with time, others would find that the new ideas had benefits and the support would grow.

Ethel returned to the podium. "Over the next few days, there will be several panels featuring this topic. I encourage all of you to attend, ask questions, and explore what it means to hold on to our identity while embracing progress." She paused continuing. "For those of you who are like me and feel a great gap of age and experience between yourself and someone as youthful as Ms. Oaks, let me assure you that she will be fully prepared before stepping into my shoes."

There was a flutter of chatter, some soft laughs, and murmured agreements around the room.

"Not only do I have every intention of continuing my time as premier for a few more years, but the minister of the Wapiti, Nancy Oaks, has agreed to serve as an interim premier as well as one of Michelle's advisers once she is premier." Ethel motioned to my mom. "Your interim premier."

Mom walked over to the podium. Her voice was soft, and even with the sound amplification spells, the audience had to stay quiet to hear her. "I've had the unique experience of being in every part of the clan, from heir apparent, to outcast, to member, to minister. I've seen clans at their best, where everyone is lifted up by strong leadership and a community mentality." She paused. "I've seen clans torn apart by petty disputes, political pandering, and poor management. As interim minister, I plan to continue following Ethel's vision, develop programs to help struggling clans and witches, as well as ease the transition between Ethel and Michelle."

Mom continued with the scripted speech, but I stopped listening because I'd heard it too many times to count while she'd been making sure she knew exactly how she wanted to say every word. Instead, I was watching the audience's gaze jump from my mom to me. The little magic show had been intended to help refute any rumors that I'd lost my powers, but I wasn't sure it had worked.

Not only were people continuing to watch me, but it was hard to hide the truth. Rumors that I lost my power had circulated for months. While I didn't need much power to be premier, I needed what I had, and I needed enough to squish any arguments that I wasn't a witch. If this demonstration hadn't been enough, I'd have to figure out something else, because I didn't want to be dealing with the issue forever.

Clapping pulled me out of my thoughts and back into the present. I quickly joined in as Mom returned to her seat next to me. While I'd had pockets of noisy supporters, Mom's applause was both evenly distributed throughout the crowd and louder. Ethel had been right. People would love her, making accepting me easier.

Ethel returned to the podium. I straightened my shoulders, knowing what was going to happen next. "Ladies and gentlemen." Ethel's voice boomed through the room. "Let the convention begin!"

Magical fireworks exploded across the ceiling, sending red, white, and blue lights glimmering as they drifted down, vanishing before they touched anyone. The crowd roared, and the orderly commencement dissolved into the beginnings of a party, with people shouting, hugging, talking, and racing for the exits.

I didn't have it in me to celebrate. The rest of my evening was going to be filled with making official appearances at every gathering the convention was hosting. That meant smiling, saying the right thing, smiling some more, and wishing I was back home with Elron. He hadn't been invited because elves weren't welcome at a witch-only gathering.

Ethel finished thanking the event host and marched over to me. Rather than one of her usually vivid outfits, she was wearing a positively sedate pale rose dress suit, her white hair pulled back in a bun.

"You did well. The overall reception was better than we hoped for, but there's more to be done."

Suppressing a sigh, I nodded. "I didn't get the tone right, did I?"

She pursed her lips, studying me. "The speech was fine, but some of the people are still trying to live like we have our own communities and never see the rest of the world. Your mission statement was strong. They need time to get used to the idea."

"Right," I muttered without enthusiasm. "On to part two, spending the night charming them."

"Precisely." The word was filled with energy I didn't have. "Now, we have time for a quick dinner before we get started."

I got to my feet and tried to remember all the reasons I wanted to be here. Yesterday, saving witches from being tortured or used as pawns in a political game had sounded so very noble. Today, it was a lot of work and being chased around by a feisty old woman.

CHAPTER FIVE

The last day of the convention was a haze. On the *Policing as a Modern Witch* panel, I fielded questions about breaking with tradition and destroying clan businesses, neither of which I was able to answer satisfactorily. Thankfully there were only a few minutes between that and my next appearance, at *Social Problems Facing Clans*. The moderator hurried me out before I could be mobbed by the participants on that one. Two hours of nonstop questioning about the time I was kidnapped by my maternal grandmother so I could carry on her legacy, or any of the other bad behavior I'd experienced as a clanless witch, was enough.

Unfortunately, I wasn't quick enough to escape uncomfortable questions at *Illegal Magic*. I gritted my teeth and did my best smile as I listened to the third question asking essentially the same thing.

"I'm afraid I don't entirely follow. You're saying that some of our own are the perpetrators of these illegal acts, malfunctioning charms, poorly enchanted items, and the like. Do you think this issue is connected to the reduced power of the clan ministers? A change in our society that you support." Her eyes drilled into me.

Ignoring the murmurs of agreement, I leaned closer to the microphone and focused on the jeans and t-shirt clad witch. "I see the issues as related but distinct. It's easy to think of ourselves as different from other groups, but we have the same problems. We have people who are discontent, willing to break the law, and willing to endanger others to enhance their own goals. I don't want to see clans abolished. I just want them to treat witches with dignity and respect. If anything, clans motivated by the health and well-being of their members should only reduce the number of witches who turn to illegal methods to provide for themselves." Ethel had drilled me on that question dozens of times, and I thought I'd hit all the right notes.

The witch shook her head. "I speak for more than myself when I say the changes you suggested to the witch community will harm clans."

"Given the subject matter of this panel, I'm afraid we'll have to disagree." My memory wasn't as clear as I wanted it to be, but hopefully recalled the right name. "Angie, the only thing I can offer is the truth. I'm not the only witch who has been treated poorly at the hands of a clan, even their own clan, and I think that must end.

"As for witches being involved in illegal magic, policing magic is very difficult. Magic is our greatest resource and the way almost all of us earn a living. For those who want more money or don't like their place in the clan, selling spells and magical goods is a logical step. Sadly, it's one that harms a great many people."

Before Angie could say anything, the moderator broke in with a cheerful voice. "We've gotten a little off topic, Do you have a question more closely related to illegal magic?"

Frowning, Angie sat down. If her scowl was anything to

judge by, she wasn't finished with me. After a few seconds, another witch raised their hand. A short woman stood up. "Are there any signs we can look for that would help us identify a witch using their magic for illegal activities on the side?"

The moderator glanced over at me. "Michelle, I think you have the most experience in this area."

I forced a polite smile. "It depends on the ability of the witch in question. You might be able to see signs of magic, but the more skilled the individual in question, the more likely it is that they've taken preventative measures to erase those signs."

As I went through the various methods, the witch nodded politely. After two follow-up questions about magical residue, the moderator selected another question. Thankfully, it went to the panelist on my left. The rest of the panel crawled by until the question and answer segment was done and I could escape.

I hurried out the door, only steps ahead of Angie. Not willing to risk a glance back and possible eye contact with Angie, I kept up the quick pace until I was safely settled into another panel. Ethel might consider this necessary PR, but I couldn't wait for the convention to be over.

Policy questions deserved quality answers, but the middle of a panel wasn't the time or place. Not to mention Ethel had been insistent that I avoid those questions. She made that sound relatively easy, but in practice, it was proving to be far more difficult. Every time I was in front of an audience, they had a chance to ask those questions, and I had to find a polite redirect.

The real problem was me. I was something of a controversial figure. This was why I got the joy of sitting on all these panels, trying to make myself seem like just another witch rather than some radical political figure.

I hurried into another room. This time I had a few allies. *Equality in Ministry* was a hot topic in our family, with my father being one of the few male ministers. He squeezed my shoulder as he sat down next to me. A moment later, my mom took the seat on the other side of him. The other three male ministers took the remaining seats. Over three hundred clans, and only four male ministers. Sad.

This was by far the least painful panel of the day. The men spent the most time speaking and answering questions, allowing me to fade into the background. After only an hour, I retreated to my room. Now all I had to do was survive tonight's dinner, and I could get home to Elron.

Far too soon, Susanna came to ensure I was properly dressed for dinner, which included redoing my hair and checking to make sure I was dressed in the prearranged outfit. Once I passed muster, it was off to dinner.

Sitting at the main table, the one where everyone got to look at you, left me feeling like I was eating inside a fishbowl. Polite but ultimately meaningless conversation filled the event.

As dessert was being taken away, Ethel stood up to say a few words. "In my many years as minister, I've been fortunate to spend time with so many wonderful witches. Looking forward to the day the ministry changes hands, I feel a rush of excitement much like that of when I became the premier. For months now, I've heard your concerns that Michelle is too young and not connected enough to a clan. When I look at her actions, I find myself reassured that she will always put our greater well-being at the forefront of her every action. In the years between now and when she becomes premier, you'll have time to get to know her as I have, through her actions and her words. I think you'll find she's qualified and passionate about serving the witch community."

Ethel surveyed the crowd. "She doesn't respect tradition or traditional values. Those exact words were said about me. Today, no one would say those words. It's easy to think that because things were done one way in the past, that is the way they should be done moving forward. But time marches on, and so must we. I have every confidence she will strike the appropriate balance between progress and traditional values."

I kept a smile on my face as the crowd applauded. A few tables had the vigor I was sure Ethel had hoped for, but several were simply going through the motions. Ethel had voiced optimism. Looking at the uncertain faces in front me, I didn't feel Ethel's excitement. Winning them over would take more than speeches.

CHAPTER SIX

A throat cleared behind me. I turned to see Susanna.

She leaned over and whispered in my ear, "The premier needs you."

I smiled and excused myself from the group with a few polite words. I could feel eyes on me as we left the reception. I held my back ramrod straight and hoped I projected a lack of concern. I didn't want anyone here thinking something had gone wrong. The moment we were in the hall and away from prying ears, though, I asked, "What happened?"

Susanna shrugged. "I wasn't with the premier. I was told to bring you to her private conference room."

I didn't bother prying for more information. If Susanna knew, she wouldn't tell me. Ethel's aids were always loyal. In other circumstances, I would have admired that, but an unplanned meeting the last day of the convention sounded bad.

I couldn't help but reach over and fiddle with my engagement ring. Most likely someone had an issue with my relationship with an elf. Elron was the love of my life, and nothing any witch said would change that, but it wouldn't stop them from trying. Too many witches only wanted a premier who was involved with another witch. They all had their reasons, but it boiled down to a simple point. Cross-species matches weren't fertile, and to them, a relationship only worked if there was the potential for offspring. Neither Elron nor I were worried about that aspect of our family, but it bothered the witches, so it was our problem.

"I don't think that's it," Susanna said.

"Huh?" I stopped twisting my ring. "Sorry, I was lost in thought."

"I don't believe the elf is an issue at this point." Her voice was neutral.

"I thought you said you didn't know why Ethel summoned me."

Her eyes met mine for a moment. "I don't, but any complaints about the elf were silenced after you…" Her voice trailed off.

Maybe it was getting stronger, or maybe repetition had desensitized me, because this time the implication didn't hurt. "You can say it. It isn't a secret. Since I lost my power."

"That has been the topic at hand. Other… issues have fallen aside. Your romance with the elf never should have been an issue, since the position isn't hereditary, but when they were looking for something to disqualify you, it was easy pickings. However, things are different now." She pursed her lips. "My point is, the talk has been about your magical abilities, not your romance."

"Thank you." That was about all I could say.

After six months of rebuilding, I was a capable witch

again. Ultimately, capable was the problem. They had stories of me showing power most of them couldn't dream of. Capable wasn't what they wanted out of me. Legendary was, and that part of me had burned away with the last demons.

"In here." Susanna stopped beside a set of matte black doors.

The steel handle was cold, and I hoped it wasn't a sign of what was to come.

Inside, two camps were separated by a convention table. On the closest side, Ethel was flanked by two of her assistants. Across from Ethel sat a witch, her golden blonde hair slicked in a tidy ponytail, a suit jacket over her red silk blouse. Her eyes were cold as they assessed me.

Keeping my expression bland, I skipped to the witch next to her. Angie's smug smile didn't bring me any comfort. Down the table were two more witches, a man with short cropped auburn hair, and another woman who looked me up and down, her jaw length ash-brown hair as blunt and impactful as her stare.

Ethel motioned me to take the seat next to her, and Susanna to join the other assistants.

The soft leather of the chair did nothing to reduce my trepidation.

"Michelle, let me introduce you to Isadora, Angie, Zach, and Marquette. They have lodged a formal complaint stating you are unfit to be in the line of succession." Ethel tapped her fingers on a stack of papers. "The specific complaint is that you do not have the power to be the premier. As such, they have requested the right to test you through Trial by Magic. They requested your presence at our discussions."

Only the hours spent with Ethel and her team allowed me to keep a neutral expression. This had been one of the possible issues they'd mention, but Ethel had made it seem unlikely. "That's a very reasonable concern, and I understand the need for a speedy resolution to this charge."

"Excellent." Ethel gave the group across the table a feral smile. "Then we can begin negotiations."

"No," Isadora said.

The finality in her voice jerked my attention away from Ethel. The cold gaze that had been directed at me was now focused squarely on Ethel. Perhaps it was the way she leaned forward, or the calm with which she spoke, but something about her had the hairs on the back of my neck standing up.

"We put forth the proper challenge. We wish to follow through. There is nothing to negotiate."

Ethel leaned back in her chair. "Yes, the proper paperwork if you are a minister. You are not. In fact, not a one of you can claim that title. The minister to whom you, Isadora, owe your loyalty, is absent from this room but has had complaints lodged against her. Those complaints put many witches in an uncomfortable position, and just this morning, another complaint landed on my desk. What you did not submit was the proper paperwork for individuals seeking to verify the qualifications of a future premier."

I kept my mouth shut. There was nothing I could say that would be better than what Ethel had already said, and I really didn't want to complete Trial by Magic. Candidates for the position of the premier and minister had died in trials. Of the survivors, more than a few had received permanent injuries. I'd come close enough to dying and to having permanent damage that neither were situations I was eager to court.

Isadora stiffened. "Are you saying you will not hear our complaint because none of us are ministers?"

"I am saying you submitted incorrect paperwork."

Ethel pushed the stack of papers across the table. "I have, in fact, already had talks with ministers, and some of the clan members, who have voiced various concerns. On several occasions, the minister brought with them individuals whose views they did not support. However, those ministers still performed their duty to their clan and made sure those voices were heard. Perhaps you should be requesting a change in clan or leadership."

I sucked in a breath as silence descended upon the table. The deflection might put an end to this issue today, but if these witches and others truly believed I was incapable of fulfilling the role of premier, it would only delay their protest.

"I have no complaint against the minister." For the first time, there were flickers of doubt in Isadora's eyes. "I know of nothing in our laws that gives you the ability to refuse our request, made through a minister or not."

"I am required to hear your complaint. Not facilitate it." Those words were clipped. "I have heard and do not agree, but I am not unreasonable."

The flicker of hope I had been nursing that I wouldn't have to participate in the Trial by Magic died. Though, if this was done outside the truly proper channels, at least as far as the paperwork was concerned, maybe we would be able to set more parameters on the challenge.

"Now we can negotiate." Isadora smirked.

Ethel scooted a piece of paper in front of her and uncapped a pen. A spell brushed across my senses as the pen stood up and wrote the date into the corner of the page. Ethel dictated to it, creating a document to amend the incorrect paperwork to be of the right type and to include certain accommodations. When she got to that part, she paused and recapped the pen.

"Rather than the unlimited Trial by Magic you

proposed, I suggest something more elegant and more focused. A Test of Power." Ethel paused. "The test will take place in front of whoever wishes to attend. If we are to do this, it will be the only time you can request such a test from Ms. Oaks. Will that satisfy?"

Isadora snorted. "An untutored child could pass the Test of Power. Trial by Magic with one of us."

I swallowed, trying to ease the tightness in my throat.

Ethel locked eyes with Isadora. "To magical exhaustion. No killing, maiming, or spells designed to cause any type of lasting injury. You will both have the ability to end the match at any point, and will be personally shielded by two ministers whose names will be selected at random."

"You coddle her," Isadora said, sneering. "Remove the rules about any type of injury and replace them with serious injury. Her parents are both ministers and should be excluded from protecting either of us."

I sat there as they negotiated the parameters of a fight I wasn't sure I was prepared to wage. I was still healing, and I still had vulnerabilities, ones I didn't have before. But being premier was more than a desk job to me. It was an opportunity to help witches and give them more freedom to live and work away from their clan.

Ethel had picked me to be her successor, but she had never promised it would be an easy path. If I truly want to be premier, this would only be the first of many tests, and likely one of the easiest. Well, not that it was going to be easy, but a fight was relatively simple compared to mediating clan disputes and trying to create fair policies.

"Both her parents and your minister will be removed from the pool of potential protectors. The rule about no spells designed to cause any lasting harm stands." Ethel said firmly.

"Agreed." Isadora raked her eyes across me. "That is, if your heir is willing to fight me."

Ignoring my trepidation, I nodded. "I'm ready." I'd hoped to see uncertainty, or even a hint of concern about the upcoming fight, but Isadora simply closed her eyes and bowed her head.

Ethel checked her watch. "Our closing ceremony is due to start in two hours. Plenty of time to refit the area for a Trial by Magic and spread the word. Isadora, I suggest you begin your preparations. Kathy, my assistant will remain with you to ensure clear communications." Ethel lifted her hand, and a square woman stepped forward.

Isadora and the rest of her group stood up. "We thank you for your just consideration of our petition." Her eyes locked with mine. "I'll see you in two hours."

They filed out, Kathy following closely. The door clicked shut behind them, and Ethel sighed. "You have my apologies. I was afraid if I didn't grant their request they would cause more trouble."

"Likely so, but now I have a duel to prepare for." I tried to keep my voice even, but I was more than a little displeased. Healed was different from ready for a duel, and no matter how polite Trial by Magic sounded, it would be a fight between Isadora and me.

Ethel tapped her fingers on the desk. "It would be ideal if you won, but a good showing should be enough to convince any doubters that you still have magic and can do more than party tricks."

"Thanks. I'll keep that in mind."

Ignoring my sarcasm, Ethel turned to address her remaining aid. "Bring Michelle's parents to my sitting room."

Great. Now they could worry too. They'd been at my side for months now, and this was supposed to be the beginning of me standing on my own again—as a healed witch.

"You'll want to prepare. My suite will be best. No one will pester you." Ethel moved surprisingly fast for a woman of her age and was halfway to the door. She looked at me with a raised eyebrow. "Are you coming?"

I hurried after her, not sure that I really had a choice.

I took a deep breath, held it, and let it out. It did nothing to slow the rapid pace of my heart.

From the stage wing, I could see the tightly packed crowd and Ethel approaching the podium. Opposite me, Isadora watched Ethel with a slight smirk, as if she already knew how this was going to end. I wished I shared her confidence. Instead, my palms were sweaty, and I kept fiddling with the wand sheath strapped to my leg. The elven bracelet I always wore was missing. Apparently, its ability to summon my wand to my hand gave me an unfair advantage.

"Before this convention comes to an end, there is one piece of business that must be addressed." Ethel paused and the crowd fell silent. Word of the trial must've spread, because I could feel the eagerness in the room. "Michelle Oaks and Isadora Baker will display their abilities in a Trial by Magic!"

Ethel's showmanship was paying off. The crowd had pressed forward, and whispers hastily passed back and forth. Taking advantage of the noise, Dad leaned close. "Remember, you don't have the stamina to outlast someone. You need to hit hard and fast. End it before you can become fatigued."

Ethel turned toward the other stage wing. "In a fight to

magical exhaustion, I present the challenger, Isadora of the Gos clan!"

Isadora tilted her chin up and swaggered onto the stage.

"And the challenged, Michelle Oaks of the Wapiti and Docga!"

That was my cue. I strode onto the stage, hoping my carriage projected confidence.

"Be careful," Mom warned me.

Already in view of the crowd, I didn't respond. As I crossed the stage to stand next to Ethel, I made eye contact with the audience. I don't know what I had hoped to see, but the eagerness was unnerving. They wanted to see this fight, whether because they viewed it as good sport or because they wanted to see me prove my magic, I couldn't say. I could give the good showing Ethel had requested.

Ethel levitated a crystal bowl next to the podium. "Two protectors will be selected at random for each participant. Ministers close to each witch have been removed from the pool." Ethel stuck her hand in the bowl and pulled out two small cards. "Latasha Farrer of the Haedus and Ingrid Burch of the Kamelos will serve as Isadora's protectors."

They were respected witches, perhaps a bit fond of tradition, but hopefully that would motivate them to be fair and honest. Ethel's hand moved back to the bowl and I held my breath.

Ethel read the cards. "Vera Allard of the Tructa and Kim Scotcher of the Aap will serve as Michelle's protectors."

I released the breath I'd been holding. Perhaps not who I would've preferred, but from my dealings with them, I was sure they would do their job honestly.

The four minsters made their way to the stage. Latasha

and Ingrid went to Isadora. Vera smiled at me, and Kim bowed her head before they flanked me. I knew what came next, so I released most of my shields. The entire room filled with a press of magic, little spells for perfecting makeup or covering a ketchup stain. Larger spells that helped make the convention accessible to the deaf or blind shone in bright gold shimmers coating the room.

"The protectors will now link to their duelist's pool of magic and create a skintight shield around them. If magic breaches the shield, the match will be paused until it can be restored."

Kim held out a hand. As soon as our fingers touched, I could feel their spell sliding through my mind and hooking into my well of power. Just as quickly, their presence was gone, but I could still feel the spell as a faint point of discomfort. That spell wasn't normally there, and it was odd brushing against it when I reached for my power.

I rebuilt my shields and added a little extra to the outer one. Ethel hadn't prohibited mental attacks, so I wanted to be prepared. While I was focused inward, power flared across my skin. The magic raised the hairs on my arms as it formed a layer on my skin. A fraction of a second later, it had quieted down, but the press of the spell and the lack of sensation it created were constant reminders that I was fully encased.

"Isadora, Michelle, take your places in the circle."

Ethel was undoubtedly speaking just as loudly as she had before, but for some reason, her voice sounded far away. I turned, and the stage behind me had been completely transformed.

A spell had changed it from wood planking to something from one of those fight shows. The blue pad that covered the area was bordered by posts and ropes. A section was open, and Isadora was already taking her place on a yellow dot in one corner. I went to the opposite corner, marked with green.

I took a steadying breath. I had a plan.

"Draw wands."

Isadora's arrogant smile fell away, replaced with cold eyes and determination.

Tugging my wand out of the sheath, I ran through the spells I wanted to cast. If I could get off a spell first, I might be able to get ahead of Isadora. If not, I'd be seeing the exact extent of my magic reserves.

A red orb floated to the center of the ring. "The match will begin when the orb turns green."

Looking past it, I focused on Isadora. She was my target.

The orb turned green.

I yanked my wand up. "*Algiz*."

As magical ropes fought to bring Isadora's arms down to her sides, I was lifted into the air. Her wand dipped down, and my feet brushed the floor. At some point, I was coming down, and the mats didn't look like they'd prevent injury. The pads might not be enough, but I could soften the wood under them. "*Orzu*."

Isadora flicked her wand upwards.

I bit back a scream as I launched ten feet in the air. It didn't matter if I was levitating, I had to do better. "*Algiz*." This round of bindings had targets: her wand hand, eyes, and mouth.

While she fought the magical ropes, I attacked the source of my levitation issue. This spell took more power, but I had hopes it would be worth it. "*Esaz Sowil*."

The spell snapped into place, blocked all outgoing magic. The levitation spell failed.

I fell. The combination of the pads and softening spell absorbed the impact, and I managed to land on my feet.

The ropes were trying their best to fulfill the task I'd set them, but Isadora kept struggling. They'd managed to cover her eyes and go across her mouth, but they still didn't have full control of her wand.

I started casting the next spell, but a surge of magic distracted me. The one way containment spell collapsed as ice formed around me. I was encased in inch thick ice. Narzel fart.

Isadora shed the ropes and began to sketch runes in the air.

Picturing the ice cracking and falling away from me, I pushed magic into the spell and prepared another. A ribbon of magic shot out of my wand as soon as it was free.

It darted across the ring and destroyed Isadora's runes.

Hoping she was a witch who needed to see her target, I cast another spell. "*Gebo*." A heavy fog coated the ring.

A wall of flames surrounded me as it burned off the fog. So much for Isadora needing to see her target. The flames were easy enough to deal with. "*Ansu Dagaz*."

As the wall of flames extinguished, their absence triggered another spell. Before I could get a probe out, a containment bubble like the one I'd used on Isadora snapped shut around me.

Tamping down the surge of panic, I got to work unmaking the spell. Partway through, my feet felt cold. Taking my attention away from unmaking the spell, I looked down to see the sphere filling with water. It hadn't come over the top of my boots yet, but it wouldn't be long.

I went back to work on dismantling the containment spell. That would take care of the water problem, but the closer I got to unraveling the spell, the more quickly water filled the space. It was lapping against my chin when I undid the last bit of the shield spell. The sphere vanished, and the water flooded across the ring.

Isadora wasn't in her corner. I glanced around the ring twice before looking up.

"Join me, if you can." She lifted her wand to the sky.

Afraid she would rain boulders down on me, I quickly cast a shield over my head.

A ball of light appeared. I had to look away, trying to blink spots out of my eyes. A wall of air hit my back, throwing me forward. I landed on my hands and knees, but the pressure only intensified. As my arms shook, I formed a layer of magic between myself and the wall. The plan was to shove enough power into the spell that it pushed the wall of air away and I could get to my feet.

My arms started to shake more. I gathered power, only now realizing how little I had left, and shoved it into the spell. It shot up toward the ceiling. The force shoving me into the floor didn't change.

My arms gave out, and I caught myself on my elbows. The probes I sent out hadn't found anything, but there had to be a spell.

"Do you concede?" Isadora shouted.

Rather than reply, I stretched the probes out to the floor below me. The spell had to be close by. Water lapped at my fingers and then wrist. I opened my eyes to see three inches of water. She was going to keep me here until the challenge was called in her favor or I gave up.

My probes brushed against a containment spell, one designed to hold the water close to me. That I could deal with. I unmade it with a few muttered runes, and the water dispersed. Though that didn't help me get off the floor.

"What about better motivation?" Isadora said.

"No, please no." My mom begged. "Gretchen, Mom, don't do this." Then she screamed.

A lifetime wouldn't be enough time to forget my mother being tortured. I closed my eyes, trying to hold back tears and ignoring the ongoing torture scene. I had to stay focused.

The probes hadn't found anything, so I looked inside myself. What was left of my magic looked clear. The link from Vera and Kim appeared to be functioning properly. Moving outward, the next spell I encountered was the barrier from Vera and Kim. It too seemed undamaged, but it was coated in a spell that altered how gravity affected me. It was unlike anything I'd seen before.

"*Nazid*," I whispered. The levitation spell worked, and the pull on my body reduced until it required hardly any effort for me to maintain my position. Now, I had to counter Isadora's spell before she realized what I'd done.

Examining it again, and with more attention, I found two weak points. I focused on them and shoved magic in until the spell exploded.

For a moment, the backlash traveled toward Isadora, but then it reversed and headed for me. I shoved every bit of power I had left into shields. It burned through them. I closed my eyes and braced for impact. Not again.

The skintight shield around me flared so brightly I could see it through my eyelids. It absorbed the backlash before it could reach me.

The glow dispersed. I was fine. It hadn't hit me, hadn't burned through me like the last backlash. I could still win this.

I reached for my magic but came up empty. I didn't even have enough magic to light a candle.

"Isadora is the victor." Ethel's words hung in the air for a moment before the crowd erupted.

I bit the inside of my cheek, trying to hold back tears as cheers attempted to drown out the dissatisfied boos. A sizable portion of the crowd clapped politely. Time seemed to slow down, forcing me to see every disappointed or overjoyed face in the audience and fake a polite expression until Ethel finished her statements and I could escape.

CHAPTER SEVEN

The entire drive home, Ethel's parting words echoed through my mind. "A good showing, but not the definitive victory we had hoped to see. Still, they saw your power, more than many in audience. It will be enough."

Hardly the most inspiring words. I especially liked the last bit. Not that it was enough, but the implication that Ethel would find a way to make it work for us.

My loss had given substance to the rumors that my power was permanently diminished. Instead of having to show why I would be a good premier and how I was being prepared for the position, we now had to deal with more questions of power. All I'd done in that fight was set us back, something I could've done without lifting a wand.

As I turned onto a gravel road, I tried to find a positive. I'd proved I had power and could use it?

Maybe, but that was unlikely to be enough.

I sighed as I parked. Things would look better tomorrow. I grabbed my bag from the back seat and headed to my apartment. A night away from witches and witch problems would give me better perspective.

A small feeling of normality washed over me as I unlocked my door. I set my bags down and flopped onto the couch. Home. Finally, I was home.

The tension I had carried for the last three days drained out of me. I had a full six months until the next convention, and not a single scheduled appearance between. The weight of being heir apparent to the position of the premier would be reduced to meetings with my mom, Ethel, and a few of the prominent witches. Compared to the frantic preparations for the fall convention, it would be a delightful vacation.

The soft sound of the door opening was followed by soft words. "Michelle? The lodge said you were home."

I push myself up. "Hey, you."

Elron leaned against the doorway, his silver hair pulled back in a braid, leaving his pointed ears bare. "You look tired." He stepped inside my apartment.

Covering a yawn, I nodded. "I may not be good company tonight."

He smiled as he crossed the room. "I planned for that." He leaned over the back of the couch and pressed a kiss against my forehead.

"Mind reader," I teased.

Elron shook his head. "You showed me your itinerary. I'm afraid to ask how many awake charms you've used in the past few days."

I winced.

"I suspected as much." He circled on the couch and offered me his hand. "I have dinner ready in my apartment. I brewed an herbal tea just for you, and if you do not want to think about the convention, we can talk about anything or nothing."

I let him tug me to my feet and followed him to his apartment. "Tomorrow is going to be brutal. I don't know why I thought I could do the convention and then go back to work the next day." Especially now that I was out of magic. A good night's sleep would help restore me, but it would be a few days until I was fully recharged.

"I presume that is a rhetorical statement." He held open the door for me.

"You presume correctly." I stepped in his apartment.

The lights were dimmed, though it wasn't so dark as to encourage sleep. Two blue candles graced the table, the cheerful flames brightening the room. Elron motioned toward a chair. "Your tea is already there," he said.

The thick ceramic mug was delightfully warm in my hands, and the barley tea inside was the perfect drinking temperature. By the time Elron brought over the food, I could feel the day's tension slipping away. The salad was refreshing after days of convention food.

"How many departments have signed a new contract?" Elron asked.

"Six, actually five. Union County never canceled their contract." I refilled my cup of tea. "I'm hoping that given a few weeks of solid performance, I can sign a few more departments. Plus, now that I've made my first public appearances as premier in training, I should start to receive a stipend for those duties."

"Do you have any work lined up, or will you be waiting for a phone call?"

"Both. I have plenty of disenchanting to do, and if there's a call for help, I'll be there." I sighed. "Rodriguez and I worked together fine. I haven't been on a job with my other clients. It's been a while since I worked with them, and I'm a little different. I don't know if they'll trust me like they did before."

Elron leaned forward. "They rehired you because they trust you. They know how much you helped their departments in the past, and they have confidence you will do so now. You worked hard to regain your abilities. Have confidence in yourself and in them."

I slid my hands under his. "I know, but it's not easy. I spent hours coming up with answers to their questions. The truth is, I don't want to talk about what happened. I don't want to think about what I could've done better or what I did wrong. I just want to move forward."

"Then tell them it's not pertinent to the case. Be polite, but firm. They don't have a right to know everything about you. Ultimately, you're a consultant, not an employee. As long as you do the job ethically, you've fulfilled your part of the contract. The officers who were truly your friends have come to visit you. They know what happened, and they understand. They're on your side."

"Thank you. Hearing that helps." A knot of worry eased. "How have you been? We didn't get a chance to talk while I was at the convention."

"I acquired a new plant for the university." A smile slowly spread across his face as he talked about the plant and how his students were managing with the collection of magical flora.

I stopped thinking about tomorrow and today and simply enjoyed the rest of the evening. Little by little, the worries faded, but even Elron's company couldn't erase the challenge and how I'd failed Ethel and myself.

"Would you like to go out to dinner tomorrow night?" Elron smiled tentatively. "I already made reservations at Italian Flair."

"I'd like a date night." I reached across the table and squeezed his hand. "I haven't spent nearly enough time with you lately. Too many lessons."

"Dinner it is." His shoulders relaxed.

As evening slid by, I enjoyed the most relaxing night I'd had in the past month, all thanks to Elron.

That night before I went to bed, I visited the altar behind the lodge. I gave thanks for the many gifts I'd received, the return of my powers, the love of a man like Elron, and the incredible family I discovered over the past year. I lit a candle for the officers I hadn't been able to save, my friends who had died, and the strangers who I had learned more about in death than in life.

With the earth beneath me, and the moon bright in the sky, I prayed for me. I prayed my failures wouldn't harm those around me. I prayed for the ability to save the people I loved from harm and heartache.

I prayed I was witch enough.

Dawn broke while I sat outside, sipping a warm cup of tea. Neither the earth nor the moon had held answers for my prayers. Prayers where I asked to be enough for me, even if I couldn't be enough to be the premier. Losing the challenge with Isadora felt like losing my position, my past sacrifices coming back to shape my future.

For a moment, the clouds shifted, one taking on the shape of a paw print, backlit by the yellow-orange of the morning sun.

Even if the witches found fault in me, the police didn't. Diminished as I was, I could still do my job with them. Oaks Consulting would always be there for me, and through it, I could save lives and do my small part to bridge the gap between the witches and the rest of the world. But, having seen how much more I could do as premier, would that satisfy me?

The sun broke through the clouds, and my phone rang.

"Oaks Consulting, this is Michelle," I answered as the sun began burning away the fog that drifted around trees and hung over the garden.

"You have to get here. They're making me leave, and I don't know what to do."

I checked the number, which I didn't recognize. "Susanna, what happened? Why aren't you calling from your phone?" Dread coiled in my gut. "Can I speak to Ethel?"

The piercing shriek of a siren filtered over the line. "The car... so much fire." Susanna's voice cracked. "They say I have to get in the ambulance. Michelle, you need to be here."

"Where? Where are you? Where's Ethel?"

The line went dead.

I swore and redialed the number. It went directly to voice mail. I swore again as I scooped up my mug and darted to the lodge. The path had to be twice as long as it had been when I walked out this morning. The door swung open before I reached it, as did my apartment door.

"Thank you, lodge." My heart thundered as I dumped out the tea. What had happened to cause a fire? Where was Ethel? Who could I call to get better information? And why couldn't I find my left shoe? I'd had a left shoe last night. It had to be here.

I got down on my hands and knees to peer under the bed. The Narzel-blasted thing had managed to slide nearly two feet back. My fingers had just brushed the shoe when my phone rang.

I snagged the loop on the back and lunged for my phone. "Hello?"

"Michelle, it's Rodriguez." He sounded grim.

With the phone wedged between my ear and my shoulder, I yanked on my shoes. "If this is a case, I can't. There's been an emergency—"

"Michelle, if—"

"Have you heard any reports about something happening to the premier? Or about a large fire?" I finished lacing my shoes. All I needed now were my purse and keys.

"The Cherokee County Sheriff's Department would like to inform you that an incident involving the premier has been reported, and you are listed as an emergency contact." Rodriguez finished in a rush.

I froze. "What kind of incident? Susanna wasn't coherent on the phone."

Rodriguez hesitated. "A car accident. So far, we have not been able to locate the premier."

"Tell me where you are. I'll be right there." I snagged a piece of paper and pen.

"That's not a good idea."

"I can help you find her. I need to help." I bit my lip to force the tears back. "Please."

He sighed. "Don't do this to yourself."

"I have to." Because if anything happened to her, I was next in line, and I wasn't ready to be the premier, not after losing a challenge, not when so few witches believed in me.

"It's in the northbound lanes on I-575, right before Exit 7." He sighed. "It's a fresh scene. I was called in when they identified the premier's vehicle and haven't done an evaluation, but it doesn't look like magic was the cause. I'm not sure what you can do."

That sucked all the moisture out of my mouth. "I have to try. If nothing else, I can help you locate Ethel. You're always telling me it's surprising how far people can wander away from a crash." I couldn't think about the other reasons they would have trouble locating Ethel.

"Michelle, listen—"

"I'll be there soon." I hung up. He could fuss at me when I got there.

The drive couldn't go fast enough. Especially since the best way to the accident was south on the highway, only to exit, get back on, and head back north. Between one moment and the next, the drive crawled by, even though my car assured me I was going the speed limit, until I reached the accident. From my spot in the right lane, I could see a tractor-trailer jackknifed across the northbound lanes and the plumes of smoke.

I focused on the road.

Two miles later, a sign proclaiming EXIT AHEAD sped by. I bit my lip to hold back tears as I got off the highway.

The wait at the lights to get back on, this time heading north, lasted at least a year. The image of the smoke and the tractor-trailer hung in my mind. As bad as it had looked from across the highway, it was going to be worse up close. Ethel's car was in there. Cars and big trucks didn't mix well.

Ethel had to be okay. I wasn't ready to be minister. The clans weren't ready for the transition. She had to be okay.

The light turned green. Seconds later, I realized the longest part of the drive wasn't coming south but back north in all the traffic trying to get around the accident. Twice I had to slam on the brakes, narrowly avoiding rear ending the car in front of me.

Distantly, I knew I shouldn't be driving, but it was too late to stay home now.

The only small blessing in this part of the drive was how little I could see past the wall of cars. Not that it stopped my visions of how the jack-knifed truck and car had collided.

Time crawled by as slowly as the traffic. Inch by inch, I crept closer.

Half an hour later, police cars with flashing lights blocked off the exit ramp and the far right lane. My eyes locked on the crash for a fraction of a second before I focused on the road ahead of me. When I wasn't driving, I could look.

The remaining traffic slowly edged around the back of the tractor trailer. I stopped behind a police car and held up the ID Cherokee County had given me last week. The officer frowned at it before waving me around. I thanked him and drove onto a wide shoulder, careful to keep my eyes on the grass in front of me. Only a few car lengths later, I parked behind a highway patrol car.

Keys in hand, I got out, and this time I had to look.

The truck stretched from the right lane of the highway, across a sizable gap to the exit lane, to where its nose was planted firmly against the side of a car. It was hard to tell how bad the initial impact had been, as the car's previous bright blue paint had peeled off from the heat of the fire. That same fire had shattered the windows and consumed the interior. Both the truck and car smoldered, even with the fire department dumping water on them. Another sedan with its front driver's side crumpled had gone off the shoulder before hitting a tree.

I stood next to my car, knees locked, tears silently dripping down my face. How could Ethel have survived that? How had anyone survived? Was Ethel missing because they couldn't identify her body?

Could I identify her body?

"Michelle, I told you not to come." Rodriguez stepped between me and the accident.

I brushed the tears away and did my best to pretend I hadn't been crying. "I thought you might need a witch."

He sighed and rubbed his temple. "You had to see it, didn't you?"

Not sure I trusted my voice, I nodded.

Rodriguez studied me. "Fine. You can stay, but you have to be here officially. I've found traces of magic but can't identify what they're for. Walk the scene with me and tell me what you can about the magic."

"Deal." I rubbed at my eyes again. It was one thing for Rodriguez to see me crying. He was a friend. Not everyone here would be, and they needed to see me as a professional. If only I felt professional.

He turned and pointed at the truck. "The reconstruction people are still working on what happened. So far, it looks like a car, whose owner hasn't been identified, cut off the truck. It swerved to avoid the car. It seems like the truck driver lost control and swerved several times, eventually going sideways and impacting the premier's car as it tried to exit the highway. Susanna said her car clipped the back of the premier's car before going off the road."

"Got it." From where the cars were, that made sense, though it was hard to see why the truck had swerved enough to lose control.

"Susanna and the rest of the people in her car have a few broken bones between them, but nothing more serious. She says they got out and raced to the premier's car. Before they could reach it, it burst into flames. By the time first responders got here, Susanna was the only coherent one. Two were in shock, and another passed out." Rodriguez glanced over at me. "She claims no one left the premier's car."

My throat tightened. She couldn't be dead. We had a plan, and her dying today didn't fit that plan. "But you told me Ethel is missing."

He nodded. "We found the bodies of a driver and a

person in the backseat. Susanna said three people were in that car. The medical examiner wasn't willing to say anything officially, but from an unofficial first look, they aren't the premier."

Two dead. Two witches I knew and had worked with for months. Two more funerals for people who should've had more life to live. This time I couldn't blame a demon, just really horrible luck. "So, unofficially, where's the premier?"

"We don't know. A bystander claims they saw a woman matching Ethel's description go into the woods." He started walking toward the car wedged against a tree. "Maybe she got out and wandered off. It's been known to happen. Maybe fire reacts oddly with old witch bones. Maybe she wasn't in the car."

I clenched my jaw against more tears. Neither of us had time for that. "What do you think?"

"Don't know." He tucked his hands in his pockets. "Susanna says the premier was in the car and didn't get out. We're working under the theory that Susanna may have missed her and Ethel wandered off. Unless you have a reason we should refocus our efforts."

That question forced me to think through the options in gruesome detail. My mind couldn't resist creating images of Ethel trapped in a flaming car. "Fire and magic can react unpredictably, but bone is bone. If you haven't found her body, I doubt she was in the car. Susanna doesn't have a reason to lie, but she could be confused from the accident. I have the number for their hotel. Someone there might be able to verify that Ethel left in that car."

"We got a name from Susanna, and an officer is following up. We have officers searching the surrounding areas. So far, no sign of her. That's all we can do for now."

"Thank you." It hurt to push the words out. "Even if… even if the outcome isn't… just—thank you."

"We'll find her, Michelle. One way or another, we'll get an answer."

"I know." That didn't stop me from being afraid of the answer. With the sun morning-bright, the earth dew-covered, and the trees quiet without a breeze, I prayed. Please, please, aid and guide Ethel. See her safely back to me.

Please, don't make me premier just yet.

CHAPTER EIGHT

"I can tell there's magic, but haven't the faintest idea what it was intended to do," Rodriguez continued in a business tone. "Can you look around?"

I wanted to say no, so I didn't have to see which spells had failed to save Ethel's life. Instead, I said, "Yes."

"Can we link so I can see what you see?" He held out a hand.

Even if I hadn't been connected to the victim, linking would've been prudent. As it was, letting him peer through my eyes was the only thing that would give my observations weight if they were needed for legal reasons. I clasped hands and switched my vision so we could see magic.

Rodriguez hissed.

Magic decorated the accident like a macabre painting. On Susanna's car, the remains of shattered protection spells lay splintered across the front. Inside, spells repelling dirt and other minor works were still functioning. At least this part of the crash appeared simple enough, magically speaking.

The same couldn't be said for the road. Fractured parts

of spells were scattered across the highway leading up to the trailer and along the length of it. After that, the magic vanished. Not because that area hadn't been touched by spells. I was sure Ethel's car had carried more than its share of magic. But magic didn't mix well with fire or water, and that area had seen both. What the fire hadn't destroyed, the water had washed away.

"Can we get a closer look at the traces on the road?" Rodriguez asked.

"Sure." Still linked, we approached a slick of magic near the police cars holding back traffic.

Visually, it was nothing more than a twisted fragment of magic. Given a bit of time, it would be absorbed back into the earth. Since I needed more information, I spun out a slender strand of my own power and lowered the probe over the spell. A sensation of regulation and speed came back.

Frowning, I touched the probe to the spell, tracing what structure was left. A bit to maintain, and a bit to know what to maintain. Someone had been using the magical equivalent of cruise control.

Before I could remove the probe, the spell twisted, closing back up into a functional spell for keeping pressure on an object. Likely, the original spell had used pressing on the gas pedal as a speed control method, and it had reverted to the simplest version of what it was supposed to be.

"Did you see that?" I asked.

"Weird." Rodriguez tilted his head. "I've seen similar spells, but none that morphed."

"Same, but given how it got here, I'm surprised it had some life left." I eyed it again. "Should I clean it? I don't want it getting stuck to an unsuspecting car."

"Please."

It only took a moment to shred the spell and watch the energy drift into the earth. Good riddance.

The next bits of magic didn't have enough left to identify, even for me. I sent those into the earth as well. After three more, with little more information than that they'd absorbed some extra energy from the crash and were rather active for spell fragments, Rodriguez called a halt.

He dropped out of the link between us and blinked as his vision went back to normal.

The change didn't bother me much, but I put effort into not seeing magic all the time. As a hedge-practitioner, Rodriguez couldn't see magic without help. I put my shields back up, and the sight of the crash overwhelmed me again. Melted plastic coated the ground by Ethel's car, the bright blue paint replaced by a coating of soot and scorch marks.

"How are you doing?"

I closed my eyes and shook my head. "Don't ask. If I think about what I'm doing, I won't be able to do it."

"Then I won't ask."

The shock and grief hadn't set in yet, not really. But it would soon, and I needed to be back home before then. "You mentioned tracking Ethel?"

"Do you think you could? We don't have any items of hers."

"Maybe. I need a few things from my car."

The walk gave me time to push my feelings back. I could feel after finding Ethel. Until then, this was business.

The tracking charm I got from my kit, an unassuming wood disk with runes etched around an opaque stone, usually needed a tie to the object it was tracking. I didn't have an item, so I had to get creative, and I carefully cast a spell linking the tracking charm to another spell.

From there, I told the spell of Ethel, a witch past her

three-hundredth year who dressed in bright colors and kept her hair in a bun. I told it of her keen wit, sharp eye, strength, and kindness. I told of who Ethel was and sent the stack of spells into the world with orders to lead me to her. The spells connected, and the tracking charm turned bubble-gum pink.

It pulled magic out of me as it raced away, streaking north. As the distance grew, first to that of a long walk, and then to a distance she couldn't have covered on foot, I fed more power into the spell. Then, between me and the lodge, the tracking spell faltered. From this distance, there wasn't much I could do other than shove more magic into it, which I did. For a moment, the spell stabilized, but then it dissolved into nothing.

"Anything?" Rodriguez asked.

Before answering, I switched my vision to see magic. The spell was well and truly gone. Little flecks of magic drifted to the ground, but nothing was left of the spell. Even the charm was gray and dull.

"Narzel blast it!" The spell had the power it needed to keep searching. So why had it shattered? "Either the tracking spell was blocked, or it hit an unrelated spell that disrupted it."

"Can you try again?"

"I could. I'm not sure it will matter." I tossed the ruined charm in my trunk. "When the spell shattered, it was searching more than ten miles north of here. Ethel didn't get that far on foot, so either the spell was looking for old traces of her, or she's in a car."

"Ten miles north? We sent everyone to the hospital in Canton." His brow wrinkled. "But none of them were Ethel. No one remembers seeing her walk away." He left off the part about the horribly burned car.

"The spell likely locked onto her things at the lodge.

She's been staying there on and off and has taken to keeping additional clothing and supplies in her room." The words tasted bitter, because if I was right, they'd eventually find what little was left of her in the car.

"I'd hoped…" He shook his head. "You should head home. We cleared the traces of magic. Our job is done."

"If you're sure." While we were working, I'd managed to switch from shock to practical working witch. I didn't want to lose that feeling. I didn't want to grieve yet. If I mourned for her, I would be accepting her death.

"Go home, Michelle. Have Elron come home and give you a big hug." Rodriguez closed the trunk of my car and opened the driver's side door. "I don't know when the department will call you again, but you need to rest."

"All I've done lately is rest and mourn. Work was supposed to put an end to those activities." One of the many reasons I'd been so eager to return to work.

"Go home, Michelle." He shut the door.

By sheer will, I kept my composure as an officer stopped traffic to let me leave. The road twisted and turned. I blocked out everything but driving. The earth had to be looking out for me because I got all the way to my apartment before breaking down.

This couldn't be. The deal had been clear. I had years before I would be premier. That way, I could have a life of my own, running my business with Elron at my side before we became the center of witch attention.

Sitting on my sofa, with soft mid-morning sun streaming through the window, I cried. I cried for me. I cried for how selfish I was to cry for myself when three people were dead and others injured. I cried for the other witches, who'd helped me so much over the past few months. Then, then I cried for Ethel, a strong woman with an eye toward the future. Rough kindness hiding behind sharp words and blinding colors. I cried because I didn't know if she'd left behind family. If so, she'd never spoken of them. If not, it was being premier that had stood in her way.

When my tears ran out, I dried my eyes and had my first clear thought in an hour. Mom needed to know. Planning the funeral and smoothing over the transitions would fall to her.

The phone rang three times before mom answered. "Hey, Mom."

"Michelle." She cleared her throat. "I was about to call you."

"I know." The last thing I wanted was to hear the news again. "I was at the crash site not long ago."

"Ah. I just listened to a message from Susanna. You know how reception is here. I missed the call, and when I tried to call her back, she didn't answer. I wish she'd mentioned talking to you." The words came out in a rush.

"Are you okay?" Because I wasn't. This wasn't the plan. This wasn't how I wanted my life to go.

Mom told someone on her end of the call that she needed a minute. "I will be. There's a lot to do, and the individuals most capable are in the hospital, which complicates matters."

"It does," I choked out.

"But, Michelle, as much as it hurts, as much as we'll all miss her, we knew this day would come. At 328, Ethel was far older than most witches. As unnatural as this is, it's the natural cycle." Mom cleared her throat again. "Susanna wasn't clear in the message. Was it an accident, or did it look intentional?"

As messy as the crash had been, I wasn't altogether sure how it could've been anything but an accident. "I found some magic, but nothing out of place. Car accidents aren't my usual work, but no one said anything about it being intentional."

"Small blessings and all that." Mom exhaled heavily. "Will you be okay alone? Should I have Landa sit with you?"

"I'd rather be alone. Ethel's de—" I couldn't say it. "We thought we had time, and we don't. I'll go out to the altar. Pray, meditate, and figure out how to tell Elron."

"If you need anything, I'm a phone call away," Mom said.

I couldn't help but smile. "I know, and I love you."

"Love you, too."

I ended the call. Around me, the room filled with memories. Sitting on the sofa as Ethel drilled the names of every minister into my head or quizzed me on policy. Suddenly, the walls were too close.

Outside, I watched the play of light as a cloud slid over the sun. As much as I cared for Ethel, her plan hadn't been without fault. A multi-year campaign and transition could be more difficult for witches than a sudden change in power. Perhaps some good would come from this tragedy. It was time for me to step out of the shadows and let myself be seen.

CHAPTER NINE

My phone landed on the grass next to me. As nice as it would've been to disconnect, today wasn't the day to be out of reach. The altar, a six-foot-long slab of stone laying across two pillars of stacked rock, didn't seem to mind the technology. Around me, the trees swayed in the wind. Any other day, I would consider it a cheerful sound, but today it had an undertone of sorrow. Their last dance with the air before winter killed their vigor.

I knelt with only a thin blanket between myself and the earth, just enough of a barrier to prevent stains on my pants. Closing my eyes, I inhaled. A wave of sorrow rose up, but with it came a knot of tangled emotions. I knew this tangle like I knew an old friend. Every time a colleague or bystander died and magic was related, a version of this reared its ugly head.

I should've done more.
I could've saved them.
It's my fault for not being a better witch.
If only I was a better witch.

If only I was less selfish, I wouldn't think of me rather than of them.

I let each one of those thoughts come to the surface, where I could battle emotions with logic. Each time I fought this battle, it was both easier and harder. This time, I couldn't have done more or saved them. But I had thought of myself first. And I already missed Ethel.

My phone rang, shattering my focus. "This better be important." I took a breath and forced a professional voice. "Oaks Consulting. This is Michelle."

"It's Natalie." She started saying something else, but a large crash and what sounded like glass breaking on her end of the line drowned out her words.

"Can you repeat that? I couldn't hear you." I closed my eyes and focused on her words, trying to ignore the strange yowls coming across the phone line.

"Magic went wrong! Can you come help?" She swore loudly. Then, I heard a muffled yelp from someone on the other end of the phone.

"Are you at the store?" I grabbed the blanket as I bolted toward the lodge. Grief and reflections would have to wait.

"Yes, hurry!" There was another crash, and she hung up.

It only took a moment to grab my purse before I sprinted to my car. I brushed away any lingering tears before starting the car and heading out.

It was only a few miles, but that was plenty of time for me to worry. As much as I wanted to think this wouldn't take long, I simply didn't believe that to be true. Natalie was a capable witch in her own right. I'd been buying my supplies out of her shop for years, and she serviced some of my equipment as well as supplied my father's clan. But there were plenty of things in her store that could cause trouble on their own or when mixed with something else. Plus, whatever had happened was clearly past her ability to manage, which hardly inspired confidence that I'd be able to fix it in a hurry.

I turned into her parking lot and was surprised to see only three cars in front of the faded brick building. I parked in a space well away from the door, pocketed my keys, and rushed inside.

The door opened easily enough, but the entryway was blocked by an opaque, magical barrier. I probed it and found a simple one-way gate spell that would allow me to enter but wouldn't allow anything to leave. A more thorough probe reassured me that there weren't any hidden spells. It was the simple barrier it appeared to be, and I was confident I could unmake it if I needed to escape. For now, I assumed the spell was in place to contain whatever was going on inside the building.

With a twist of my wrist, I felt the familiar weight of my wand settle into my hand. Now that I was properly armed, I stepped through the barrier, feeling the magic slide across my skin and leave behind tingly nerves. Before my eyes could make sense of what I was seeing, I heard the same strange yowls I'd heard across the phone. They were followed by a shouting, female voice, the sound of glass shattering, and the angry hiss of flames.

Blinking rapidly, I took in the overturned shelves, the herbs strewn across the floor amongst glass shards, and the liquids splattered everywhere. On my left, the corner that usually housed purified cloth was an inferno, sending flames all the way to the ceiling. A scowling, angular woman I didn't recognize was shooting a fountain of water out of her wand. The flames hissed where the water met them. Wand steady, she sent a nervous glance over her shoulder.

My gaze drifted across the rest of the room as I tried to figure out what the woman was so concerned about. I didn't see Natalie, but on the other side of the store, a man was wearing a stainless-steel mixing bowl as a helmet and holding a broom as if it was a baseball bat.

"No!" I recognized Natalie's voice but still couldn't find her. She must've been in the back of the store. "Get back here, you damn cat!"

The man frantically motioned for me to get down, but I was here to solve problems, which meant I had to see the problem first.

A ball of yellow fire darted along the floor, dodging around puddles of liquid. A blue-tinted glass bottle tumbled to the ground. The fiery orb jumped into the air, rotated 180 degrees, and hissed. A fraction of a second later, the flaming sphere sprinted between aisles, turned, and ran directly at me.

It was at that moment that I realized there was a cat under all that fire. Through the flames, I couldn't tell the exact color, perhaps a brown tabby, but it still had all its fur and didn't seem to be burning as much as it was afraid.

I lifted my wand, but I didn't have a spell in mind because I still wasn't sure what exactly I was seeing. A cat that was on fire but not burning was a new one for me. The main problem, though, was its constant motion, so a simple containment spell should solve this problem.

"No containment spells!" Natalie shouted as she darted out of the back. "They just make the fire hotter."

So much for that idea. Thinking back to the witch who'd been using her wand as a hose, I conjured water. "*Gebo tan fehu.*" A small cloud, dark and heavy with water, appeared over the flaming cat. Big raindrops hissed as they fell into the flames. The cat screeched, darted around the end of an aisle, and headed toward the back of the store.

Great. Now it was trying to run away from the water. I took off after it, hopping over wet areas and broken glass.

Ahead of me, the bottom of the aisle was filling with a yellow-green smoke. I probed it, but there were so many different things interacting that I couldn't tell exactly what had been created.

For once, luck was on my side, and there was a gap between two sets of shelves. I slowed down, stepped to the right, and checked to see what was ahead of me. The aisle was free of any odd yellow-green smoke, so I abandoned my previous path for this one.

As I picked my way around a large red ceramic jar that had a big crack running up the side, I tried to figure out what to do if the water didn't put out the cat. Since the animal had appeared uninjured under the flames, the fire had to be magical. Magical fires could be unpredictable. Some of them could be extinguished by water, but others, well, they required special handling. Just like their natural counterparts, magical fires might need to be deprived of oxygen, smothered, or simply left to burn themselves out. It all depended on what the fuel source was. Until I could get close to the cat and figure out exactly what type of fire we were dealing with, I was hoping the water would work.

"Narzel blast it," Natalie murmured from nearby.

I froze. "Do you need help?"

"No." She heaved a sigh. "I just walked through a spell that dyed my pants black."

Going up on my tiptoes, I could just see Natalie over the shelves. Her gray hair was a wet mat laying limply around her face. Her mascara had run, giving her black, smudged eyes, and one eyebrow had been mostly burned off, leaving only a few hairs. "What caught the cat on fire?"

"I think it was something in a cauldron that came in for a warranty checkup. I sneezed and knocked the cauldron off the workbench. When it hit the floor, it captured the cat inside. When I lifted the cauldron up, Timothy was on fire. I tried a containment spell, but that made it worse, and at that point, he started running around like crazy. It didn't take me long to call you." The flames in the corner crackled, and Natalie winced.

There was a loud hiss and the telltale sound of another glass bottle crashing to the floor. "Is there anything Timothy really likes or really hates?"

"He isn't fond of water or fire. He'll do just about anything for fresh fish, but I'm all out of that."

A distinctly male bellow had both of us darting for the back of the store. I leapt over a murky, green puddle of something and hoped I wouldn't have to spend my entire day cleaning this place up after I figured out what to do about the cat. I edged around a display and planted my feet, unsure of my next move.

The wizard using a mixing bowl for a helmet was wildly swinging the now-flaming broom. While I wanted to help, I couldn't figure out how to get close to him or what he was trying to attack. He turned toward the wall and put some muscle behind his weapon.

"No!" Natalie screamed, reaching out as if it would stop him.

The broom whooshed through the air, colliding squarely with a wall of dry herbs. I didn't even have time to swear before the entire floor-to-ceiling display went up in flames. Only a breath later, the fire jumped to the lacquered wood shelving beside them. If it weren't for the cat involved, I would have voted for evacuating this place and calling it a loss.

A hair-raising yowl split the air. I winced as a flaming sphere of cat launched itself off the highest shelf and arced overhead. My rain cloud was nowhere to be seen, so the flames must've burned through it. As the cat soared across the room, it left a wake of blackened ceiling tiles. It was time to change my tactics.

"Are you trying to destroy my shop?" Natalie screeched at the wizard.

I went after the cat, ignoring whatever reply the wizard made. Near the center of the store, a display case toppled over, and I figured the cat couldn't be far from there. Since water didn't work and the flames fed on containment spells, it was time to get creative.

I held my breath as I tiptoed through a dense, orange cloud of some strange mixture of magical supplies. When I was well clear, I sucked in smoke-tainted air and continued searching for the cat. The problem was that most of the ways I could get rid of the flames were likely to hurt Timothy. Ideally, I could figure out what spell had gone wrong and fix it. However, I would have to get the cat to hold still so I could thoroughly investigate the flames, and I didn't think that was likely to happen.

Of course, maybe I didn't actually need to know what spell was causing the flames if I could simply remove the fuel. There were quite a lot of magics that would start flames, contain them, shape them, and intensify them, but most couldn't sustain the fire for very long. Therefore, suffocating it would work. Usually, I would just make a containment spell, suck all the oxygen out of it, and set that over the flames, but in this case, that would kill Timothy. Somehow, I suspected Natalie wanted her cat alive at the end of this.

I carefully edged around a growing hole in the ground that had been caused by half a shelf's worth of bottles tumbling into the spot.

On second thought, maybe she would be happy if I killed the cat.

"I'll drown you if that's what it takes, you flaming beast." That steely voice didn't belong to Natalie or the wizard.

I took a hard right and found Timothy cowering in a corner with walls of water all around him. The flames were a solid three feet tall, and big plumes of steam were emanating from every side of Timothy's watery cage. But the angular witch, who'd been so determinedly extinguishing the purified cloth a few minutes ago, looked like she was ready to summon an ocean if that's what was needed to contain Timothy.

In a rare turn of luck, the flames had retreated from the cat's head and neck. I pointed my wand at Timothy, not bothering with runes because it would be too awkward to frame the spell. Instead, I visualized a gap that air couldn't cross, limiting the air that could feed the flames. The empty space went from the cat's neck to the flames twisting at the end of his tail, under his feet and up until it completely separated the highest flames from the rest of the room. That wasn't a containment spell as much as magical separation of air, which made it impossible for oxygen to move through the space and to the flames.

I held my breath as the spell solidified and waited to see if the flames would react. For a long count of five, they did nothing. That was enough for me. I activated a spell to suck the oxygen out.

As the first bit of air went hurling out of the squashed oval of space around Timothy, the flames roared up, encouraged by the artificial breeze. Then, they slowed down, and the top of the fire settled to just under two feet. I poured more energy into the spell that was pulling the air away from the fire, willing this to work.

I could feel the air moving out again. The flames had shrunk and were slowly fading in color. I put more magic into the spell as the flames got smaller and smaller. Finally, as I was panting with the effort to keep the air moving, the flames flickered out completely. I quickly ended the spell, making the space around the cat a completely airtight environment so the flames couldn't reignite.

Timothy collapsed onto the floor, eyes wide, panting even more than me. I wasn't sure if he even saw the walls of water anymore. Poor little guy.

With the flames gone, I carefully extended a slender strand of my power and probed Timothy, looking for any spells or residue that could give me a hint as to what caused the fire to begin with. The air around him was empty, but as soon as the tendrils of magic touched his fur, a tingle raced back to me. He was covered in warped bits of a fire charm. It felt like a corrupted version of the standard charm that came on most cauldrons. However, this one had transferred to Timothy and ignited.

The good news was it was easy enough to strip off. I yanked at the knots of magic that were holding the spell in place, and it collapsed. The residual energy flowed back into the earth. I probed Timothy again, and he was just a cat. A scared cat, but a cat who still had all his fur even after setting half the shop on fire. Since he was free of the charm, I released the magic holding the vacuum around him.

I glanced at the witch beside me. Sweat was dripping off her temples, but her wand was as steady as ever. "Excuse me, ma'am, but you can let the spell go. The cat is fine now."

Her eyes never left Timothy. "Are you sure?"

"Absolutely."

She turned just enough for me to see her raise one very skeptical eyebrow.

"*Sowil*," I muttered under my breath and flicked my

wand. A light containment spell encapsulated Timothy. The flames didn't come back. His eyes drooped then closed. He hadn't even noticed that he was effectively captured. "He's just a very tired cat now."

"If you're sure..." She eyed the cat.

"I'm sure." The walls of water fell limply to the ground. The containment spell kept Timothy dry, and he didn't even open an eye.

"Is he alive?" Natalie came up next to me, her voice rough.

"Yep, but I'd take him to a vet for a better evaluation."

As Natalie hurried forward to check on her pet, I surveyed the shop. There were fires everywhere, half the shelving was turned over, and assorted colors of smoke were slowly moving throughout the room. I had serious doubts that much of the inventory could be saved.

However, Natalie had been good to me back when I was clanless and a lot of witches didn't want to have anything to do with me. "*Dagaz ehaz.*" With that, the fires went out. The one nearest to me cooled so quickly that I could put my hand against the wood in a matter of seconds.

"Thank you," Natalie said softly. "I couldn't manage the set of spells you used on Timothy. And I can't thank you enough for putting out the fires."

"Do you want me to stay and help with the rest?" I tried not to cringe at the thought. It was going to take days to adequately clean this place, never mind the actual repairs, before she could reopen.

Natalie patted my shoulder. "You've done enough. I know a clan that specializes in this type of stuff. I'll call them. You'll send me a bill?"

A half-burned shelf in front of us crumpled to the ground, smashing all of its contents. "Or you could figure out an appropriate discount on my future orders, and we'll call it even."

"Deal." A quick handshake cemented the agreement. "Now get out of here. I have a shop to fix and Timothy to take care of."

She didn't have to ask me twice. I tweaked the spell on the door enough to let me pass, walked out to my car, and collapsed into the driver's seat.

Now, I really needed a comforting tea. Maybe if I asked nicely, the barista at Roasted Beans would give me a double pump of mental fortitude in my latte.

CHAPTER TEN

Before I could start my car, the phone rang. I groaned.

"That better not be another emergency." Sighing, I dug the phone out of my purse. "Oaks Consulting, this is Michelle."

"It's Rodriguez. Can you get down to The Creamery? I have a problem that I need your help with."

No way. It simply wasn't possible that I had a third emergency today. "You're kidding, right? I just finished dealing with an emergency at Witch's Warehouse."

"Not joking at all. I've been down here for the past thirty minutes and the magic is past my scope. I've called you eight times, and dispatch called twice for magical back up. They said you were busy, and they didn't have anyone else to send. If I could've gotten someone else, I would've. I'm sorry."

I silently swore. This day. "I'll be there as soon as I can."

"Thanks, Michelle." He hung up before I could change my mind.

I set my phone down in a cup holder. This was the day

of sorrow and never-ending emergencies. My magical reserves were holding up fairly well, but the emotions of the morning had settled over me. Mourning wasn't a great energy booster.

There wasn't even a good excuse, like Friday the thirteenth or a full moon. Nope, it was smack in the middle of the lunar cycle, not new, not full, nothing interesting. For whatever reason, everything was going wrong, and I had to be one of the people to swoop in and fix it.

Cursing under my breath, I backed out of my parking space and headed over to The Creamery. It was only a few blocks away, and the short drive wasn't nearly enough time to recover from my morning.

Before I knew it, I was parked in front of The Creamery, and Officer Rodriguez was standing in the parking lot waiting for me. Just like before, I didn't take anything but my keys and wand with me.

I approached him, trying to look chipper and friendly even though I just wanted to go home and hide until the day passed. "You were a bit vague on details over the phone. What's the problem?"

Rodriguez scrubbed a hand over his face. His black hair was windblown, and his normally golden complexion was a bit pale. "I wish I knew. It's my third call today, and I'm not at my best."

I patted him on the shoulder. "Mine, too. I don't know what's going on, but I'm ready for this craziness to wear off."

"Agreed." He looked back at The Creamery, where a boy, late teens or early twenties from the look of him, was standing nervously by the door. "I think we're going to need more help. The people in there seem to be suffering from some sort of unintended effect of today's magical ice cream."

I groaned. Please, please, don't let the effects be anything like what they were at Happy Paws. I directed the prayer to the earth, moon, sun, sky, and anyone else who was feeling benevolent and was listening. Finally, I worked around to what I needed to focus on. "Reminds me of Happy Paws. Do you think these two situations could have anything in common?"

He shrugged. "Maybe. We won't know until we wade into the magic."

"Ask for back up, medical support." From the shadows I could see through the window, there were at least four people in there, and I still didn't know exactly what kind of magic I was dealing with.

Rodriguez shook his head. "Why don't you go over and talk to the employee? I'll make that request and join you in a few minutes."

Looking over at the guy, who kept glancing between us and the customers, I sighed. "Deal."

As I headed toward the door of The Creamery, I hoped this was less exciting than the rest of my day had been. Somehow, I didn't think I was going to get that lucky.

The lad pushed open the door and hurried out to meet me, letting the door swing shut behind him. His brows were pulled close together, and his words tumbled out so fast they ran into each other. "Are you the witch? The officer said you'd be able to help. I really don't know what happened. I was the last one here last night, and everything was fine."

I held up a hand. "Slow it down." He took a deep breath, then a second one. "That's better. Tell me what last night has to do with today, and tell me if you noticed anything odd."

He sucked in a third breath. "So, I closed last night,

which meant I set the machines to make the ice cream overnight. It's a slow process, automated, so it's not a big deal. We get recipes for what the next day's batch will be. This was one I've done before, Sweet Dreams. It's supposed to let them see the best outcome of happy things they've dreamed about, wished for, you get the idea."

I nodded and hoped he kept talking at this nice normal pace rather than the spillage I'd gotten a moment ago.

"Last night, everything was fine. There were no problems with yesterday's batch. I poured in the milk, sugar, all the ingredients. I checked the expiration dates on everything. The first bottle of Sweet Dreams mix I grabbed was expired, so I put it in the bin for magical disposal and got a bottle that was in date. I followed the directions exactly. I made this last month, and several times last year. It's never done this before." He finished by grabbing my arm and tugging me inside the building.

I stumbled after him, and as soon as I could get my feet under me, I braced myself and carefully removed his hand from my arm.

"Look at them! There's something really wrong." His voice went up.

"I can see that." I said it before my mind had fully cataloged what I was seeing. I said it so he would stop trying to convince me that something was wrong and let me figure it out.

All seven of the people in the shop seemed to be at the mercy of their supposedly sweet dream. I was pretty sure the girl wrapped up in a spider web didn't think it was that sweet of a dream. In all likelihood, neither did the couple who were staring into their bowls of ice cream and shaking. I could just barely hear the woman whispering, "My teeth, not my teeth."

Another young couple seemed to be having some sort

of negative reaction as well. The guy was breathing in great gulping gasps, and the girl had her hands crossed over her chest. The floor looked wet under the man who was gasping for air. At the table in the far corner sat a young boy and a woman, presumably his mother. The woman sat absolutely still, her eyes fixed vacantly on some faraway point. Her son shivered violently, then screamed, only to repeat the process.

I moved around to get a better look at the group. Make that eight people. In a corner that was oddly dark for this time of day and the lights in the shop, there was a little girl, knees clutched to her chest, eyes wide. "No, not the dark," she whimpered.

"What do you think?" Rodriguez asked softly from behind me.

"I think we need to help the guy who seems to be choking before he hurts himself, and then we need to figure out what caused this." The Creamery employee started talking again, but I spoke over him. "Do we have backup coming?"

The boy shut up, looking rather offended. I didn't much care. I had a job to do.

Rodriguez suppressed a smile. "They said it would be a little bit. They're still cleaning up a different problem." He turned to the boy. "Jim, wait outside. Do not leave the area, but don't come back in unless we ask for you."

Jim opened his mouth like he was going to protest, then seemed to think better of it, snapped his mouth shut, and walked outside.

When the door swung closed behind him, Rodriguez turned to me. "Where did you say you wanted to start?"

"With the guy who's choking."

Without any further conversation, I worked my way over to him. When I was standing next to him, I took a deep breath and slowly let it out. I didn't drop my shields, but through them I tried to simply feel the energy.

Around me, there were weak pulses of magic, and some stronger ones, but there wasn't a particular origin for them that I could determine. Obviously, the ice cream had magical components, and that was part of it, but I didn't know if that was the only thing at work here.

I cracked open my shields and extended a tendril of magic. Rather than start with the guy, I first focused on the ice cream, letting the probe hang above the bowl. While I could feel some sort of magic, I couldn't figure out what it was.

I lowered the probe until it touched the ice cream. There was a mix of all the things I expected to find in ice cream, like milk, sugar, and flavoring. However, I could also feel a mass of spells. They were stronger than I'd thought they would be, strong enough not just to make people see something, but to believe it was happening to them.

Pulling back the tendril of magic, I gently touched it to the man's shoulder.

For a moment, I was swept away in the sensation. There was water all around me. I couldn't get to the surface. I was running out of air. I had to breathe. I opened my mouth, and water came rushing in. Now I was choking, drowning, and there was no way I was going to survive.

Except I was standing in an ice cream shop. That thought was enough to break the connection, and instead of feeling what he was feeling, I was back to seeing and feeling the magic. The spells in the ice cream had sunk into him, making him believe one of his deepest darkest fears. And, with the strength of the spells, he wasn't only seeing the dream but experiencing it. Somehow, I didn't think this experience was going to help him get over his fear of drowning.

With the way the spells were tangled and warped from their original intentions, I was wary of trying to simply unmake them. Not only would it take a long time, but there was a chance I could get sucked into his nightmare. Instead, I extended my magic so it could latch into different parts of the spell and yanked it apart. The spell dissolved. The remaining energy floated down to the floor of the shop, and from there into the ground below.

The man came back to himself with a gasp. "Where am I? What happened?" He looked at the ice cream, then across the table at his date. He groaned. "She's never going to go out with me again."

Rodriguez clapped him on the shoulder. "You never know. I got great relationships on terrible first impressions." The guy nodded. "Now, if you could come with me, I'll explain some of what's been going on and give you some tips on how to turn this into a second date." Rodriguez led the man away from the table.

I stepped around to be next to the woman. After taking a few breaths and putting some mental space between myself and whatever I was going to feel when I touched the magic, I very gently brushed her shoulder with a probe.

As with the man, she was in the grips of a very bad dream. This time, I didn't get the details, but I could tell she was standing in front of an audience, and she wasn't wearing as much as she would've liked. I yanked at the magic, and it fell away.

The girl shuddered as she woke up from the dream. "Ugh. It was supposed to be a good dream. Wait, where's Reg? And who are you?"

I held out my hand. "I'm Michelle Oaks, witch and magical consultant for the local police."

She shook my hand but didn't even come close to smiling. "Nice to meet you. What happened?"

"Something went wrong with the ice cream. My colleague and I are here to help. If you'll walk outside, I believe Reg will be there, as will my colleague, who can give you some more information about what will happen from here." I really hoped that was enough direction, because I didn't want to talk to all of these people. I had done enough dealing with people for one day. I wanted to finish this job and go home.

Apparently, she had the same feelings I did. She got out of that chair and power-walked to the door.

With this table cleared of people, I studied the ice cream. Outwardly, it didn't look particularly special. It had a very faint blue tint, and a light, somewhat vanilla-inspired smell. To my eyes and nose, there was nothing remarkable about the ice cream.

While I would have to figure out exactly what had happened to the ice cream at some point, for now, the first priority was getting the innocent people out of here. The girl crying in the corner tugged at my heart, but I knew it would be much easier to have her mother there to help calm her down, so I went over to the woman who was staring fixedly at the ceiling.

As soon as I touched her with a probe, I knew what had happened. She was convinced she was paralyzed. She couldn't move at all.

Well, I knew how to fix this. Yet again, I shredded the spell. She woke up.

"Oh, that was awful." She rubbed her face and then looked up to me. "Thank you."

"Um, you're welcome?" She seemed far more coherent than the last two.

She gave a wry smile. "It's my nightmare. I'm paralyzed, but I know what's going on around me. Now, could you help my kids?"

"Sure." I moved around the table so I could kneel next to her son. It hardly took a moment to feel his dream. This poor child thought he was falling over and over and over again. I ripped through the dream, and the boy hurled himself into his mother's arms. She cradled him close, whispering reassuring words to him.

With those two taken care of, I walked over to the oddly dark corner where the girl was huddled. I didn't even have to touch her to know she was afraid of the dark. As soon as I ripped the spell away, the shadow shrouding her vanished too. She scrambled back over to her mom as quickly as she could.

I followed her more slowly and picked up the mom's purse as I guided the three of them to the door. Jim helpfully held the door open for us and even took the woman's purse from me. I smiled at him before heading back inside. As the door closed behind me, I heard Rodriguez began his speech all over again.

Since I was close to them, I went over to the girl who kept saying her teeth were falling out and the guy across from her who was trembling in his seat. It was easy enough to pull both of them out of their nightmares and hand them over to Rodriguez for further information.

From there, I went over to the last person, the girl wrapped in spiderwebs. At the table close to her, a bowl of ice cream was absolutely empty. The other bowls had been missing a few bites, so I suspected the more of the ice cream a person ingested, the more the nightmare would affect them.

I had just ripped the magic away from her when I heard a crash and a splat behind me. I whirled around to see a poltergeist zipping through the air. On the floor was a broken bottle of something very magical.

"You're spoiling my fun!" he yelled. He hurled another bottle onto the floor. The glass shattered, and more magical liquid joined the puddle.

Part of the bottle slid across the liquid, coming to rest a short distance from my foot. The label on the glass read *Turtle Tracks*. I wasn't entirely sure what magical turtle tracks liquid did, but I was reasonably confident I didn't want bottles of magical ice cream stuff mixing on the floor.

The girl was sitting on the ground crying. I tugged her to her feet and started marching her towards the door, trying to avoid stepping in any of the liquid. With my other hand, I summoned my wand.

The poltergeist threw a third bottle. "Take some Winter Wonderland, you witch!"

"You got that right." I pointed my wand at him.

The poltergeist went still, the chipper expression fading from his translucent features. "Why you gotta spoil my fun?"

I kept pushing the girl towards the door. "What was the first bottle you threw?"

He grinned wickedly. "Why, that's the bottle of Sweet Dreams the lad thought he was adding to the ice cream mix last night. I switched them while he wasn't looking. I also changed the amount he should add. He put in four times the amount that should've gone in that much ice cream. Can you believe that? How careless!"

I shoved the girl towards the door. Thankfully, she kept stumbling in that direction. The door opened long enough for her to get yanked out and for Rodriguez to step in.

"Set the remaining bottles down, and we can talk

about this nicely." That was going to be my one and only offer.

For moment, he seemed to be considering it, then he grinned. "Nah." He hurled the last bottle at me. "Enjoy some Strawberry Fields!"

I dodged to the side. The bottle shattered right behind where I'd been standing. I had had enough of this poltergeist. I focused on him and the air around him. "*Fehu!*"

He, and six inches of air in every direction, turned to solid ice. The block containing the poltergeist hung there for a fraction of a second and then started to fall. But I'd been expecting that. "*Nazid.*" This slowed the block's fall until it was moving no faster than a feather drifting down. It finally touched down on the counter with a light thump.

I ended the levitation spell and turned to Rodriguez. "Did you get that?"

He frowned. "I heard the confession. I'll make a note in the report that the boy wasn't at fault, and I'll have the poltergeist transported to magical lockup."

I felt magic stir behind me.

"Uh, Michelle, which bottles did he say he threw?"

"The unexpired bottle of Sweet Dreams Jim thought he was adding to the ice cream, Turtle Tracks, Winter Wonderland, and Strawberry Fields." I pivoted, and my mouth dropped open.

Four giant chocolate turtles stretched their necks out to peer around the ice cream shop. Behind them, five snowmen who didn't look particularly kind spread out. A swirl of air condensed into a cloud that I suspected was a "Sweet Dream," though who knew what it would be now that it had combined with the other magical additives. Not to be left out, Strawberry Fields contributed about twenty basketball-sized strawberries.

Rodriguez was next to me with his wand out. "What do we do?"

"This is a first for me." I tightened my grip on my wand. "I haven't had such good luck with containment spells against magical mishaps lately. I'm willing to entertain options."

Before he could answer, the cloud that I could only assume was Sweet Dreams zoomed across the room, colliding with both of us.

I wasn't in The Creamery anymore. I was little, maybe seven or eight, and I was running down the stairs, chanting "It's Christmas! It's Christmas! It's Christmas!" over and over again.

My dad was at the bottom of the stairs. He caught me as I jumped. He held me up high, and I laughed. Then he cuddled me close before setting me on my feet and following me the rest of the way to the Christmas tree. Mom was already there, lifting the stockings off the hooks over the fireplace.

But this wasn't real. My dad had never been around for Christmas when I was little. This was a dream, a bittersweet dream.

"It's not real." I was a little girl, whispering while looking at my parents.

"It's not real." A bit more force behind the words this time. The image of Christmas with my family wavered. "It's not real!"

I was back in the ice cream shop, standing next to Rodriguez, with a small army of turtles, snowmen, and strawberries headed in my direction. I might not be able to capture all of them or know how spells reacted to them, but there was one thing I could do that was sure to get rid of all of these creatures in one go.

I shook Rodriguez.

He came back to himself with a shiver. "Thanks."

"You can thank me later. Shield as hard as you can."

Without hearing an answer, I started building the spell in my mind. I needed an eating spell, one that would consume all the magic in the room. It couldn't affect anything outside the walls of The Creamery, but all the magic inside was fair game. It would eat until it consumed all the magic, and then it would push the energy into the earth.

Sucking in a breath, I forced the spell through my wand. A dark hole showed up smack in the center of the puddle that had spawned all of these creatures. I snapped my shields into place, adding layer upon layer to them as quickly as I could.

A turtle melted into a puddle of chocolate and caramel as it slowly oozed into the hole. A snowman vanished in a flurry of flakes. Three strawberries exploded but didn't leave anything behind. The berry goop simply vanished, the magic that had been creating them flowing into the vortex.

For a moment, the spell brushed across my shields, but it couldn't get through, and it moved on. I felt a focus on Rodriguez, and I thought it left him alone, but I wasn't sure.

It sucked down the cloud of dreams. Then, one by one, the rest of the turtles, snowmen, and all of the strawberries followed. In a matter of seconds, there was nothing but the vortex. The edges wobbled, and it collapsed in on itself. I felt the magic gather into a single concentrated point. Then it exploded downwards, thrusting the energy into the earth as it shattered into a million pieces. None of the spells it had consumed remained.

I looked over Rodriguez. I couldn't say his color was

any better than it had been before, but he didn't look like he'd been drained of his powers. "Did you make it?"

"Yeah. I'm fine."

"You don't sound so sure."

He straightened his shoulders and stood up a little taller. "I'll be fine. I just want to go home and forget this wretched day happened."

I laughed, I cried a little, and I laughed some more. "Me too, Rodriguez. Me too."

A couple of minutes later, Mary Bells and a small fleet of ambulances showed up. I helped them load up everyone who'd been in The Creamery. They also took the poltergeist. In a flurry of movement, they swept out as quickly as they'd swept in.

I stood next to Rodriguez as the cars carried everyone away. "I may be known for my astonishing bad luck, but this day is a record, even for me."

"Me too. I think it's just one of those days." He rubbed the back of his neck. "Maybe the next job will be something simple."

"You jinxed us." I groaned. "Now the next case is going to be really bad."

He didn't have to say anything because his phone rang.

Yup, it was one of those days.

CHAPTER ELEVEN

Thank the earth for small blessings. Rodriguez's phone call hadn't been another emergency. I eyed the time as I drove back to the lodge. After this day, I needed to clean up, which would make me late for date night. Narzel was having all too much fun with my life.

If I'd been thinking more clearly this morning, I would've canceled dinner, but the day had gotten away from me. Somewhere along the way, the pain of Ethel's death had dulled, but that could've been the fatigue talking. Sorrow aside, I had to admit, Ethel wouldn't want me to miss anything because of her death. She'd want to charge ahead with my wedding, take the witch community by storm, and do a bit of social reform along the way. That had been our plan, and now it was mine.

Besides, I'd already missed the dinner Landa served for overnight guests, and after a day like this, I wasn't going to suffer through my own cooking. As long as I didn't cry over dinner, it would all work out.

I cleaned up in record time, and according to my car's clock, I would only be a few minutes late. For once, luck was favoring me. The drive went smoothly. I parked at the far end of the lot before heading into dinner.

Italian Flair channeled its name into its style. Strings of lights hung over the outdoor seating, with shrubs sculpted in the shapes of elves, dwarves, nymphs, satyrs, and all sorts of races growing out of Roman pots. I walked between stone columns twice my height as I entered the building.

The satyr at the host station smiled at me and bowed his head. "Welcome to Italian Flair. How may I assist you?"

"I have a reservation, Elron Oaks." After one unfortunate incident with a bed and breakfast not believing he only had one name, he now used my last name to make reservations. I'd have to ask if he intended to take it as his when we married.

The satyr raised a hand, and a waitress appeared. "Echo will seat you and be your server."

"This way." Echo led me through the restaurant. Even without the warm brown undertones in her skin, the spring of purple Hyacinthia tucked in the tidy bun would've marked her as a nymph.

Unlike many restaurants that had solidly bought into the dark mood lighting, in Italian Flair pendant lights illuminated every table, and soft overhead lights gave the rest of the space a welcoming glow. More than crisp white linen or the live orchids on every table, I appreciated being able to see my food and dinner companion.

Echo halted next to a table for two in the back that was surprisingly unoccupied.

While I checked my phone, Echo filled our water glasses. As soon as she walked away, I called Elron. As rude as it was to make a phone call in a nice restaurant, Elron was never late.

His phone rang until it clicked over to voice mail. Odd.

I hung up without leaving a message. Today had made me jumpy and suspicious, that's all. Elron was fine and would be here soon.

He wouldn't be in a car accident.

That was just today's horrible events toying with my mind.

A sharp clank of silverware on china cut through the conversation. I kept looking at my phone, trying to will Elron to show up or communicate.

Cutlery clacked against china again, followed by a gasp.

I poked at my phone morosely. Was it so much to ask to actually have dinner with my fiancé tonight? Then to go home and cry about, well, all of it? Because tomorrow I had to be strong again. I had to be the witch with permanent solutions to magical problems, the next premier, ready to be in the spotlight.

Cutlery scraped across a plate with a hair-raising screech.

Irritated by the constant annoyances, I swung around. Everyone was staring at a circular table in the center of the room seating six. With a shriek that would've done an opera star proud, a man scrambled away, knocking his chair over in the process. The rest of the table didn't waste any time in following his example.

At first, I assumed they'd found a bug in their food, but as I was turning away, a glint of light caught my eye. A spoon hopped onto an empty bread plate with a clack. A second spoon followed, and with a scrape of metal across ceramic, started to dance.

Around the table, the rest of the cutlery came to life. The forks gathered together and started what I could only describe as a line dance. Two knives started to fight one another, sending sparks into the air.

I had to close my mouth. Dancing and fighting flatware that seemed to be doing all of this on its own was a new one. It only took a moment's thought to extend a tendril of magic. Sure enough, they were spelled.

Wand in hand, I pushed away from the table to head over. The spell shifted under my probe. The dancing forks paused, as did the rest of the flatware.

Across the room, Elron lifted his hand in greeting.

The forks leapt off the table, closely followed by the knives. The spoons shot up, shattering the light over the table. The same man shrieked and seemingly broke through the shock holding everyone in place. People darted in every direction as the flatware on adjoining tables joined in the fun.

A spoon launched itself at me. I batted it away with my wand. "One nice evening. Was that too damned much to ask?"

Another light shattered. A stuffed shell splatted on a woman's face. I tracked the flight path back to an intrepid group of spoons who were using a salt shaker as a fulcrum.

Apparently, an uneventful evening was not in my future. Narzel blast it all.

The front door swung open, and Echo bellowed, "Everyone out!" The words reverberated throughout the room.

It was a great plan, it really was, but all I could envision was the flatware loose on the streets, puncturing tires, setting up traps for the unaware driver on the road, and finding their way across the entire city. If I managed nothing else, I had to keep the flatware in this building. Easier said than done, especially without using more magic than I had to spare given how the day had gone.

A shield spell across the door would do, though I couldn't think of the runic name for flatware fast enough, so that part had to be done with visualization and willpower. I channeled the rest of the spell through my wand and runes, amplifying the power I put into it. "*Sowil esaz a perzae ansu.*" Hopefully that would work.

A group of three people dashed for the door and I held my breath, hoping the shield would work properly. They went through without so much as a hitch in their step. Success enough for me.

Something warm and vaguely slimy thumped into my cheek before sliding down to land with a plop. Ravioli. Of course the flatware would hurl it at me. I was the only one holding still.

I looked around for Elron but had lost him in the dash for the door. He was a smart elf and could take care of himself. Turning around, I headed for my table and phone, dodging a flying breadstick along the way. If I had to handle this mess during what should've been my off time, so did Rodriguez.

Phone pressed to my ear, I kept a sharp eye out for more flying food. At a table across from me, the flatware pieces had teamed up and was building a trebuchet, with the apparent intent of getting a sizable meatball airborne. My wand was in the air when movement at the edge of my vision caught my attention. A gang of spoons were working on pushing open the door to the kitchen. "Oh, no. None of that."

"None of what?" Rodriguez said. "Why do I hear screaming? I thought you were at dinner."

"I am, or was." I kicked the spoons away from the door, and they scurried off, bowls drooping. Until today, I hadn't known I could feel bad for kicking a spoon, but I did. "You know those magical problems we had at Happy Paws and The Creamery?"

"Haven't forgotten yet."

"Same problem at Italian Flair." Almost everyone had gone out the front, though I still didn't see Elron.

Rodriguez groaned. "Really?"

"Don't give me that. It ruined my date. The least you can do is call reinforcements and help me deal with this."

"I'll be there in twenty, and I'll get some officers there to cordon off the area sooner."

"Thanks." As I hung up, a terrifying thought occurred to me. Everything in the dining room had come from the kitchen. What was going on back there?

"Narzel blast it." There was at least one outside door in the kitchen too. I had to block it. Before I went through the door to the kitchen, I quickly cast the same barrier I'd cast before, letting people pass but not flatware.

With that done, I took a deep breath and shoved the door open. It banged off the wall as I stepped through. At first glance, the kitchen was free of the pandemonium of the dining room, except it was empty. Not that I was the world's best cook, but last I checked, food didn't prepare or plate itself. There should've been cooks, waiters retrieving dishes, and any number of people back here. Instead, industrial-sized pots bubbled on the stove, and something smoked from inside a pan on an eight-burner range.

All of which would've made sense if this area was awash with rioting flatware, but other than some lettuce on the ground and the burning whatever on the stove, it appeared to be in perfectly functional condition. The hairs on the back of my neck stood on end.

Twisting around, I looked behind me, but I still didn't see anything. Sucking in a deep breath, I reminded myself all I had to do was shield the back door, and I could get out of here. Simple, right?

A whoosh of air had me darting to the side, which was the only reason I took the blow on the shoulder instead of the head. A metallic clang filled the room as the bowl crashed past me and onto the ground, flinging lettuce across the room as it went. It rolled on its rim, picking up speed instead of losing it, until it managed to flip itself right-side up.

Now the bowls were in on the action? That couldn't be good.

My eyes slid over to the huge pots of boiling water. Normally, I'd be looking at those thinking about all the glorious pasta they could produce, but now… boiling water was dangerous.

I backed up a step. The bowl rocked toward me.

The back door. I just had to block the back door.

I spun and darted around a workstation I didn't have a name for. No one with my lack of cooking skills was familiar with restaurant kitchen equipment. There, on the other end of the lengthy bench, was the door. Three knives—chef's knifes, not cute butter knives—stood up in the middle of the walkway.

With their appearance, I decided I was close enough to the door. The spell went quickly this time, in large part because I'd done it twice already, but added to the day's work, the drain on my magic was a concern. With the building sealed off, I could call my work done and join the masses outside. This could become someone else's problem. Cleaning up this mess wasn't in my contract with the county anyway.

The center knife of the three hopped toward me.

Then again, it was my problem if being stabbed was a possibility. I took one cautious step back.

The knives jumped forward.

Common wisdom was not to run from predators. It made them hunt you. My racing heart was sure running was the answer.

There had to be a way, a non-magical way, to neutralize these knives. I risked a glance over my shoulder. The salad bowl scooted along the ground a few feet behind me. Maybe running was the right answer—if I had a proper distraction.

Keeping my movements slow and steady, I inched away from the knives. They bounced forward, matching my progress. I kept my wand up, just in case. It was better to run out of magic than get a knife to the—well, any part of me.

I paused with the salad bowl only a foot behind me. This was it. I took a deep breath and hopped back, lined up, and punted the bowl at the knives. I took off toward the door to the dining room, only sparing one quick look back. The knives were too busy fencing with the bowl to chase me.

For once, luck smiled on me, and I made it through the door without further incident. Not that matters had improved much in the dining room. Gangs of flatware and dishes leapt from table to table, using breadbaskets as barricades as they waged war on the tables and chairs. The absolute madness of the scene aside, I had to admire their ingenuity.

It crossed my mind to snag a serving tray as a shield, but then one of them rolled through an enemy line. I abandoned the idea.

Thanks to their focus on each other, I managed to avoid most interaction with the magically improved items. One fork tried to bite my shoe, but I flung it into an enemy camp. They pounced on the newcomer with clear glee. It was all going as well as could be expected until I spotted the door.

In the rush, I'd forgotten about the outdoor seating, which would have the same dinnerware as the dining room and nothing keeping it from running off to cause trouble. I cast the shield on the door. Previous escapees couldn't be helped, but it would prevent additional runaways.

A meatball flew in front of me from the same group who'd been using themselves as a trebuchet earlier. They had three trebuchets now and were holding off attackers handily.

As much as I wanted to go out the front and find Elron, as far as I knew, I was the only one here with the power to corral magical dinnerware.

With a sigh, and dodging another meatball, I darted around a group and made it to the patio door. I didn't bother looking out to see what was waiting for me. It wouldn't be a gang of chef's knives, and that was the current bar of horribleness I wanted to avoid.

My phone rang, and I tugged it out of my pocket with my left hand. "Oaks Consulting, this is Michelle."

"It's Rodriguez. I'm almost there, but officers at the perimeter are reporting escaped items causing problems. Can you get on that?"

I shoved the door open with my foot. "I'll do what I can. Only leaving the building now."

"Now?"

I didn't bother to answer. If the mayhem inside had been bad, outside was worse. Former customers and a few employees were running around screaming. Bright police lights flashed red and blue around the parking lot. Even before my injury and power reduction, I wouldn't have been able to fix this.

Of all the excitement, and there was a lot of it, a

familiar silver haired elf at the other side of the patio caught my attention. Elron lured a dinner plate over to him, which put it in reach of the ivy. In a second it was bound up so tightly it couldn't move. As I got closer, I spotted flatware, bowls, a serving tray, and even one pitcher caught in the vine.

"Now that's a handy way to solve the problem." The area looked relatively clear, so I dismissed my wand and gave my hand a break.

Elron smiled at me. "The ivy was willing enough."

A spoon leapt off a table at me. I caught it and hurled it into the greenery, which captured it as quickly as it had the plate. "So I see."

He gave me a quick hug. "Sorry I was late."

"Given what happened, I wish we'd both been later."

A centaur in police uniform trotted past with a serving tray rolling after it. With one well-placed kick, it split the tray in half, and the officer continued on its patrol. The two halves of the tray flopped to the ground and didn't move.

"Do you have a plan?" Elron motioned to, well, all of it.

"Maybe." I spun out a tendril of magic and probed the serving tray. Breaking it had damaged the spell but not removed it, so simply damaging all the items wasn't an option. However, I was able to determine that the magic was only on the surface, not inside. Rather like the magic at Happy Paws. And, given the similarities between the two events, likely from similar sources.

I moved the probe to the items Elron had captured in the ivy. The spell was stronger on some of them than others. That could be due to differences in exposure to the magic that started this, or they could be using up the energy in the spell and, over time, would return to perfectly ordinary items. Since I didn't know of any spells that had unlimited power, the second seemed more likely to me. Not that Rodriguez or any of the police would like that answer.

"Given enough time, I think the spell will wear off. If we could round them up, we could treat them with a spell remover. Though I don't have any with me." And didn't have it in me to make one. Honestly, sealing the building had used what I had had left this evening.

"We need a null," Elron mused.

"That'd be great. Do you know of a local one?"

Nulls were rare. I wasn't sure exactly how rare, but rare enough that finding one in the general population was remarkable. Especially since the government loved to conscript them. They loved having someone on hand who could drain all the magic from an area. Trouble was, most of them lived in major cities and only moved when their government overlords told them to. Not because the nulls were heartless, but because someone always wanted them, and with the government behind them, they were safe.

"No."

And that was likely the end of that idea. "We can mention it to Rodriguez, but even if there's one in Georgia, I doubt they could get here in time to be helpful."

Elron shrugged. "Given the situations you've encountered lately, having a null around for a few days could be useful."

"No argument from me." My phone rang again, and I fished it out of my pocket. It was Rodriguez. "Are you here yet?"

"Just parked. Where are you?"

"We'll meet you at the front of the building."

"Copy." The line went dead.

Elron opened the gate and ushered me out with a bow and a playful smile. "My lady."

"Why thank you, good, sir." I rested my left hand on his arm and summoned my wand into my right hand.

As we walked away, a strand of ivy lifted from the ground and waved goodbye.

Elron slowed. "Thank you for your assistance, and be kind to anyone who comes to retrieve those items."

The ivy bobbed in a motion akin to a nod and sunk back to the ground.

"That never gets old." I could do plenty of cool things. Magic was nifty like that, but talking to plants wasn't one of them.

"Nor does seeing you levitate an object."

"Child's play, but fun."

The rest of the light conversation was lost when we rounded the corner of the building. A fork wobbled across the pavement in front of us.

That shouldn't have been able to escape. Not that my opinion mattered much when the fork was so clearly outside the building.

CHAPTER TWELVE

A man held up a tie knotted around a fistful of flatware. "Nice haul, if I do say so myself."

Elron grabbed the fork before handing it off to a nearby flowerpot.

Why hadn't the spell worked? It should've worked. I edged around a woman sternly lecturing her purse, which had been, well, wiggling at the start of the scolding but was now still, to the front door. Both doors had been propped open with rocks from the flower beds, and past them, a small army of dinnerware beat against the shield, so they weren't crossing at will. The spell was mostly working.

I turned back to the woman. "Excuse me, ma'am, but may I ask what's in your purse?"

She looked at me and then at her purse.

"Michelle Oaks. I'm a witch who works with the police."

"Well, the water pitcher bit my husband's jacket as we were leaving. It tried to bite us, so we stuffed it in my purse." She hesitated. "It wasn't just us! A spoon was in a lady's hair. My husband even found a fork in his pocket!"

She kept talking faster, as if without the additional details I wouldn't believe her.

"It must have been terrifying. Could you hold onto that pitcher for a little longer? We're working on how to contain all of these items."

She nodded, and her fingers tightened on her purse strap.

"Thank you, ma'am." I stepped away before she could tell me more stories. They'd all be about the same. The spell had worked, but only against items that weren't attached to a person. If a fork or plate had been in contact with a person, it got out just fine. Not the wild success I'd hoped for, but at least the majority of the items were trapped inside.

"Oaks! There you are." Rodriguez strode through the crowd, several of which were following him. "What can you tell me that I don't already know?"

"Not much, and there's even less I can do to fix the problem." Likely not news to him, but galling to say nonetheless. It was Happy Paws all over again.

He sighed. "Here I was hoping for better news."

"You're lucky I was here at all. If it hadn't been for a dinner date, we'd both have gotten this call, and it wouldn't have been limited to a few forks in a parking lot." My stomach growled.

"Gratitude has limits." Rodriguez locked eyes with me. "I had plans too, and they didn't involve this any more than yours did."

I wanted to argue, but I couldn't. "What is it about this town that attracts all this? Is it really like this everywhere and I never noticed until I started working with the police?"

"No idea, but it would be great if it was someone else's problem for a bit." Rodriguez looked past me to the door, and his eyes went wide. "They really are animated."

"Annoyingly so. Like at Happy Paws, I can't pull the magic off of all of them. It would take too much effort. Given that these spells aren't on animals, I think you could let the spell run its course. It should wear off in twelve to twenty-four hours. At least that's my best guess." I glanced over at Elron. "Tell him your idea."

"A null." Elron didn't bother to expand.

Rodriguez shook his head. "I tried to put in a request for one after Happy Paws, and again after The Creamery. I even tried calling the FBI directly. I was told very bluntly their nulls have better things to do than sit around small towns waiting for minor magical emergencies."

My eyebrows shot up. "They really said that?"

"Yup."

"Wow."

Rodriguez shrugged. "It was a good thought, Elron."

"Though not useful," Elron said.

That sounded like my cue. "What do you want me to do here, Rodriguez? It's been a long day. I don't have it in me to use magic to capture the dinnerware." I summed up how the shields worked and what I'd done. "Oh, and I'll only charge you half my normal rate. I was already here, and even if I didn't work with you, I would've done something."

"Thank you." Rodriguez rocked back on his heels as he looked around. "Go home. Have a nice night, give me a report tomorrow. Tomorrow afternoon. We'll be rounding these things up for hours. No reason for you to be here. I'm not even sure if there's a reason for me to be here."

"You're sure?" It was a mess, and I felt bad leaving him alone to face it.

"Yup. I'll talk to the perimeter guys, let them know

you're clear to leave." Rodriguez rubbed his face. "It's gonna be a long night."

"If you need me, call. For this mess, still half my usual rate since I'm leaving you to deal with it."

"Thanks." He flashed a tired smile. "Now go before something else goes wrong."

"Got it." I took Elron's hand and we went. Not together, since we'd arrived in two cars. I went directly home, stomach protesting at leaving without food but glad to get away from the mess. Elron had promised to meet me at the house with takeout in hand. I planned on cracking open a bottle of wine and pretending like we'd planned to have our date night at the lodge.

Elron arrived only ten minutes after me, though how he'd managed carry-out rather than drive-through on that timeline was a mystery I'd leave for another time. He even found lilac statice flowers for the table. Turned out, red wine went nicely with burgers, even if his was mushroom rather than beef. In between bites, we recapped our day. Between the news of Ethel, which seemed to have happened days ago rather than this morning, and the emergencies at Witch's Warehouse, The Creamery, and Italian Flair, I did most of the talking. But I got to enjoy the last of my burger with cheerful tales of the greenhouses.

After munching down the fries, the conversation lulled. In quiet moments, memories and thoughts of Ethel swirled through my mind, but the day had numbed me from the pain. I didn't have tears, simply sadness. More than anything, I wanted to look forward. The accident that had killed her was a cold reminder that life could change in an instant.

"Can we talk about wedding plans? After everything…" Reaching across the table, I wrapped my hands around his. "I need to look toward something good."

His brows pulled together. "I am not sure this is the best time, given… but if it is what you wish."

"We are planning this wedding." I stared him down.

"Spring, as we said before." Elron took a deep breath. "Two years from now. It's quick, but with modern technology, getting all the invitations out in time should not be difficult."

I held my breath and counted to ten. "Yes, modern technology does make it easier to get invitations to people. So, with that in mind, spring of this coming year."

Elron's mouth gaped open. "That only—only six months away!"

"Quick, but with modern technology it should be easy enough." I managed to say it with a straight face.

His mouth moved, but sound didn't come out.

"Small, immediate family and friends." I pushed forward while I had the chance. "Perhaps have both an elf and witch marry us? It would be a nice touch. We'll want flowers. Given your job, I'd think something magical would be ideal. Oh, and casual. As sexy as you'd look in a suit, it's not your style."

"How long have you been planning this?" He finally figured out how to talk again.

My smile had a feral edge. "Oh, darling, planning weddings is what little girls do."

He paled, grabbed his wine, and drained the glass.

I snagged the bottle before he could refill. After all this time, I wasn't letting him drink himself silly before we had a solid planning session. "We already agreed to an outside wedding. Any ideas for the flowers?"

"What?"

"Flowers, what would you like?" This time I hid my smile.

His eyes went wide. "Well, there are so many choices. Roses are classic."

"But not very us."

"I suppose not." He didn't sound sure. "I know a good flower shop. We could visit tomorrow."

"Gladly." I grinned. "I want to pick the flowers for my bouquet tonight."

Elron sighed. "What about tulips?"

"Magical or mundane?" I should've forced him into this conversation ages ago. It was devilishly good fun watching him squirm.

"Sunflowers!" Elron's words tumbled over themselves so quickly they ran together. "There is a magical variety that gives the appearance of a small sun hovering over the center of the flower."

"A little bright for a spring wedding, but lovely symbolism." I tapped my fingers on the table and took rather too much pleasure in watching him squirm. Looking at his wide eyes and white-knuckled grip on the empty wine glass, no one would know the man had been married before. Maybe elven weddings were easier to plan.

I suppressed a snort. Right. Invitations sent years ahead, gifts in the making before invitations went out… Nope. They weren't any easier, at least not for the formal weddings.

"Or rhododendron flowers." Elron grabbed the wine bottle out of my hand.

"I don't know… remember that day in the rhododendron maze?" I really shouldn't torment the man, but six months of dodging questions, and I couldn't resist. "What do they mean?"

He set the bottle down and looked at me with clear

blue eyes filled with hope and a hint of pain. "Everything is better with you."

"Rhododendron it is." And it didn't matter if they could dance and sing. In fact, after today, I'd rather they didn't.

Elron pushed away from the table. "It is, you know."

"Is what?" I couldn't see or hear past the silver of his hair, the blue of his eyes, or the love in his voice.

"Better with you." Cupping my cheek, he leaned down and brushed his lips across mine.

A sharp knock cut through the moment.

We froze.

"Michelle, we need to talk." Mom's voice shattered whatever was left of the romance.

I groaned. "She won't go away."

Elron smiled slightly and brushed his knuckles across my cheek. "There will be other moments."

"But I was enjoying this one," I grumbled as I answered the door. "Mom, I wasn't expecting you."

Mom pushed her way in, followed by Dad, Susannah, and two other aids. "Given—" She took a deep breath. "Given the events, we need to talk. Oh, hello, Elron."

Dad shook his head. "I told you to call."

"A call would've been nice. Doing this in the morning would've been better. Today was, well, along with everything else, filled with magical mayhem that needed my attention." I snagged Elron's glass of wine off the table. Whatever we were going to talk about would require fortification.

The aids marched past our awkward family moment, refreshment tray and papers in hand. Without more than a nod in my direction, they set up in the living room.

Elron shut the door. "Shall we get started?"

Before moving so much as an inch, I gulped the wine, which was a poor use of a nice red.

As we shuffled to the living room, he leaned down and whispered in my ear, "We'll do this quickly so they can be on their way."

"Smart man," I whispered back before settling next to him on the love seat.

Mom and Dad took the sofa, with Susanna perched next to them. The puffy-eyed aid whose name I couldn't remember set the papers in front of mom while the other set out the tea. The mini vanilla scones were from Landa's kitchen, and I took three. After we were settled, they retreated to the kitchen, one of them loudly blowing her nose.

"To what do I owe the pleasure of your company at—" I checked my watch, "nine-thirty?"

Mom shifted uncomfortably. "Susanna should start."

Susanna bobbed her head before focusing on me. "Word of Ethel's death has spread quickly. I've been fielding calls all day from ministers who do not believe, given how events have unfolded, that it is appropriate to follow with Ethel's plan of Nancy easing the transition between Ethel and you. They want to vote in a new minister immediately."

"How many calls?" Not that I had a strong position to push back a movement against me. And did I want to? Was I helping witches in general if I pitted clan against clan in a bid to gain power? That was the point behind accepting the position of premier—being able to help witches avoid the outdated and inhumane customs that some minsters insisted on inflicting upon their clan.

"Enough." I put more bit behind my words. "A number."

Her lips flattened. "Sixty, but you know for each clan

that called, another two share their views but are afraid to speak."

"Afraid of what, exactly? Me holding a grudge? I don't have any power over them. Even as premier, there are limits to my power. Maybe I'm woefully under-informed when it comes to politics, but given my precarious situation, fearing me is senseless." Across from me, Mom and Dad were doing their best blank faces. A hint of doubt crept in. "Right?"

Dad sighed. "No one wants to be on the wrong side of the premier."

"Which I'm not, and no one is sure if I'll ever be at this point."

"That's not precisely true," Mom cut in. "You've been named the next premier. Paperwork filled out, and signatures gathered just as they've been for thousands of years. They even worked in an addendum about my tenure, which was rare but not unheard of. The question is if enough clans will press the issue to cause a problem."

"Sixty isn't enough." That much I knew. Which would've been more comforting if I had any idea how to handle this situation. It wasn't a magical emergency. It was people, and those were harder to wrangle than forks flinging meatballs.

Susanna shook her head. "The issue isn't the sixty questioning your leadership but the thirty who've called to question why you aren't in custody, being the clear benefactor of Ethel's death."

"What!" Only Elron's grip on my leg kept me sitting. "I didn't want her dead! I'm much better off if she lives the rest of her long life and then turns over the position."

"I told them as much, but if everyone with a reason to want a different premier bands together…" Susanna didn't say it.

Not that it mattered. Everyone in this room knew the rules and could do the math. If everyone who didn't want me to be the premier banded together, it wouldn't be difficult for them to get the 140 clans needed to push a vote on the subject. A vote that was unlikely to benefit me in any way.

I drained half the glass of wine before coming up for air. This was where I had to make a decision. Fight or don't. It was all up to me.

Elron's hand closed over mine. "That is enough."

"No, it isn't." But I let him take the glass anyway. Drunk wasn't the way to decide my future.

"Michelle," Dad's voice was soft, but the words weren't. "This is the life. It isn't like working with the police. There's no one else. All the decisions come down to you. Whether you're tired, sick, heartbroken, it doesn't matter. You still have to be the premier. Or you don't, but this is your last chance to back out."

"I…" I didn't know what to say.

Mom sat next to Dad, back ramrod straight, hands folded in her lap. Her thoughts didn't show on her face, but it was all too easy to slide back to my grandmother, her mother, torturing her in an effort to find me. Grandmother hadn't cared about Mom, a simple medial witch, but my power? That she wanted for her, the clan, and to become the next minister. And if torturing her daughter was what it took, well, that was the cost of the future.

"If I step down, which will do nothing but fuel the rumors that I had a hand in Ethel's death, who will take up the mantel? Who will fight to allow more men to be minister? To allow people to easily leave clans and bring justice when a minister abuses their position? Because these ministers like their power. They won't choose a premier who cares as much about the abuse of power or lack of integration with the rest of society."

And I knew. I knew that wanting a job wasn't the same as being the right person for a job.

"In this world, you're a radical," Susanna said bluntly. "They'll find a nice traditional minister and shove them into the office. Nothing will change. Perhaps the new premier will undo the progress Ethel has made."

"Then we fight."

I'd said those words before, with fever and fire behind them. Today, only fatigue and pain backed them. Fatigue and pain.

Three sharp knocks at the door held up any replies.

Almost as one, the group turned to the door with puzzled expressions. Which was refreshing, given how many people were currently in my apartment ruining what part of the evening the nonsense at Italian Flair hadn't already ruined.

"Were you expecting company?" Mom asked.

I gave her a pointed look. "No."

Three more knocks.

With a heavy sigh, I marched over and yanked open the door.

Isadora paused, hand poised to knock again.

"What are you doing here?" Defeating me publicly hadn't been enough?

"I didn't do it." She grabbed my shoulders, nails digging in through my shirt. "You have to believe me. I didn't do it. I didn't kill her."

The smeared eyeliner, heavily creased makeup, and hair tumbling out of its ponytail was a far cry from the woman I'd faced at the convention. That one had been a shark in a suit. This Isadora had the look of a woman who'd fought off a shark and barely escaped.

"You're hurting me." I kept my voice calm.

She let go and backed up a step. "Sorry, sorry."

I gently ushered her in and led her over to the table. "Take a breath and tell me what happened." I got her seated and cast a longing look at the empty bottle of wine. I really wished Elron had let me finish the glass.

Isadora's hand shook as she slid her phone across the table.

She still hadn't noticed the rest of the people in the room, and I wanted to keep it that way. As subtly as I could, I motioned for them to stay back. "What is this?"

"Read it."

A bright red headline filled most of the screen. "Isadora Baker is wanted in questioning in the death of Premier: Suspect magically capable and dangerous."

"They think I killed her."

I scrolled down. It only got worse, all but saying Isadora had killed the premier, though it was light on details as to how Isadora had managed to create a car accident that only killed one person or if they'd even located Ethel's body.

A lump formed in my throat, and tears gathered in my eyes. I swallowed hard, pushing back the emotion. Problems like this needed cool and collected thinking. Too bad I hadn't had that since breakfast.

When I finished reading, I pushed the phone back to her and waited until she looked at me and I could lock eyes with her. "Did you kill Ethel?" It hurt to say those words.

"No! No!" She grabbed my hand, squeezing too tightly. "You have to believe me. I don't like you, but how would killing Ethel help me? If she's dead, you're the premier. I wanted you gone! Now that can't happen."

According to Susanna, it could, and the woman I'd

battled was smart enough to know that. "Unless enough band together for a vote."

She blanched. "They haven't done that in nine hundred years! A hundred and forty ministers can't agree on lunchtime, never mind more important matters. Why do you think we have a premier?"

"To prevent little witches like you from causing trouble. Only Ethel was too lenient and you killed her for it," Susanna said as she charged over.

Isadora knocked her chair over in her haste to get up. "No, I didn't. I wouldn't." She backed away, eyes wide as she finally saw all the witches in the room.

"You did!"

"I wasn't even there! Cars crash. Horrible things happen, but it wasn't me." Isadora spun around and grabbed my hand. "You have to believe me."

Oddly enough, I did.

CHAPTER THIRTEEN

"Susanna, stop. Accusations without proof don't help anything." I pitched my voice to cut through the room, and it did, with everyone focusing on me. "Sit down in the living room while I talk to Isadora. Mom, join us?"

"But, what if she tries to hurt you?" Susanna didn't say 'like she did the premier,' but we all heard it.

Isadora's grip tightened painfully on my hand.

I snorted. "Don't mistake her besting me in the Trial by Magic for me being defenseless. I trust if it comes to it, you'll rush to my defense."

Susanna's lips flattened to a thin line. "As you wish."

Mom shooed the other aids over to Susanna, and Dad drifted into the middle of the room until Mom waved him over. Elron had already assumed he'd be involved and positioned himself behind my chair.

I used the time to free myself from Isadora's grasp and shake feeling back into my hand. The events didn't add up to me. Susanna claimed the witches blame me for Ethel's death. Isadora shows up claiming she's a suspect. Maybe we'd both be suspects, but then Mom should be on the list too. And why would the police be looking at Isadora in the first place?

"You'll help me?" Isadora's voice wobbled.

I sat down between her and my mom. "Tell them what you told me, and we'll talk."

She showed them the phone. "Zack, Marquette, and I were driving home today. We'd stopped in Woodstock for dinner. While I was in the bathroom, I heard a woman mention the witch who killed the premier, so I checked my phone. There it was, a picture of me. I took the car and drove here as fast as I could. I didn't know what else to do. My clan minster would turn me in, guilty or not, and I couldn't put Zack and Marquette in any more danger. You have to believe me, I didn't do this. I was at the hotel when I heard about Ethel's accident. It's why we delayed leaving."

"Say I believe you. Why do you think the police are looking at you?" Mom asked.

Isadora shrugged. "Maybe the Trial by Magic?"

"Can you think of any other reason?" I watched her closely.

"No." She shook her head. "My minister and I don't get along, and she'd love to be rid of me."

"That's it? That's the only person who might be holding a grudge?" I couldn't let it go. It took effort to plant evidence, magical or mundane. The police had to have a reason to want to talk to her.

Her shoulders slumped. "I spent the drive over replaying every moment. I don't know why I'm a suspect."

Police I could work with. Police wanting to question her, I could manage and control, to an extent. "Mom, get one of Ethel's lawyers here."

"What? Why?" Isadora's attention darted from Mom to me.

I took her hand in mine, hoping this way she couldn't cut off circulation to my fingers. "You have to talk to the police, but you don't have to do it alone or risk a tense situation when turning yourself in. I'm going to coordinate a meeting between you and officers I trust." She tried to yank her hand away, but I held firm. "You came to me for help. This is how I can help."

"By turning me over! That's not help, it's suicide." She looked at Dad. "You know what they do to witches!"

That was mostly true. It wasn't easy to hold a witch in jail. We tended to get expedited trials and swift executions. Another one of the many reasons witches didn't want to work with the rest of society. A reason I'd like to change. "Doing it this way ensures everyone is on their best behavior. You'll have a lawyer and the next premier with you. You'll talk to police I trust. This is the only way."

"No, it's not." Isadora sighed. "But it is the smartest option."

I smiled, which may not have been as reassuring as I'd hoped from the way she clutched her phone. "I'll do everything in my power to make this uneventful and easy."

"Make your phone calls." She sagged against the chair back and closed her eyes. "Take my phone so I'm not tempted to use it."

"Done." With her phone in one hand and mine in the other, I stepped away from the table.

Elron followed me. "Are you sure this is wise?"

"No." I found Rodriguez's number. My finger hovered over the call button. He wasn't going to like hearing from me again tonight.

"Then why are you helping her?"

"Because I wished someone had helped me when I'd had trouble. Because the premier has to help. That's the job." I gazed into his worried eyes. "Don't you see? She—

they need me. And not that long ago, I could've used someone like me in this job."

"You can't save them all."

"I can save her." I dialed Rodriguez's number.

The worry in his eyes faded as pride took its place. "If anyone can…" He gave a small smile and went back to the table.

I hoped I hadn't just made a promise I couldn't keep. I hoped she was worth it.

"Michelle, what could you possibly need? Magic running wild at the lodge?" Rodriguez grumbled. "I'm only now finishing at Italian Flair."

I winced. "You know I wouldn't call unless it was important."

"I'm waiting."

"Rumor is the police are looking for a witch, Isadora Baker. I can arrange a meeting." And with those words I wasn't Michelle Oaks, police consultant, but Michelle, presumed next premier. That realization took my breath away for a moment.

Seconds passed before Rodriguez spoke. "When?"

"Sooner would be better."

"So, tonight." Rodriguez swore. "I'd like sleep tonight."

"Me too."

He sighed. "The lodge, I'm guessing? I'll need half an hour to get myself and a few other officers there."

This time I hesitated, unsure of my new role. "She's scared, Rodriguez. She's agreed to answer questions, but the press about her has her spooked."

"That's our fault. Damn rookie sent out the wrong information. We want to talk to her. I hadn't heard anything about her being a suspect or the police being concerned about interacting with her, at least not until after that press release."

"Good to hear."

He sighed again. "I'll be there soon. And Michelle, be careful." Without explaining what he meant by that, he hung up.

"Thank for the warning," I grumbled. Like I didn't know the jobs of consultant and premier didn't play well together. Lines that needed to be solid ended up blurry.

I slid my phone back in my pocket, took a deep breath, and turned back to the table. Elron had resumed looming over it from a few feet away. Mom and Dad were keeping an eye on Isadora, who still had her eyes closed, but her foot tapped the floor. I sat.

Isadora's eyes opened. "Well?"

Mom leaned forward. "I have a lawyer on the way here. We're in luck. Thanks to the convention, Rhiannon is in town. She'll be here soon."

"She's a shark. Or a dragon." Isadora's fingers twisted together. "I've seen her in meetings. Brutal."

"And now she'll be your shark." I forced a smile. "The police will be here in half an hour. We'll set you up in the living room. My contact assures me the police didn't intend for the press release naming you as a suspect to go out."

"Frankly, that doesn't fill me with confidence."

I shrugged. Nothing I said would make her feel better about seeing herself publicly named a suspect in Ethel's accident and, at this point, her presumed death.

Mom filled the gap in conversation. "As soon as Rhiannon is here, she'll take over dealing with the police. Listen to her. She'll be on your side and there to help you."

"Got it."

"It's going to be fine. My contact is honest, and Rhiannon will make sure they don't force you to say anything you don't want to say." I patted her hand. "While we wait, I need to talk to Susanna. I'll be in the living room if you need me, okay?"

Isadora nodded.

Giving her a reassuring smile, I left the table, Elron and my dad not far behind. With each step, I tried to put Isadora's problems out of my head and refocus on the clan problems. But the accident, the location of Ethel's body, and the strange magic erupting throughout town were no more willing than Isadora's problems to fade to the background.

It was too much. Logic and strategy were distant memories. The day's events had reduced me to reacting, but being the one to decide how to handle clan problems was new, and I didn't have years of previous reactions to fall back on.

"She's guilty. We all know it." Susanna's bitterness pushed the words out in a rush. "I don't know why you're bothering to help her. Not with the trouble you're in with the clans. How this helps you is beyond me."

"If we all know Isadora is guilty, then why did you barge in here claiming the clans believe Michelle is guilty?" Elron said icily. "Pick your villain. Given their previous interactions, it cannot be both of them."

Susanna huffed. "Helping her won't endear you to the ministers."

"According to you, nothing will strengthen my position. All that's left for me to do is resign and fade into the night." I watched for a reaction that would give me insight to her motives.

Displeasure sat on her face the same as it had before. "As I've said, circumstances are not in your favor."

"Then we change the narrative." Dad stared at her. "Surely we can salvage this—that is, assuming you still want the job, Michelle."

"I do, and I know what the problem is. Ethel named it before she died."

That got Susanna's attention, interest breaking through the sullen displeasure.

I took a deep breath. "They don't know me, and what they know of me doesn't fill them with confidence. To most witches, I'm not the person who spearheaded the largest spell in modern history, but the girl who was broken by the power she channeled and may yet be crippled by that experience, magically, mentally, or both. They think I want to use their power, but I'm not strong enough to hold the reins. They don't know me. They don't know that I'll fight with them and for them. Until they do, they'll assume the worst because why would they credit me with abilities they've never seen?"

That's when it hit me, what I needed to do to reassure the minister. "A press conference on The Witch Network. We can do it live. They'll show it over the regular broadcast and can replay it. I say how sad I am that the mantle has passed to me. I reassure them that the investigation is ongoing. I show them I'm here. I'm not in hiding. I'm ready, and I can be their premier." If I didn't step into the spotlight now, I'd lose my chance.

"It could work," Dad mused. "You don't focus on the nuts and bolts of the accident but how you'll handle the event as a whole. You give them a glimpse of what their world will be like with you as the premier."

"Do it with pomp and style. Everyone loves a good show," Elron added.

Susanna looked between us sourly. "It could work."

"Set it up. We have a lot to do, and I'd like to get some sleep tonight." I stared at Susanna until she tugged a phone out of her pocket. "Hair, makeup, wardrobe, the works. You know the drill."

"Our people should still be in town given what's happened. I'll get them here." She had a quick word with the other assistants, and then the three of them were on their phones.

My head swam. I leaned forward, elbows braced on my knees. This was it. I was going to fight, not for what I most wanted, my life as a consultant, but for where I felt I was most needed. My reward? Spending my days managing a bunch of bickering witches who didn't like or respect me much.

Dad knelt in front of me. "I'm proud of you."

"I'm scared."

He nodded. "You can be scared, but remember, Elron, Nancy, and I, we're here for you. Both our clans support you. You're not doing this alone."

Elron dropped to one knee beside him. "Whenever this new job overwhelms you, we can run away to the woods and spend time with elves."

"I'm sure the witches will love that." I sighed. "Can you help me write out what I'm going to say? My brain is cooked, and I won't remember without notes."

"Of course," Dad said.

Elron nodded his head. "I will ensure the event has the pomp it needs."

"Thank you." I searched for better words but couldn't find them. "Thank you."

Two sharp raps at the door brought all conversation to a stop. Mom marched over and opened the door to a stout woman with her blunt chin-length hair straightened to perfection and a high shine on her pumps. The slate gray suit and cutting smile completed the look. Paying no attention to those of us at the far end of the room, Rhiannon settled herself next to Isadora at the table, shoved a plate to the side, and got to work.

From there, it was a blur of activity. Witches poured into the room with various tasks related to getting me ready for my first solo press convention. The activity paused when Rodriguez came in, followed by Officer Kent, a dark elf, and an officer I vaguely recognized from the accident scene. Thankfully, with Rhiannon here, all I had to do was make the introductions and remind Isadora to listen to Rhiannon.

I would've liked to have stayed to hear the interview, but my speech wasn't finished. Besides, I doubted I'd learn anything useful from Isadora. While she was certainly capable of causing the accident, I couldn't figure out a motive and didn't think she was the type to take action without a reason.

With that situation under control, I retreated to my bedroom, where Dad helped me with the speech while witches worked on my hair, makeup, and clothing options. If anyone had asked me—which they didn't— I would've said there wasn't a perfect outfit for saying, "Sorry Ethel's dead, but I'd like to take over her position and power." Turned out, a deep plum suit with a black shirt was the perfect outfit.

Dad took the speech notes, promised to have the prompter ready, and fled before wardrobe could kick him out. Only minutes later, my reflection gazed back at me from a full-length mirror. The somber and competent reflection looked like someone I would trust.

They rushed me past Isadora, whose tears had dried. She was regaining some of her own shark tendencies under Rhiannon's care.

From my apartment, they herded me outside, which didn't seem at all right to me until I saw it. Witch lights illuminated the altar, and the newly set-up podium beside it. The lilac statice that had graced our dinner table now lay across the altar, a reminder to the loss of Ethel that had to be Elron's idea. With the light concentrated on me and the rest left to darkness, it would be a quiet moment, one that gave the illusions of catching me honoring my predecessor.

"Remember, Susanna will introduce you. You'll step into view, wait a moment, and then start the speech," a witch reminded as she positioned me at the very edge of the light.

"Right."

Zach, the same Zach who'd supported Isadora, manned the camera. Over his head, glowing letters spelled my name, followed by my first prompt. *Walk*.

All I had to do was look serious and follow the prompts. Should be simple. It wasn't like live broadcasts ever went wrong.

Susanna took her place behind the podium.

Zach held up three fingers. Then two.

In what felt like the blink of an eye, the countdown was over, and Susanna had already done part of her introduction. The words came to me over a long distance and only faintly at that. I'd done this before, stood in front of a camera, leading up to and at the convention. But none of those had been live or as important.

"Now, a statement from your next premier, Michelle Oaks." Susanna carefully stepped between the podium and altar as she left.

Walk flashed brightly, so I did. Hand tightly gripping the bottom edge of the podium where the camera couldn't see, I struggled to follow the prompts.

"This morning in a tragic turn of events, the Premier Ethel's car was involved in an accident. The police investigation is ongoing, but initial reports indicate the premier did not survive." I swallowed twice, praying my voice wouldn't crack as I continued. "As the proposed transition Ethel and I had planned no longer works under these circumstances, adjustments have been made. I am ready to assume my position as premier, with Nancy Oaks serving alongside me for the first year to ease the transition."

Mom had agreed, and I think she had even been relieved that she wouldn't have to do the job for very long.

The prompter flashed brightly.

"To further cement my commitment to you, and to honor our traditions as we move forward, I will be assembling a council of eleven ministers to guide me. While no one can replace premier Ethel, I hope their experience can fill the void left in Ethel's absence." I held back a sigh of relief. That was the worst of it.

"If you would join me in a moment of prayer." I took my place, kneeling beside the altar.

To my dismay, I couldn't think clearly enough to put together a useful prayer. Instead, all I did was desperately plead that Ethel not really be gone. That I had more time before I had to give up my business and the life I so enjoyed. That I could have a little more time to figure out how to balance what I wanted with what I had to do. There had to be a way I could do both, if only I had time to work it out.

I stood up, not sure if that had been the right length of prayer for the press conference. It didn't matter. I had to get off camera. A sour taste filled my mouth at my own hypocrisy, asking everyone to pray for Ethel when I knelt and thought only of myself.

"And the broadcast is over," Zach announced. "Camera is off!"

I sucked down great gulps of air. Over, it was over.

Susanna appeared in front of me, her pinched expression replaced with a grin. "I didn't think you had it in you, but I was wrong. That will win them over."

Mom and Dad came over and managed to nudge Susanna to the side. "You've made it hard for anyone to call for your replacement. It should do the job for now."

"They'll criticize me for not making a statement this morning." And for anything else I'd done wrong in their eyes, no matter how real or imagined. But even Ethel had said that was part of the job. A terrible part.

Dad shrugged. "We'll make a statement, say you were waiting to get more information from the police, that you'd hoped to be able to offer them a full explanation but investigations take time."

"Do you think they'll buy it?"

Susanna shrugged. "It doesn't matter as long as they don't make too much of a fuss. Once you're sworn in as Premier, you're the guiding force, the great mediator between clans, the steady spot in the madness. The politics won't matter as much."

"I guess that's good news." With the adrenaline fading, fatigue was taking its place. "Can I be done for the night? It's been a long day."

Mom nodded. "I think the police are still interviewing Isadora at your place."

"She can shower at my apartment." Elron took my hand and gently tugged me away. "Bring a change of clothing for her and hangers for this suit."

A shower sounded like heaven.

Nearly an hour later, I escaped back to my own now blissfully empty apartment. I had Elron and my mom to thank for it being empty. They'd shooed everyone out. Even Isadora, though she'd tried to come thank me for helping her. According to a quick chat with Rhiannon, she and the police were square. That was all I needed to know for the night.

Safely tucked in my own bed, I let myself feel. At first the grief was distant, dampened by a day that felt as long as some years. Then it came back, with a few tears at first, and then sobs. For a lot of witches, Ethel was the face of her office, a symbol, but she'd been my mentor, supporter, and friend all rolled into one. I'd never thought I'd be taking her place like this. Not this soon.

Eventually, I fell asleep, but dreams of Ethel haunted me through the night.

"Michelle?"

"You're dead," I mumbled. "Leave me alone so I can sleep."

"I assure you, I am not dead, and it is past time for you to wake up."

The voice wasn't right. That didn't sound at all like Ethel, but like a man. I bolted up, blinking at the light pouring through the window. "Elron?"

He handed me a mug of tea before taking a seat at the foot of the bed. "You missed breakfast, and I worried."

"No." I checked the clock and groaned. "I've got twenty minutes to hand Rodriguez reports on yesterday's cases."

"Landa packed a bag of muffins. They are on the dining room table." He got up and headed to the door. "I must go. I am expecting a delivery at work. I will see you at noon at Fab Flowers."

"Wait!" I scrambled out of bed and tugged him down for a quick kiss. "Thank you. Be safe, and I'll see you later."

He chuckled. "You are the one who needs to be safe." He tugged the door shut behind him.

I rushed to get ready and was bouncing down the

driveway when I realized I'd forgotten my tea. "Narzel blast it." Arriving without reports was one thing, but without reports and caffeine? Hard pass.

Roasted Beans was on the way, and plus, they would put a pump of energy boost in my tea. I could even get a drink for Rodriguez while I was at it.

CHAPTER FOURTEEN

That's what I told myself right up to the moment when I pulled into the parking lot and saw the drive-through line wrapping around the building. It might not be as quick of a stop as I'd wanted, but it would still do the trick. Rather than sit in my car as I waited, I parked and headed inside. At least this way I could get a secondhand pick-me-up while my tea was in progress.

I pushed open the door and was assaulted by absolute chaos. It took me a moment to sort it all out. In the chair closest to the door, a woman with her face buried in her hands sobbed violently. The man across the table from her was frantically making list upon list on a tiny scrap of paper, the words running into each other.

On the other side of them, a man was screaming into his phone. Three people were laying on the ground behind him, asleep from the look of them. Behind the counter, one barista was slumped across the cash register, shaking ever so slightly. Two other baristas were darting back and forth frantically but didn't seem to be noticing when they spilled drinks or something fell on the floor. The last barista was frantically scrubbing the cappuccino machine, but it didn't look dirty. If anything, it looked like she'd been doing the same task for quite a while.

They were far from the only ones. On the other side of the store, a large man was pacing back and forth, talking to himself. Near him, another woman appeared to be asleep on her feet. At the tables behind them, four people behaved as oddly as the rest. Two girls were sharing a table, and they seemed to be typing so fast the computer couldn't even register the keystrokes. The other two tables each had one person, a scowling elderly woman and a crying young man.

I cracked open my shields, intending to extend a tiny tendril of magic, but I didn't even get that far. The entire room was overflowing with some type of magic, similar to what I'd seen at Happy Paws and The Creamery. Like those jobs, I would need help.

Trying not to attract any attention, I backed out the door, closed it quietly, and then fished my cell phone out of my purse. Rather than hope my usual contact Officer Rodriguez was available, I simply dialed 9-1-1.

A crisp, female voice floated across the phone. "Cherokee County 911, what is your emergency?"

"Hello, I'm Michelle Oaks, a witch and consultant with the Cherokee County Sheriff's Office. I'm calling because there seems to be some type of magical emergency at Roasted Beans, the coffee shop in the old downtown district. I'm afraid I don't know the exact address."

"Don't worry about the address, I can pull that up." There was a short pause. "Ms. Oaks, I have verified your status with the sheriff's office. Is there anyone you would like to have respond to this call?"

I knew who I wanted, but I wasn't really sure what was needed here. "It would be ideal if Officer Rodriguez could get here. Other than that, backup of any kind, preferably officers with some magical sensitivity, and certainly with magic nullifying handcuffs. I have not yet ascertained the cause of the incident, but there are about fifteen people in this building, and all of them are going to need some type of magical assistance."

"I'll see if Officer Rodriguez is available."

"Thank you." A car pulled out of the drive through line, tired of waiting. I squinted, trying to see through tinted glass doors. I hadn't thought to look at the drive-through window or considered how many people might have been infected by whatever was going on here and then driven off to cause trouble somewhere else. Hopefully, it was localized inside the building, or this would be quite the mess.

"Do you need me to stay on the phone until backup arrives?"

"No. I'm going to see if I can solve some of this."

"Good luck."

"Thanks." I had a feeling I was going to need it. I hung up the phone and tucked it in my purse, my mind already focused on the job.

If I wanted to do my best to contain this, I couldn't let the people who were in the drive-through leave until I was sure they were safe. Since I didn't have a badge, I doubted the drivers would all listen to me just because I said so. While I might be able to come up with the power to put a big shield spell around the building and parking lot, that wouldn't leave me much for the rest of the emergency. Plus, it would take even more energy to construct the spell so the police could get in but no one else could get out. That meant I would have to get clever, and probably irritate a few people.

Keeping one eye on the entrance in case another car

came in, I walked across the parking lot until I could see most of the cars in the drive-through line. With a twist of my wrist, I summoned my wand. Then I focused on the ground under the cars. "*Orzu.*"

The ground softened under the cars, and their tires slowly sank. When they were deep enough in the earth that I didn't think the cars would be able to force their way out, I solidified the ground. "*Fehu.*"

Then I circled around to the last two cars that were next to the windows and repeated the process with them. This would irritate the drivers to no end, but it was easy enough to undo once the problems here were resolved.

With the people in the drive-through dealt with, I walked over to the entrance to the parking lot. Using my wand, I carefully drew the words "POLICE LINE: DO NOT CROSS" in the air. When I was satisfied with the spacing of the letters and it fully spanned the entrance and exit, I pointed my wand at it. "*Wunho.*" The letters began to glow red.

That was all I could do out here. I stopped by my car and locked my purse inside. Tucking my keys in my back pocket, I braced myself for what I was about to find in the building. I opened the door with my wand in my hand, ready to cast a spell.

If anything, it had gotten more chaotic. The crying was louder. There was an argument breaking out between the man who had been pacing and the formerly asleep woman.

Taking a deep breath, I sent out a tendril of energy to the person closest to me, the woman still slouched over crying. My probe didn't find anything in the air around her. If I thought any of these people were rational, I would've asked for permission before probing them for magic, but I didn't think they were in their right mind because of whatever magic had been done to them. I carefully touched the probe to her shoulder.

Ah, there it was. The magic was inside of her. But it seemed to be moving, as if the spell hadn't really settled into being. Even though it was in flux, I got hints of what it was trying to do. It was creating the emotions. It was actively making the woman feel sorrow.

I pulled the probe away from her and directed it towards the man. He was still frantically writing his list over and over and over again. At this point, the paper was almost blue from pen marks. I repeated the same process with the probe, first hovering above him and then touching him. As before, I didn't feel anything in the air around him but got a sense of the spell as soon as the probe made contact with his skin. It had the same unfinished feel as the spell on the woman, but this one seemed to be creating obsession with his current task.

Someone grabbed my arm, breaking my concentration. I lost track of the probe, and my shield snapped into place. I pivoted, looking at the elderly woman with a hand clenched around my sleeve. She had curly blue hair and an expression that meant business.

She scowled at me. "What are you doing? Don't you know we need help?"

"Ma'am, I'm doing my very best." I didn't even get a chance to continue before she started scolding me.

"All you have done since you got here is stand right there and stare at those two people. That does not help. We need help. Something is wrong." Her eyes went wide at the end.

I took a deep breath and reached over to try and pry her fingers off my sleeve. "Ma'am, please let me explain. I'm a witch. There's a magical disturbance at work in this coffee shop." And that was as far as I got.

"I don't care if you're a witch! You need to help us." Her fingers tightened as she spoke.

I took a deep breath, trying not to get frustrated with this poor woman who was clearly at the spell's mercy. "I am trying to. You are interrupting me."

She let go of my sleeve and grabbed my hand. The spell pushed against me, and I could feel it morphing inside her. This time, it had ramped up her anxiety and brought her to this state. There had to be something I could do.

I tuned out her renewed scolding as I tried to figure out a spell to help her. Maybe if I just put her to sleep. "*Mannaz.*"

I may have put a little too much behind the spell, because she collapsed as if she'd been stuck with a tranquilizer. I caught her and slowly lowered her to the ground, leaning her against the wall by the couple I had been examining before she had interrupted me.

A roar came from my left.

I whirled around, wand in hand. The man who'd been pacing and arguing with the woman had his head thrown back, his throat working as he roared again. I'd heard that roar before, and it chilled me right down to my very bones.

Before I could do anything else, his shape twisted, and his clothes ruptured at the seams, falling to the floor. Where he'd been, there was now a fully grown male black bear. He opened his mouth, showing off an impressive set of teeth, and roared for the third time.

Beside him, the woman collapsed to the ground. I couldn't tell from here if she was passed out or asleep again, but it really didn't matter. This day, which hadn't started great, had just gotten exponentially worse.

Then my brain kicked back into gear. I was standing in a room with more than fifteen innocent people and a werebear who was a victim of magical influence, and he was angry. I had to contain him before he caused problems for anyone else.

I shouted the very first spell that came to mind. "*Sowil!*"

A containment spell popped into being around the black bear. He swung his head away from the woman in towards me. I wasn't sure that part was progress, but he seemed to be captured for the moment.

Taking a deep breath, I quickly glanced around the room. The man who'd been yelling on the phone was peeking out from behind the counter, along with three of the baristas. One of them was still collapsed across the cash register. No one else had reacted. They were so heavily influenced by the magic that they hadn't noticed the bear.

I returned my gaze to the bear as he lifted up a giant paw. The claws at the end of his toes were truly terrifying claws. He swatted at the containment spell.

This spell should've been immune to physical damage. No mere bear should've been able to get through it. Or that's what I told myself.

The spell wobbled as his paw impacted it. When he moved back, I could see four gashes in the spell where his claws had ripped right through it. Yep, this day officially sucked.

He poked his nose at the shredded remains and managed to shove part of his face through. He leaned forward until his shoulders were touching the spell. After a moment, the spell just melted away.

This time, I tried the same spell that had worked earlier, though I threw a bit more power into it. "*Mannaz!*"

He sat back on his haunches and shook his head. Then he shook his head again, as if disoriented. Well, that was an improvement over terrorizing people. Though I wasn't going to feel good about him until he'd been rid of the spell and was back to himself again.

The werebear might have stayed sitting, but the woman woke up. Upon seeing the bear, she let out a scream that would've done a banshee proud. With that, what portion of the sleep spell that had been working was broken. The bear lunged to his feet, stretching out his nose as he did so.

Since I was oh-for-two on spells, I had to figure out something else quick, because the last thing I wanted to see was a werebear eat a woman because they were both under the influence of magic.

I wracked my brain for something else. "Ropes," I whispered, trying to remember the rune. "*Algiz!*"

The magical ropes snaked around the bear, and in a fraction of a second, they had him tussled up. All four of his feet were tied together, and his snout was tied shut.

I held my breath, hoping that this spell would finally hold him.

Something hit me from behind, knocking me forward. Three quick steps later, I regained my balance and whirled around with my wand in the air.

A slender man in a police officer's uniform with pointed ears and gray brown skin yanked off his sunglasses. "Sorry, Ms. Oaks. Couldn't see you through the door. What seems to be…" He finally spotted the bear, and that seemed to answer that question for me.

My gaze followed his. The ropes were holding the werebear, so at least that spell was going well. I turned my attention back to Officer Kent. I was rather surprised to see him on this particular call, as it was still the middle of the day, and he was a dark elf. They didn't usually do so well in bright daylight, which was why he been wearing sunglasses. "I'm surprised they sent you."

He made a face. "On call, and I live fairly close.

Dispatch said they are having trouble all over town, and I was the closest one with 'magic.' Do you know what happened?"

"I'm not sure. I stopped by to get a cup of tea and found the place like this." I found my eyes drawn back to the werebear. "Okay, the bear was still in human form, but you get the idea."

Officer Kent took in the room, from the woman I'd knocked unconscious, to the couple at the table who were still doing what they'd been doing since I got here, to the three catatonic people. The man who'd been screaming into the phone was still huddled behind the counter, as were the three baristas. The three people remaining behind the werebear were either typing or crying as they had been before. It was very unsettling that most of the people hadn't even noticed the bear.

"Have you managed to ascertain what's affecting these individuals?" Officer Kent asked.

"Not really. It seems to be some type of spell that has yet to settle into specific form. I suspect they ingested it, but I'm not sure yet. Oh, and it reacts unpredictably with magic. So, I don't know how long those ropes on the bear over there will last."

As soon as I said that, Officer Kent got out his radio and started requesting medical teams and a team to take care of an out-of-control werebear. I hoped that last request wasn't one he made every day.

While he was busy, I kept my eyes on the bear. So far, the rope seemed to be holding, but I wasn't going to probe them and potentially mess up whatever balance they had with the magic inside of him. The woman was passed out again. That was one less thing to worry about right now.

"Ms. Oaks," Officer Kent said, "do you think you can remove the spell from these people?"

Before I could answer, a woman barged through the doors to the coffee shop. She was absolutely as neat as a pin. Her hair was carefully combed, no single strand out of place, crisp creases in her slacks, and a suit jacket over her red blouse. Though the angry scowl dominating her face was more compelling than her suit. "Officer, I need to report a crime. Someone sunk the tires of my car into the road, and it will not move."

"Where was this?" Officer Kent glanced at me.

I tipped my head away from the woman, hoping he'd get the hint and excuse the two of us to talk for a moment.

"In the drive-through." Her voice went up in pitch. "If I can't leave soon I'll be late to a meeting with a client."

Officer Kent lowered his voice. "Ma'am, give me just a moment. I need to consult my colleague, and then I can address your concerns."

He stepped over to where the three catatonic people were still laying on the floor. I followed while the incredibly tidy lady glared at us.

"Was there something you want to say, Ms. Oaks?"

I look him straight in the eye and hoped he'd understand exactly why I'd done what I'd done, or I might be getting a trip to jail tonight. "I needed to ensure that no one left the premises after being exposed to the spell. Since I have yet to figure out what's causing this problem, I was worried it could be transferred to the people in the drive-through, and then both your fellow officers and I would get to chase it all across town. So, to prevent that scenario, I sank the cars. I can reverse it, but we need to clear all those people before they leave, right?"

Officer Kent closed his eyes and took a deep breath before looking at me. "Ms. Oaks, are you sure you can get those cars out without doing any damage to them?"

"Yes." I mean, I'd never actually freed that many cars

before, but I'd used the spell plenty, and it had always worked in the past.

"All right, then. I'll deal with the angry drive-through customers while you figure out what's going on in here." Rather than give me time to argue with him, he marched back over to the woman tapping her foot.

With a sigh, I looked down at the three catatonic people underfoot. Maybe I hadn't handled everything properly, but I couldn't figure out what else I should've done. I didn't have the same authority he did. I didn't carry a badge. I was a witch.

That's right. I was a witch, and it was my job to figure out what happened to these poor people. With that thought, I actually saw the three catatonic people. All three of them had their eyes closed. Since I could see their chests moving from time to time, they seemed to be breathing just fine. From the way they had fallen, slightly on top of one another, with limbs tangled, I thought it looked like they had been suddenly reduced to unconsciousness.

Plus, there was a puddle of coffee under the three of them. That made the sudden collapse assumption even more likely. People didn't willingly drop coffee they'd just purchased. Even if they did drop the coffee, they didn't lay down and take a nap in it.

One of the coffee cups burbled out a bit more of the dark fluid. Now that was a waste. Leaning over, I snagged it off the ground. Two stars and the word energy caught my attention. That was how the shop marked drinks if they were getting a pump of a magical ingredient. Though a boost of energy didn't explain why these people were unconscious.

Or maybe it did. There was always a chance for magic to go wrong. Sometimes when it went wrong, it went very, very wrong.

On a hunch, I picked up another one of the coffee cups. It also mentioned energy, so I picked up the third. In an extremely surprising turn of events, it also had a note for an energy boost of the magical variety.

Now, two could be coincidence, but three was most definitely a pattern. I glanced around the shop. There were actually quite a few coffee cups still around, as if people started them but didn't finish them or weren't aware enough to put them in the trash. Cracking my shields open just a little bit, I extended a tendril into the cups. A spell swirled, a much more concentrated version of what I'd felt in the man and woman I'd probed. The spell seemed to be in the process of changing from an energy-boosting spell to a sleeping spell. That would explain a lot.

I carefully set the three cups on the shelf and hurried over to the table with the crying woman and the man still frantically making a list. Even without probing the two cups, I could feel the magic as I picked them up. The woman's cup listed a magical boost of joy, while the man's cup mentioned a quarter shot of disinterest.

So far, everyone had shown essentially the opposite reaction to what was listed on the cup near them. The guy had asked for a little disinterest and gotten a lot of obsession. The woman had asked for some joy and ended up sobbing. My three sleeping beauties over there had asked for some energy. In fact, I was willing to bet that almost everyone in the shop had consumed a beverage that was supposed to have one effect and was instead having a very different affect.

The bear growled. I set the man's cup down and whirled around, wand in the air. He was still safely tied up, but his eyes were darting around, and he looked a little confused by the situation now. I'd be willing to bet a fairly hefty sum of money that he had requested some calming in his drink.

The door swung open again, and this time Officer Kent and a woman I vaguely recognized stepped in. It had been a while, and she had changed her hair, but if memory served, that was Mary Bells, a medical witch, which was absolutely perfect considering the problem.

Officer Kent quickly introduced us. "Michelle Oaks, this is Mary Bells, one of the medical witches who respond to community disturbances. Dispatch sent her over after you told them how many people have been spelled."

Mary smiled at me. "It's good to see you."

I shook her hand, returning her smile. "I wish this could be under better circumstances."

She nodded. "You have an idea what happened to them?"

"Actually, I do." I leaned over and grabbed the two cups off the table. "Both of these coffee cups, as well as three belonging to the sleeping people over there, list a magical additive. I think something went wrong with the additives, and they're causing very extreme reactions that oppose the original intent. So, if you read these two cups, they should have gotten a very small amount of indifference and some joy. Instead, he seems to be under some sort of obsessive compulsion, and she's sobbing."

Mary Bells took the cups from me. She stared at them and then held a hand over one. A second later, she jerked her hand back and rubbed it on her pants. "Well, there's definitely some unstable magic in there. You think it affected everyone in here?"

I sympathized with her. It wasn't a pleasant sensation. "Everyone who consumed something with a magical additive." I hated this next part, but it was a necessity. "It's possible there are people around town suffering from this, too. I don't know how long it's been going on, but anyone who got a beverage in the drive-through would be well away from here before the effects started."

Both Officer Kent and Mary Bells muttered unpleasant things under their breath. Finally, Officer Kent said, "That might explain some of the calls we've been getting today."

Mary Bells nodded in agreement. "I do appreciate you taking care of this so far, but I think I can manage. I'm going to have ambulances transport all of these people to the hospital for further treatment and have this place shut down until the health department can sort out exactly what happened."

I couldn't help but look at the poor werebear again. "Are you sure? It's a lot to handle. I can help narrow down the search for the health department."

Mary shook her head. "If you can free the drive-through customer's cars, I can take it from here. I can even handle Mr. Bear over there. As for narrowing down the search, there was a case just last week where a coffee shop had recently switched suppliers for their magical syrups, and the new batch wasn't up to the same standards and had some interesting effects. My guess is it's something like that, but the health department will have to be in there anyway, so there's no point in you doing their job."

"All right. I'll go free those cars and get out of your hair." I shook both of their hands again. "Hopefully the next case will be a little less of an emergency for all of us."

Officer Kent and Mary agreed. After saying goodbye, I went outside. The cars in the drive through were exactly as I'd left them, though the passengers were now under the watchful eye of another police officer. In just a couple of minutes, I freed all of the cars. It was no more difficult than sinking them had been. That was something I should keep in mind for future cases.

With a friendly wave for both Officer Kent and Mary in case they happened to be looking out the door, I headed back to my car. I wasn't so sure I wanted that tea with a shot of energy anymore.

In fact, as I slid into my seat, I thought it would be quite nice to go home and make some tea myself.

My phone rang, and I groaned. Please not another emergency.

CHAPTER FIFTEEN

It was another emergency, or rather the same emergency, but a mile down the road.

I hadn't gotten there in time. Mary Bells had been right. People and drinks were spread across town, causing trouble, and the worst of it was a mile away. With a groan, I headed to the next call. Being premier had to be less stressful than this.

As nice as that sounded, today I was still Michelle of Oaks Consulting. And my next case was on the left.

On my way, I tried to call Elron. Twice his phone sent me to voice mail. "Narzel fart," I muttered as I took the left into the parking lot. "Hey, I know we were planning on meeting with the florist at noon, but I'm not going to be able to make it. Could you reschedule and call me back? Thanks and love you." I hung up and pulled in behind Rodriguez's car.

Midmorning on a weekday wasn't usually a busy time for a strip mall and restaurants, but today, four police cars edged in a beefy pickup truck with half a shrub stuck in its grill. An officer on a speaker asked the driver to exit the car. Even from here, I could see the rude hand gesture the driver pressed against the window as their answer.

Rodriguez sauntered over. "Fancy seeing you here on this fine morning," he drawled.

"Missed you at Roasted Beans." I summoned my wand as I got out of the car.

"Sorry, I was having too much fun getting a human who thought they were a soccer ball who could roll down the highway all on their own restrained and into an ambulance. Funny thing, I found a Roasted Beans cup in her car." Rodriguez tipped his head toward the truck. "It sounds like this guy visited everyone's favorite shop of horrors too."

"Oh, that's great. One of their drinks forced a werebear into an uncontrolled change." I locked my car and shoved my keys in my pocket. Thanks to years of working with the police, I knew the drill. If this party traveled, I'd be in a patrol car. "What's the story?"

"Driver passed a car in a no-passing area. An officer tried to pull them over but they kept driving. It was an average car chase until the driver hopped out and flung a stop sign and three golf clubs at officers. According to reports, the brownie's powers are out of control. They levitated a hubcap and bits of road debris before getting back in the truck, with the levitated items following them, and took off. So, here we are. Most the officers here are human. This is the sixth call of this type, and the department is stretched thin."

That explained why the officers were keeping their distance. What brownies lacked in stature, they made up for in powers. The hearth, home, and farm abilities included levitation and magical strength disproportional to their size. I'd never heard of a gang of brownie thugs, but I wouldn't want to meet them in a dark alley. "If we can get him out of the car again, it would be easier."

"I'm open to ideas. I set out spike strips at the entrance before we forced him in here. He levitated them into the grass."

"Then we try a more direct method. Do you have a knife?" Brownies weren't the only people who could levitate stuff.

Rodriguez slapped a folding knife in my hand. "All yours."

"Thanks."

I knelt behind a patrol car, unfolded the knife, and tapped it with my wand. "*Nazid*."

The knife floated out of my hand.

Smiling, I directed it down until it was hovering a few inches above the pavement and then sent it on a path to the truck's rear driver's side tire. When it was level with the tire, I made a jabbing motion with my wand. "*Tewaz*."

The knife slid into the tire. Perfect.

The truck lurched into motion, back tires screeching as it took off. The motion shattered my hold on the knife. The back tire went flat. The truck slowed, but then the back end leveled out, and it kept going. The troublesome brownie was levitating the side I'd punctured.

I bolted toward Rodriguez's car. As soon as I got the door shut behind me, we took off after the brownie. "Sorry about your knife."

"Department issue," he said, his voice terse as he swerved around a panicked sedan halted in the entrance of the shopping center.

Between the wildly swerving truck and police cars, I couldn't blame the drivers for being confused. Nor could I blame the three motorists who laid on their horns when the truck barreled onto the street without hesitation. I grabbed the Oh, Narzel handle over the door and hung on.

"Any bright ideas?" Rodriguez asked.

"Puncture more tires?"

"We can see how well that's working."

"There's got to be a limit to how much he can levitate."

"You held up a car."

"Car, not truck."

"Sure! That's the distinction that matters right now!" he yelled as he stomped on the brakes as we slowed for a hard right.

"Fine. I'll end it," I snarled. "Warn the other officers they'll need to stop quickly."

While he got on the radio, I pointed my wand at the road in front of the truck. "*Orzu.*"

The truck took the turn and rolled into the soft road, sinking in to the running boards in hardly more than a second.

"*Fehu.*" I solidified the road with the truck in it, which couldn't be doing the road any favors.

Enough cars cleared out of the lane to our left that Rodriguez could go around. He parked us on the driver's side of the truck. I hopped out of the car as an officer bellowed instructions for the brownie to exit the truck.

The window shattered and chunks of glass went flying at the officers.

"*Gebo fehu.*" Moisture from the air surrounded the glass and froze, sending it crashing to the ground harmlessly.

The truck door popped open, and the brownie hopped out, coffee staining his jeans and white t-shirt. True to Rodriguez's story, a hubcap trailed along behind him, as did several golf balls, a Roasted Beans mug, and a phone.

"You!" The brownie pointed at me, and a golf ball hurtled in my direction.

I froze it as I'd frozen the glass. Another followed, and I did the same.

"Why can't you let a man morn his lost marriage in peace?" He shuddered, toppled onto his butt, and bellowed, "Why'd ya leave me, Darcy?" His levitating pile of junk fell to the ground.

"Give me the nullifying cuffs." Their main purpose was to block magic, but they worked just fine on other powers too.

Rodriguez handed them over without a word.

Wand in one hand and cuffs in the other, I marched over to the brownie and grabbed his hand.

He yanked back and glared at me through his tears. "You'll not be wanting to do that, lass."

I snapped the cuff closed. "Try me." I snarled.

The hubcap rattled as it lifted off the pavement.

"Do it." I met his wild eyes with my resolve. "I'll make you eat it."

The hubcap thudded back to the ground.

I closed the cuff around his other hand and locked them, activating the nullifying effect. "Now, I'm sorry about Darcy, and I'm even more sorry to tell you that your morning coffee drugged you. You've been causing trouble and are going to go with the police and paramedics and get help." Deciding it was as safe as it was going to be, I dismissed my wand.

He looked past me to the officers. "Where did they come from?"

"They came to help you," I said gently. With the cuffs on, he seemed different, as if by blocking his abilities, the effects of the corrupted magic were also blocked. "Let's get you up and to a hospital."

He staggered to his feet. "Do ya think my Darcy will come visit me?"

"I don't know, you'll have to ask the hospital staff." I handed him over to an officer.

"Oh, I will. Darcy also cares for me when I'm sick." He let the officer get him settled in the car.

Turning back to the car, I raised my wand. "*Orzu ansu*." The ground softened, and the truck lifted out.

"*Fehu*." With that, I solidified the road. The truck, listing to the side from the flat tire, sat atop it, ready to be towed away.

"Thank you," Rodriguez said softy.

"He didn't want to cause trouble."

"I know. I heard you took care of the source."

"For all the good it did." While no one had been hurt dealing with the brownie, it could easily have ended in tragedy.

"I know we were supposed to meet today, but I think we're both going to be on call dealing with other incidents."

"The reports," I groaned. "I haven't finished them."

"Me either." Rodriguez tried to grin, but a yawn interrupted it. "Tell you what, I'll drop you off at your car, and we can go over reports tomorrow."

"I'll have them done by then, I promise."

Rodriguez winced. "Before either of us make promises we can't keep, let's see how the rest of the day goes."

"Deal." I returned to his car, checking my phone. Still no message from Elron, so I tried calling him again. He didn't pick up.

I eyed the clock. Assuming he hadn't canceled our appointment with the florist, I had just enough time to get there as long as I didn't have to rush to another emergency. "Any cases you need me for?"

"I don't think so. The rush seems to be over." He sighed. "I need a break."

"Same."

He pulled up next to my car. "Until next time?"

"You know it."

Rodriguez waved and drove off.

As if those words were taunting the universe, my phone rang. I answered without checking who was calling. "Oaks Consulting. This is Michelle."

"Ms. Oaks, we need to review the plans for Ethel's funeral."

"What?" It took a moment for my brain to match the voice with a name. "Susanna, what funeral arrangements? Last I heard, we didn't have a body. The medical examiner was going to have to do some extensive testing to see if one of the difficult to identify remains was hers, and until we have proof she's missing, she's presumed dead, but not officially dead."

Her voice shifted from business as usual to sympathy. "I have it on good authority that one of the burned remains is that of the former premier."

That was news to me. "I'd like to see that paperwork."

"As I said, it's in process."

"If there isn't any paperwork yet. Then why would I plan a funeral?" I rubbed my temple, sure I was missing something.

Susanna sighed. "We need to be ready. It can't look like you're delaying the funeral of the previous premier. What would people think? The moment we have definitive news, we need to have a funeral to announce."

"Fine. I'll review it tonight, but right now, I'm Michelle of Oaks Consulting, and I have to do that job."

"You're going to be the premier!"

"It does look that way, doesn't it?" I said dryly as I

turned on my car. If I left now, I'd only be a couple of minutes late for the florist.

"This is your job." Susanna's voice crept up in pitch. "The transition from ordinary witch to premier is where your focus should be."

I sighed loudly. "It will be my job. Right now, police contracts pay my rent and buy my food. When I see a paycheck for being premier, then we'll talk about my priorities." I hung up on her protests.

The phone rang again while I was pulling out of the parking lot, but I ignored it. Susanna had gotten all she would from me right now. I had flowers to pick.

The drive over went smoothly, more smoothly than I'd expected. Usually after channeling as much power as I had this morning, and yesterday for that matter, fatigue settled in. Only I didn't have the tired empty sensation I'd expected. Sure, I could tell I'd used magic, more than I had in months, but I had plenty left, and more trickled in as I took stock.

Huh. Dr. Stiles had been right. Practice was what stood between me and the power reserves I'd once had. Oh, it would be months or years before I was fully back to my old self, but this was a vast improvement from a week ago. Too bad I hadn't practiced more before the Trial by Magic. I might've been able to win.

With that sour thought, I parked in front of Fab Flowers. Elron's car was clearly absent. I dialed his phone again as I headed for the shop with a multicolored display of iris tucked under an OPEN sign. Inviting enough, though it would be even better with my fiancé.

The call went to voice mail again, and I hung up. Two minutes past our appointment time, I pushed open the door.

Coolers showing off brightly colored flowers dominated one wall. Tables topped with vases and arrangements of every size and for any occasion should've looked graceful, but two large ones had toppled from the table and shattered on the ground.

"I told you to *go away*!" A woman yelled.

My eyes followed a trail of flowers past the counter. A tidily wrapped, but now squished, set of red roses lay under the pass-through.

"I miss you," a man pleaded.

A twist of my wrist, and my wand was in hand. I pushed through the pass-through, edged around a steel-topped table, and shoved open the door to the back room.

Flowers of every type and size dotted the floor in clumps. More than a few of the bunches had been ground underfoot, likely by one of the two satyrs. Probably not by the lady, feet tapping nervously from her position atop another worktable, but the male. He gazed up at her as he shoved a rose in his mouth and started to chew.

"Can I help?"

The satyr on top of the table blushed until her cheeks matched the soft pink of her sundress. "Ah, you must be Michelle. Fern, proprietor of Fab Flowers. As awkward as this is, I would be delighted to have your aid in removing *him* from this establishment."

"You know my name!" Rose petals flew out of his mouth. "You used to love telling everyone about your boyfriend. Couldn't wait to brag about me! I'm more than a *him* to you!" He made a grab for Fern's feet.

She yanked back her hoof and planted a solid kick in his shoulder.

He yelped and stumbled back, crushing more flowers under his hooves. "Why'd you do that, Fern? You love me."

"Don't Fern me. When I asked to go steady, you said no, and after five months of hoping you'd see me as more than a casual date, I dumped you. It takes more than love." She didn't take her eyes off him, but her tone shifted. "Michelle, the phone is on the wall beside you, if you could be so kind as to call the police."

"Sure." I took my eyes off them long enough to find the phone. I snatched it off the cradle and mashed the first number. A cup from the trash can under the phone caught my eye. From this angle, I could only make out a third of the logo, but it was all I needed. Roasted Beans strikes again.

"Fern, was he drinking coffee when he came in?" I turned back to them.

Him was in midair, having leapt for the table while I wasn't looking.

"*Mannaz*!" I pointed my wand squarely at him and shoved extra power into the sleep spell.

Him dropped to the floor with a thump and flowers sliding across the ground.

"That is enough for one day." I finished dialing 9-1-1.

Fern hopped off the table, nudged him with a hoof, and started gathering up her flowers, trying to hide her tears behind her work.

I turned around, giving her what privacy I could while I explained the situation to the operator. Given the power I'd put behind the sleep spell, Him wouldn't be waking up any time soon. By the time I hung up, an ambulance was on its way, and Fern had a giant pile of flowers on the floor and a smaller pile on the table.

"An ambulance?" she asked as she sorted a dozen roses between the two piles.

Dismissing my wand, I leaned against the door frame. "There's something you should know." Outlining why Him (who's name turned out to be Alekos) had acted oddly filled the time until the ambulance arrived.

The paramedics didn't bat an eye at their unconscious patient. As it turned out, they'd been at Roasted Beans and two other related incidents today. In their words, Alekos would be their least troublesome passenger of the day. Though they did make me go over the spell I'd used three different times. To reassure them, I handed over a business card with strict instructions to pass it on to the hospital staff so they could call me if they had any questions.

By the time they left with Alekos gently snoring on the stretcher, Fern had turned the shop sign to CLOSED and deposited all the ruined flowers in a bin labeled "Plant Clippings Only."

"I should've asked if you wanted to file a police report, make Alekos pay for the damages." If I'd been less annoyed at work problems colliding with my personal life, I would've thought about it more clearly.

Fern shook her head. "It isn't as bad as it looks, and I know him. Without the magic, he never would've done this."

"You're sure?"

"Yes." Fern tugged a stool out from under the table and sat, chin leaning heavily on her hand. "I know we had an appointment, but do you really want to talk about flowers now?"

"Why don't we reschedule."

"That would be good." Fern summoned a faint smile. "I promise not to have any ex-boyfriends destroying my shop next time you're here."

"Same time next week?"

"Sure."

"I'll tell Elron."

Fern walked me out and locked the door behind me. Frankly, I didn't blame her.

My phone rang. I check the caller ID. Elron. How

timely of him. Since I wasn't sure what to say after he missed all my calls and our meeting with Fern, I settled on the very useful, "Hello?"

"I am sorry, but I will not be able to make it to the appointment." A voice in the background overpowered his for a moment. "Please pass my apologies along to Fern and do what the two of you can without me."

"I take it your day hasn't gone well either?"

"No. I have a situation with a fey student and kudzu." The frustrated spill of words stopped. "Either? I thought you were doing paperwork this morning. Were you called to a case?"

"Three."

"I see." A flurry of voices filled the background. "Alas, without my attention, the kudzu has resumed engulfing a student. I would very much like to try to have dinner, the two of us, tonight. Could you meet me here, and we can go to the pizza place you like?"

"It's a date."

"Delightful. Stay safe."

I ended the call and settled into my car. All of this, and I still hadn't gotten my morning tea or finished those reports. Determined to get a little bit of work done, I headed back to the lodge.

Narzel must've been taking the afternoon off, because my phone didn't ring once on the drive, and I got home in time to enjoy leftovers from the lunch Landa had served the guests. I even avoided any witches who could be lingering around looking for me.

The paperwork went as well as it ever does, and I sent off all of the reports before getting back in my car to meet Elron for dinner.

In a marvel, the call-free afternoon continued. I

should've been thrilled. Instead, it left a tingle of unease running down my spine.

Ignoring the feeling, I pulled into a visitor space and started the long walk to the door. The tingle came back.

"Don't be paranoid," I told myself. This wasn't a case or a risky situation filled with danger. Meeting my fiancé for dinner at his work was the most normal thing in the world.

A surge of magic raked across my senses.

That had to be from one of his magical plants, right?

Another surge, this time with the patterns of a spell.

"Not a plant." I sprinted for the corner of the building. My purse fell from my hand as I summoned my wand.

I prepared to put on a burst of speed as I rounded the corner, but instead, I skidded to a halt. Three witches, or that's what they felt like given the magic in the air, surrounded Elron. All had black masks pulled over their faces. My elf was doing his part, his sword a blur in the air as he tried to skewer the masked figure in front of him. And he would've managed, but the witch kept throwing up shields to deflect his swords.

The other two attackers looked to be doing joint spell work, with hands clasped as they sketched runes in the air. I couldn't tell exactly what spell they were casting, but it didn't matter. Nothing they were doing could be good for Elron.

With a quick blast of power, I erased the runes hanging in the air. My wand lowered to their hands, and with a spark of magic, I shocked them. They broke apart.

"*Algiz!*" Magical ropes tightened around the witches who'd joined together to cast a spell.

That lasted all of a second before the witch fencing with Elron undid the spell while blocking his sword.

"*Fehu!*" I fed the spell more magic than it needed. A sturdy layer of ice encased the three witches.

Elron backpedaled, giving himself more room.

I frantically searched for another spell, one that would hold all of them and not require too much magic. After all the spells I'd flung today, magic was in short supply. Even when I'd been fully rested, I hadn't been able to defeat Isadora.

"Call the police!" Elron shouted.

My fingers brushed across an empty pocket. I swore. For once, I'd put my phone in my purse, which was on the other side of the building where I'd dropped it.

Water poured off two of the witches, and steam curled away from the third.

Narzel blast it all. I needed a better spell. Or a good enough spell to buy us some time. "*Sowil.*"

The containment spell wouldn't hold for long. Maybe I could try to put them to sleep, like I did the satyr? Going into battle, smart witches would adjust their shields to block such a spell. Of course, these might not be smart witches.

"Did you call the police?" Elron edged around the witches on his way to me, being careful to give me a clear shot at them if they tired anything.

The ice melted off of two of them. We had seconds at most, and I didn't have a good plan. "Don't have my phone."

Elron swore.

The containment spells disintegrated, and a spell shot toward Elron.

Dredging up as much power as I could, I flung my own shield around him.

The spell splashed across Elron's chest before wrapping around him. I'd been too late.

I raised my wand.

"I wouldn't if I were you." The witch who'd deflected his sword stepped forward, her voice cool and calm, as if this was a business meeting and not an attack.

"Why not?" I kept my wand up and started running through the runes for a stronger shield spell.

She smiled.

That's when I felt it. Icy daggers piercing my skin, twisting around my heart. I shouldn't have felt it; the spell wasn't on me, it was on Elron. "No."

"You shouldn't let others know your weakness." She jabbed her wand at Elron.

The ice spread from around my heart to the rest of me, but it wasn't the spell. She knew. She knew my life was tied to his.

"What do you want?"

I'd do anything to save him. Anything.

CHAPTER SIXTEEN

"Drop your wand."

My fingers opened before I thought about following her order, and my wand fell to the ground. Being wandless wouldn't stop me from casting spells.

The spell around Elron's heart, that stopped me. It narrowed my focus to the woman and elf in front of me, the rest of the world a blur.

A muscle in Elron's jaw twitched, but the rest of him hadn't moved since the spell hit. Maybe it was more than the promise of death curled around his heart. It could be holding him in place too. Any other time, I'd probe the spell, but I'd seen spells react to probes before, and I wouldn't risk Elron's life.

"Drop the sword."

I felt the clang of the metal colliding with the pavement in my bones.

The witch nodded. "Elron is going to walk over here, nice and slow, and get in the van. Michelle, if you so much as twitch an eyebrow or command a drop of magic, he dies. Now, walk, elf."

"As tough as dragon hide and unrelenting as the ocean." Elron stepped forward.

"None of that." The witch's wand jerked. "Or I'll have to come up with a fitting punishment."

I pressed my lips into a thin line and watched the love of my life get in the van with two witches.

"Wait for our call." She darted inside the van and pressed a charm against his neck. He collapsed.

"Elron!" I lunged for my wand.

They rolled away, not with a squeal of tires, but a purposeful lurch, and were around a building and out of sight before I could do more than curl my fingers around my wand.

The knives of ice around my heart faded away. Either distance had dampened the effect, or they'd removed the spell from Elron. It didn't matter which. I knew what I had to do.

I ran back to my purse even faster than I'd run toward Elron. My hand shook as I dialed the phone. "Gordon? It's Michelle. I know it's been a while, but I need your help."

Bless him, he didn't ask why my voice shook, he didn't ask if I was okay. He asked where and what happened and promised to be here as fast as his cruiser could make the trip. He'd even send Jerry to check the scene.

I managed to stutter my thanks. It took three tries to hang up the phone because the more I tried to hold my hands steady, the more they shook.

The university police found me a few minutes later, holding Elron's sword and sobbing. A voice in my head kept telling me to be strong, to be logical, to think this through and figure out why the witches captured Elron rather than simply killing him.

At some point, Jerry sat down next to me and handed me a box of tissues. "Gordon's on his way. I checked the magic, but I'd like to hear what happened." He stretched his feet out and crossed his ankles.

"Remember that case with the mayor? You watched them take me away in an ambulance? I've hardly ever been so embarrassed. Me, a grown man and capable hedge-practitioner, and there I was, beaten by flying chihuahuas of all things."

"They were a menace." I dried my eyes. It was hard not to smile at that memory. Between the fireballs and their ability to dart through riot shields, we'd all been happy to lob curses at the breeder.

"You never once teased me. I don't think I ever thanked you for that." His rumpled uniform's fit accentuated his thin frame.

I blew my nose. "Nothing worth teasing. Confronting a new magical creature, even one as seemingly harmless as a flying dog, has risks."

"That it does." He tipped his head toward me. "What happened?"

And with that, I knew he wouldn't ask why I broke down. He wouldn't tell me it was an over-reaction. He wouldn't look at me next week and think less of me. So, I told him. At first, the words came slowly, but somewhere in the middle I found my rhythm. The Michelle telling the story wasn't the same one who'd stood there and watched her love be abducted. That Michelle was mourning Ethel, wedding planning, in love with an elf Michelle. This one, the one who could tell the story without crying, this was Work Michelle: police consultant, killer of demons, and next premier.

Gordon arrived as I was relaying the spell, the one meant to stop Elron's heart. He stepped out of the cruiser, a solid block of a man who just looked like he would protect you. And he would, but these days, most of his time was devoted to overseeing the Magical Response Unit in Cobb County. On the way over, he took in the scene before focusing on me.

Under the assessing gaze, my throat tightened, and I lost my grip on Work Me.

"Sergeant, Michelle was just telling me how the assailants took Elron." Jerry snagged Gordon's eye and gave a slight shake of his head.

Gordon tucked his hand in his pockets. "Please continue."

I had to swallow twice before I could say it. "They put a spell on him, one that could kill him. I think to stop his heart, but I didn't probe it to be sure." Work Me got through most of the story without breaking. "He said... doesn't matter. They forced him into the car, placed a charm on him that made him collapse, and drove away."

For a moment, neither of them spoke. With a creak of leather, Gordon knelt down, his face kind. "We need to know everything. What did Elron say?"

I could feel the tears gathering. "Please don't."

Gordon simply looked at me.

I swallowed. Procedure. On his side of things I would've asked too. "We have a saying. I told it to him once, and he used the words when he proposed. It's about our love. He used part of it today. 'As tough as dragon hide and unrelenting as the ocean.'" The tears I thought would fall didn't. I'd said the worst of it. The last words he said, words of love, and I hadn't been able to say them back.

"Do you feel up to walking the scene with us?" Jerry asked softly.

"Yes." Because I would move mountains and walk through fire to keep him by my side. "We should start where I parked."

It took over an hour to go through it, let Jerry check the

magic, and fill out paperwork. But after that first telling, it was easier. I'd already looked at my actions, where I felt I'd failed, and with each retelling, I went over my actions again. Maybe I could've used more magic, more aggressive or even deadly spells, maybe if I'd known then what I knew now, I could've saved him. But I hadn't, and with the knowledge and magic I had, I'd tried my best.

If I got Elron back unharmed, that would be enough.

"We could try tracking him. I should've done it as soon as they got in the van, but I wasn't thinking clearly." That's when I saw it, the shadow in Gordon's eyes.

"You can't." He kept his voice gentle. "You can't work the case of your missing fiancé."

"I have tracking charms in the car." I said it, even though I knew it wouldn't matter.

"Michelle, you can't, and you know why."

I sucked in a deep breath. "If you can use the charms, you're welcome to them." It sounded lame, even to me.

"We'll take them." Jerry glared at Gordon. "We can always use tracking charms."

Gordon nodded but didn't look happy about it.

"Thank you."

"We are going to do everything we can to find him." Gordon met my eyes, and in him was a man who'd move mountains. "We will find him."

"I'm counting on it." That was all I could say without tearing up, and tears wouldn't help Elron. "I'll get those charms for you."

Jerry met me at the car, Elron's sword in his hands. "Usually we'd keep it for evidence, but there isn't much we can do with it. Take it home with you. I collected his gloves to use with the tracking spells."

I nodded too many times and laid it across the back seat. Thankfully, my eyes had dried up, or I would've cried again, and I'd filled my crying quota for the year this afternoon. Still, I closed the door softly and felt a little better for having the sword.

Popping the trunk, I dug through my extra supplies. While recovering, I'd made buckets of charms, so I was better stocked than usual. I pressed a bag of fifteen charms into Jerry's hands. "I know why you can't use them on this case, but it should help."

"It will."

I closed the trunk and stood there, not sure what to do.

"You have your purse?" Jerry asked.

"Phone, wallet, everything."

"Wand?"

"That too."

"Then go home. Call your mom, or a friend, but don't wait for news alone. I promise, I'll call as soon as I know something." He opened the door for me.

"Thank you, you don't know…" I looked down at the gum-smeared pavement so I didn't have to see the sympathy in his eyes. "Just thank you."

I drove away, pointedly not looking at the cops still going over the parking lot. Elron wasn't here anyway. He was gone, but I was going to find him. Move mountains. Walk through fire. Carve through dragon hide. Be as unrelenting as the ocean.

CHAPTER SEVENTEEN

At the lodge, I detoured through Elron's apartment, grabbing his hairbrush before going to my workroom. I set three tracking charms next to it and got to work. A few runes and scraps of wood later, I fused three together, multiplying the power of the spell. If that plus my remaining power couldn't find him, magical tracking wasn't going to find him.

A glance at my phone reassured me that I hadn't managed to miss any messages, but I double-checked that the volume was all the way up just in case.

One steadying breath later, I activated the charm and placed one of Elron's hairs across it. I made sure my adjustments to the charms were working as intended and that it had clear directions on who to find before feeding it every bit of magic I could muster. The spell flared silver as it bolted through the world.

I held my breath.

It turned north and a tad west, following the highway, and raced away.

The spell was working. It would find Elron, I'd call the police with the tip, and I'd have him back by dinner.

Only the spell slowed.

I reached for more magic but didn't have anything to give it.

The spell faded to nothing.

"No! No!" I slumped into the chair. "It should've worked."

Just like the tracking spell for Ethel. They both should've worked.

Unless... unless it was me. I was the problem. My spells didn't work like they did before. My magic, my abilities, they weren't really back. It's why the tracking spells didn't work, why I hadn't been able to save Elron, why I couldn't make sense of the magic at Ethel's crash, why I'd lost to Isadora.

It was me and my magic.

What else could it be?

My thoughts spiraled around that thought until my phone beeped.

Low battery.

"Me too." I plugged it in beside my bed and mixed a potion to boost my magical recovery and help me sleep. It wasn't until I was in bed that I realized I'd added the boost to my magic.

Habit, though it wouldn't matter. My magic wasn't going to bring Elron back.

Morning light woke me before my alarm went off. As much as I wished there was a moment when I didn't remember how badly I had failed Elron, I knew as soon as my eyes cracked open what I'd done.

I checked my phone before and again after taking a shower. People liked to say no news was good news. What they really meant was the worry wouldn't change the outcome. I had plenty of reason to worry and only one reason not to.

I was alive.

As long as I lived, I knew Elron did too. And given how little harm the witches had done during the abduction, I doubted they'd harm him while he was of use to them. Shame I didn't know what they wanted him for.

Out of obligation, I texted my family and Susanna, which I should've done last night, but I hadn't been thinking clearly. As expected, they told me they'd be right over.

I spent all of breakfast convincing them I was fine alone and had work to do. The last part was the truth. I had yet more reports to finish for Rodriguez.

While waiting for my second cup of tea to steep, I called Jerry.

"McKade."

"It's Michelle. Tell me you have news, anything you can share." I squeezed my eyes shut and prayed for good news.

"You know I can't tell you anything."

"Jerry, it's me, please."

He hesitated. "All we have is some video of the van headed up 575. We lost them before Canton and don't have another lead. You didn't hear that from me."

"Thank you."

"I'll call if I have something." He hung up.

The cereal I'd eaten sat like little shards of rock in my stomach. I shouldn't have been surprised. The group had been too quick, too clean about it.

I headed back to my workroom. Piles of disenchanted items narrowed the space. I really should take them to Regional Disposal Experts. I half-heartedly extended a probe. The boxes didn't have a drop of magic in them.

Dad had helped me relearn. He'd disenchanted several of these with me and checked my work for weeks later. If my magic was deeply flawed, he would've noticed. He would've worked with me to pick apart every part of my spellcraft until we found the problem.

A bad spell or two, sure, but my magic wasn't flawed. Mom, Dad, Dr. Stiles, Ethel, and everyone else who'd helped me get back to my normal life would've noticed.

I sat in my chair, closed my eyes, and turned my attention inward. The pre-bed potion had done the trick, not that I'd cared last night, and most of my magic had regenerated. I didn't see or sense any spells or contamination, but to be safe, I did a quick purification ritual. It didn't take much magic, and I felt about the same after.

If it wasn't my magic but a bad spell, it could even be a bad batch of tracking spells, so I made several new tracking charms. While crafting them, I checked every reagent and every rune. Then I took one of the new charms, one that I was as sure as I could be was perfect, and tried to track Elron again.

I held my breath as the spell lifted off. It zoomed north, and for a lovely thirty seconds I thought it would work. Then the spell dissipated into nothing just like the last two.

"Narzel blast it. Why won't you work!"

Unsurprisingly, the charm and hairbrush didn't answer.

"It's fine." It wasn't, but I didn't know what else to do right now. I could attempt a different type of tracking spell, but until I had an idea as to why the spells kept failing, I didn't know what spell to try. All of which I could ponder while finishing the reports.

With a sigh, I rolled over to the computer and got started. Because my focus was on Elron, it took twice as long as it should've, but I still managed to finish them by lunch. Not that lunch was inspiring. Microwave noodles never were. Had Mom been here, she would've scolded me for eating standing up by the sink.

I played back everything, the convention, Ethel's accident, the cases, all of it. The answer to why witches abducted Elron was in there, if I could find it. Only I got stuck on the crash that killed Ethel. The tracking spell hadn't worked on her, but they also thought she wasn't in the car.

It didn't add up.

I stared at my phone, willing it to ring with news. Unsurprisingly, it didn't oblige.

With a sigh I snatched it off the desk and dialed Jerry's number.

The line went from ringing to live. "I don't have any news yet."

"What? No greeting, no pleasantries, nothing? I don't even get a hello?"

"I don't have anything new on the van." Jerry sighed. "We're reviewing video from the university, trying to determine who was behind this attack. You turned down the officer who'd wait with you in case of a ransom call. In fact, you said we'd be of no use. Unless you're calling to tell me you have a recording of a ransom call, I don't know why we're on the phone."

I winced. I'd said that, but he didn't understand why. "Can you be my friend for a minute?"

He hesitated. "Narzel. You have exactly a minute."

That was all I needed. "Right now, I'm in line to be the next premier. The only witches who'd abduct my fiancé are those who don't want me in power or want control over me. The ransom is going to be me or my actions. You'll tell me not to do what they ask, but I will, because I love him."

"Michelle…"

"I know."

"We can trace the call, put a tracker on you, get video, whatever it takes. You're underestimating us."

I closed my eyes and wished... well, I just wished. "Let me know if you find him."

"If you change your mind, call."

"I will." I ended the call. The phone felt like it weighed fifteen pounds, dragging my hand to my lap. I couldn't have the police hovering over me. It was the same reason I'd kept everyone else away. I couldn't have people around. Not now. Not when I would do anything, break any law to get Elron back.

Until then, I had another call to make. It was easier to call Rodriguez. He wouldn't be asking why I wasn't cooperating.

He answered after the second ring. "I was about to call you."

"Oh?"

"Report came back from the medical examiner. One of the bodies we pulled from the car was identified as Ethel. I'm sorry, Michelle."

"I thought…" I wasn't so sure now. Susanna was the only one to survive the crash. Maybe her memory wasn't as clear as I'd thought. Accidents had a way of changing memories.

"I'm sorry." He repeated. "Given this report, it's clear she never left the car. We think the bystander was confused by the accident, and that's why they said Ethel ran into the woods."

"But…" I didn't know what I'd wanted to say. Ethel was dead, and now the maneuvering to determine the next premier would really begin. "When did you get the report?"

"Ten minutes ago."

And last night, Elron had been abducted. They could be connected, but why? Why would someone want to kill Ethel and take Elron?

They were two different types of leverage. With Elron they could get to me. Killing Ethel accelerated the timeline, either putting me in the premier's position sooner or forcing a vote to push me out. Of those, the second was far less likely. "And the medical examiner is sure?"

"He's sure. DNA sure."

"Thanks, Rodriguez."

"Call if you need anything."

"I will, and you do the same. I'm still working." I had to. I had to keep going. If I stopped, I wouldn't be able to move.

"You're sure?"

"Yes."

"Then I'll call."

"Good." I hung up, my mind churning. It didn't fit together. Ethel and Elron. But it should. There had to be a reason they were both targeted. And it had to be the same person. But why?

It felt like I should know the answer, but it was just out of reach. Buried under days of being surrounded by problems and only seeing one path. A path shadowed by heartache and fatigue.

I went back to the beginning. Ethel's crash and death. First the accident, with traces of magic everywhere. The reports that she'd gone into the woods, but no one could find a geriatric witch who wasn't known for her walking speed. Two bodies were burned beyond recognition. Then, one of them ended up being Ethel.

And somehow that connected to Elron's abduction.

They didn't add up, but I knew a source with more information about the crash. I typed a message to Susanna, asking her to come to my apartment. She and the rest of the premier's staff had taken rooms at the Lodge after the accident. I'd been avoiding most of them, not sure what to do while the situation was in flux.

Hardly two minutes later, she knocked on the door. I let her in, sitting next to her on the couch. For the past six months, Susanna had been Ethel's constant companion and one of her most trusted assistants.

Susanna shifted uncomfortably. "What will it take to gain Elron's freedom?"

"I'm afraid I don't understand." The words came out before I even had time to think about a proper response. Countless hours of Ethel's drills, and they'd worked. If only I'd been able to tell her how well she'd trained me.

"That is why you asked me here, is it not?" Susanna motioned to the empty seats. "I couldn't think of another reason for only the two of us to meet."

"Ah, but I could." I let her squirm for a moment. "Tell me about the accident."

She shook her head. "It's too painful to remember."

"Susanna, tell me about the crash." My voice hardened. "I'm not asking as Michelle. I'm asking as the next premier, and your boss."

"Do you really need to hear this from me?" She didn't look up.

"Yes, I do." Maybe this was cruel of me, but she was the only one who'd given a coherent statement.

Susanna inhaled slowly. "My memory is spotty. I was in the front passenger seat. I remember seeing a car pass us and then Ethel's car. They were swerving. That's the last thing I remember until I smelled smoke.

"The premier's car was upside down and already on fire. Then the car's fuel tank leaked or ruptured, or something. The fire got so much worse. I couldn't get close enough to save anyone.

"We tried a spell to stop the fire, but the car was shielded from spells and the magic on the car mingled with the flames. We couldn't get another spell to override that mix." Susanna fingers twisted together.

"Can you remember any other details?" I leaned forward.

"They packed me into an ambulance as quickly as they could. All I remember is watching the car burn." She swallowed. "It burned them."

I blinked back tears. Crying didn't lead to well-thought-out investigations, and I had to think, not feel. "Thank you, Susanna. I appreciate you going through the events with me."

She nodded.

"You were right. The police have identified one of the bodies from the car as Ethel's. They'll be making the announcement soon." I don't know how I said it without crying, but I did.

Susanna's lip wobbled, and tears slid down her cheeks.

I handed her a box of tissues. "We need to work on my statement and next moves to secure my place as the premier."

"They're sure?"

"Yes." No matter how much I wished they were wrong. "Take an hour, then inform the staff and work on our plan moving forward."

She nodded as she dabbed her eyes. "Thank you for telling me now."

"It was the least I could do." I smiled slightly. After a few more pleasantries and a stab of grief I did my best to suppress, I showed her out.

As soon as the door shut, I took ragged breath after ragged breath. For some stupid reason, I'd thought I could talk about Ethel's death without grief. I couldn't. I might never be able to because deep down so much of this felt like it was my fault.

If I hadn't gone after the demons, if I hadn't spent months recovering, if I hadn't asked for more time before becoming premier, if I'd been more of what she needed and less selfish, this wouldn't have happened. I would've been introduced at the spring convention. I would've been at full power. Ethel would've had time to execute her transition plan as intended. Ethel would be alive, and Elron would be by my side.

Instead, she was dead, he was captive, and I didn't know why.

I couldn't see the connection. I couldn't even see if Susanna's story matched the crash. I didn't remember it clearly. I'd been shocked. Even when I'd checked for magic, I'd focused so tightly on my work I hadn't really noticed the rest of the scene.

Rodriguez would have the file, along with all the pictures and statements. I could even visit that stretch of road.

I grabbed my phone and started to dial Rodriguez's number but stopped. He wasn't likely to let me take a file, but if I showed up he'd let me read it.

With that settled, I checked to be sure my phone's volume was all the way up, grabbed my purse and headed out. First, I'd check the road, and then I'd visit Rodriguez. One way or another, I was getting answers.

My silent phone mocked me.

If I didn't hear from Elron's captors soon, well, I'd come up with another plan there. I refused to believe I was out of options.

CHAPTER EIGHTEEN

Even though I didn't remember the accident scene very well, my memory of where it had taken place was crystal clear. I pulled off the shoulder on I-575. This morning, the only traces of the accident that remained were rapidly fading spray paint on the asphalt.

Of the parts of the road that I considered dangerous, this wasn't one of them. It was near an exit, which always added a bit of excitement, but the road was basically straight and only angled slightly downhill. For an area known for its rolling hills and curvy roads, this was as straight and flat as it got. Of all the places I would've predicted a fatal accident, this wasn't one. Had it really been as simple as driver error?

That could explain the accident, but not the failed tracking spell. They didn't usually dissipate into nothingness.

"Sweet bones of Narzel, the tracking spells." Grief, fear, doubt, all of those had clouded my mind until I couldn't even see the most obvious connection between the two incidents. Tracking spells that faded to nothing. One that malfunctioned when the target was dead only feet away, and the other when the very much alive target was on the move.

Someone had to be interfering with the tracking spells. If I'd taken a person and knew a witch would be on my trail, I'd have done the same thing. Though delaying the discovery of Ethel's death didn't make sense. There had to be a reason, but I didn't see it yet.

The one thing messing with the tracking spell would do was distract me from looking at the magic fragments at the scene. Those magic fragments couldn't have come from a spell that tried to tame the fire. When that type of spell failed, the fire ate it. No, those had to be the remains of a spell that contributed to the accident. Maybe even caused it.

That's why it had shattered beyond recognition. The collision and fire had blasted the remains into tiny pieces. Casting a spell like that would require being near the accident. Close enough the police should have a record of that person as being a witness.

With a much better idea of what I was hoping to find in the police report, I returned to my car and got back on the road.

The drive took more time than I liked, and Rodriguez wasn't even there. I did manage to talk another officer into letting me see the file. He sat me at Rodriguez's desk with strict orders that I couldn't copy or remove anything in there. Those were rules I could live with.

I started with the photos and diagrams. The car Susanna had mentioned was really a truck. This didn't seem like a detail I would've forgotten if I'd remembered enough to know what that vehicle did to cause the crash. And the rest of her story didn't exactly match what happened either. Sure, the car had rolled over, but the gas tank hadn't exploded. Instead, the gas had leaked all over the car and then caught on fire. Terrifying, but very different from a true explosion.

Then I dug into the witness statements, where I found mention after mention that the truck had suddenly started driving erratically. The truck driver claimed it had to be a mechanical problem because he lost control of the steering. As far as Ethel's supposed escape, no one but that one bystander ever saw her leave the car. One person mentioned a sand-colored SUV had stopped for a few minutes but left before the police arrived. And that was it. Everything.

I went back through the witness statements again, checking names and races. Not a witch in the group.

So, who had cast the spell that impaired the truck? The only witches the police had record of being there were those on Ethel's team. Even if one of them wanted her dead, there were easier ways.

That thought had me switch over to the medical examiner's report. Ethel's body had been burned so badly they'd had to cut into bone to get a good DNA sample. Oddly, the most readable sample came from the outside of the bone, not the inside. The medical examiner noted this was unusual, that typically in these cases, the inside of the bone yielded the best sample. I added that tidbit to the pile of odd things in this case.

The pile of papers seemed to stare up at me, almost taunting me in inconstancies. I really needed the name of the witch who cast the spells at the accident. That person either knew where Elron was or knew who took him. Given the lack of communication with his abductors, I couldn't help but wonder what they had in store for him. Or if they knew about my connection to him and how our lives were linked.

"Fascinating reading, isn't it?" Rodriguez leaned against the desk.

"Something like that."

He studied me, his dark eyes boring into me. "You didn't tell me about Elron."

"I didn't want to talk about it." I closed the file and moved out of his chair.

"Not to the locals, or to me." He raised an eyebrow. "Why don't you want the police involved? You lobbied for witches to be more open to interacting with law enforcement."

"Are you asking as a friend or as a cop?"

Rodriguez settled into his chair and leaned back so he could look me in the eye without tilting his head. "Right now, a friend."

"This time it isn't politics. Nothing going on there you can't figure out." I moved a chair from in front of his desk to beside it. I took a deep breath. "They could have Elron because our lives are linked. Mine to his. Kill him, and I die too. That can't go in a file. I can't have people taking aim at the man I love when I'm the one they want." I left out the part that I was all but immortal until Elron died. Besides, it would serve me right to brag about my invulnerability only to find a loophole large enough to die through.

"That's a good reason to keep your mouth shut." Rodriguez leaned forward. "Do you think you can keep that a secret for the rest of his life? What, another fifteen hundred years or more?"

"I haven't been thinking that far ahead."

"Clearly." He tapped his fingers on the desk. "You're going to need a reason you live extra long."

Of all the ways for this conversation to go, this wasn't what I'd expected. "I figured I had a solid two hundred years to come up with an answer. Besides, as unhappy as people are with me becoming premier now, I think they'd be a lot less happy to hand over a lifetime appointment to a woman who'll live five normal lifespans."

"Fair point." He pondered for a moment. "Do the kidnappers know?"

I shrugged. "All I know is they have him, and I'm waiting for a phone call. Or to fall over dead."

"Hmm." He leaned back. "Makes sense you wouldn't talk to Jerry or Gordon."

"They're good men."

"Beside the point and you know it."

I didn't bother to argue. It didn't matter if they were good men or not. Any reason I gave them for the abduction had to go in a report, which was why I mentioned being in line to be premier and not the life link. "Either they'll call or kill him. It makes the situation rather simple. It's also not why I'm here."

Rodriguez shook his head. "Fine. You were looking at Ethel's case. Any connection?"

"Maybe. The tracking spell I tried for Elron fizzled out the same way the one did for Ethel."

"So potentially the same person."

I nodded. "And the more I look at it, the less right the accident looks. That magic… I'd never seen a spell shatter like that before, but a high speed collision and a fire could account for most of the oddities."

Rodriguez flipped through the report, opening it to Ethel's autopsy. "This bothered me."

"Add it to the list."

"Trouble is, we don't have enough. It's suspicious, but that doesn't make it criminal." Rodriguez flipped through the photos of the accident.

"If I could find the evidence—"

"The evidence half a dozen of this department's

personnel, as well as four GBI agents and one Highway Patrol officer missed? If you could find something we missed, we'd have to verify it before acting." Rodriguez closed the file. "Friend to friend, you're better off trying to figure out who took Elron."

"The best lead I have is the tracking spell I tried on Ethel."

"Damn."

"That sums it up nicely."

I closed my eyes for a moment. The thoughts swirling were as clear as mud. Nothing fit, and I was too deep in the grief and anger to put it together. "Do you have any work for me? If I can't fix this, I'd at least like to feel useful."

He glanced back at his workroom. "I've gotten as much evidence as I can from our recent magical items. Could you dispose of them?"

"Gladly." At least this was simple enough. The entire lot could go to Regional Disposal, and they wouldn't be terrorizing the town again.

It took us four trips to stow everything in my car. I thanked Rodriguez and promised to call when it was done. He went back inside, and I sat there, looking at my keys. One little run to Regional Disposal wasn't enough to get my mind off things or distract me for long. Thirty minutes and I'd be back to watching my phone and hoping they didn't kill Elron.

Someone knocked on the window.

I screeched as I twisted around, my wand settling into my hand. Rodriguez stood outside the car, a sheepish look on his face. I shoved the door open. "Other than scaring ten years off my life, what do you want?"

"Change of plan. We have a case."

"What kind of a case?"

"Magical mayhem, what else?"

What else, indeed. I grabbed my purse and a bag of supplies before trotting over to his car. He flipped the siren on, and we were off. Finally, a good distraction.

The radio buzzed with reports of out of control magic at the high school science fair. Each bit of information that came over the radio sounded less believable than the last. More of the tainted magic was on the loose. Though that didn't explain the reports of a bear prowling the gym, but I figured that part would sort itself out when we got there.

We slowly drove through a panicked herd of parents, teachers, and students to reach the door. After a quick debate, I left my gear in the car. I might need to be light on my feet, and a duffel made that difficult.

People swarmed Rodriguez, all of them shouting their own version of what happened. Since I wasn't in uniform, they left me alone. I caught Rodriguez's eyes long enough to tip my head toward the gym. He nodded and went back to trying to escape from the mob.

I summoned my wand as I approached the door.

The square woman guarding it moved directly in front of the door. "You can't go in there." A sooty smudge obscured her name tag.

"I'm with the police, here to fix the incident." I held up my wand.

Her eyes swept over me from head to toe and back again. "Badge?"

I'd left it in the car. One of these days I'd get used to carrying it. "Witch and consultant. If you'd like your gym to go back to normal, let me in." I bared my teeth in a smile.

One brow arched, but she stepped aside and held open the door. "Be careful, it's a different world in there."

Rodriguez came up behind me. "Hurry, before they follow." He grabbed my arm and pulled me into the gym.

The door closed behind us with a thud that wasn't at all ominous.

I'd wanted to know what the teacher meant by a different world, but I wasn't going back out to ask. Not when a miniature helicopter crafted from wooden sticks swooped down at me.

I ducked. It zoomed past me and angled up. The double-height entry had plenty of room for the helicopter to go up, though it would do well to avoid the banners listing every championship the basketball, volleyball, and wrestling teams had won in the past fifty years.

A quick look didn't reveal any other threats, unless trophy cases or the pedestal of the school mascot counted. On the floor, navy blue letters proudly proclaimed Home of the Grizzly Bears. I had a sinking feeling about the reports of the bear. Especially since the jumbo paw prints walked a curved path past the empty pedestal.

"I think the magic feels the same as what we've encountered before." Rodriguez waited for a reply. "Michelle?"

"Remember those reports of a bear?" I pointed at the pedestal.

Rodriguez looked at the empty space and the words on the floor. "Oh. I'd forgotten."

"Forgot what?" I spotted the helicopter making another pass. "*Sowil.*"

A containment spell snapped into place around the helicopter. It slowed before hitting the side and hovered in the center of the spell.

"I went to a different local high school, but I should've remembered. Creekview's mascot is the grizzly bear." Rodriguez eyed the doors leading out of the atrium.

"You know, I thought my life couldn't get worse. Dead—maybe murdered—premier, clans plotting against me, abducted fiancé, but this is worse." Animated grizzly worse.

He looked ill. "Just check the magic."

It went against every instinct to look away from the doors. Trusting Rodriguez to warn me if a grizzly turned up, I spun out a thread of magic and probed the helicopter. It was tainted with the same twisted magic that had been the cause of all of our emergencies lately. "Same stuff."

"Then we neutralize the worst of it, clear and close off the building, and tell the school to hire a specialist."

"I like that plan." Mostly because it was likely to leave me with enough of my magic for the next emergency.

Rodriguez nodded. "Which doors are less likely to have a grizzly behind them?"

To my right, two sets of double doors led to the gym floor, which was all I could tell past the giant posters obscuring their windows. On the left, a sign indicating the bathrooms dangled above a single set of double doors. From what I could remember of gyms, that door likely led to locker rooms and weight rooms too. "Bathroom door." If I was a bear awakened by magic, I'd go toward the interesting stuff on the gym floor.

"Left it is."

Before leaving, I set a containment spell across the doors to the gym. Last thing I wanted was to have stuff follow us and have to go through the building multiple times.

On the other side of the single set of doors were several other doors. We split up, each taking a bathroom. Wand leading the way, I nudged open the door to the ladies room. A pair of hooves filled my vision, and I jerked back. The hooves landed against the door with a solid thud, shoving it closed.

I waited, trying to decide if a student had been defending themselves or if this was another problem caused by tainted magic.

"Did you get it?" A high pitched voice drifted through the door.

"Don't know." The reply was more thoughtful. "Didn't get a good look at it."

I leaned forward and rapped on the door. "I'm with the police and can help you out of the building."

Silence followed my announcement.

Rodriguez had gotten into his bathroom without any trouble, though for all I knew he was wrestling the grizzly in there.

The door opened enough for a young girl with brown eyes and black hair to peer out. "Can you get us out?"

"I can." I tried to give her a reassuring smile. "Right now, if you come out."

She looked back into the room before nodding and tugging open the door. Her coat matched the black of her hair, and those were definitely her hooves that had nearly gotten me. She side-stepped, using a hand to hold open the door. "It was the only safe place we could find."

A younger centaur with equally black hair held back by a bright pink flower headband peered into the hall before walking out. A slender fey with her green skin tinting gray followed her out. One human-looking girl left the bathroom, and another took the door from the centaur so she could join her sister. The last human left the bathroom, the door closing softly this time.

"Is that all of you?"

They nodded.

"Okay, we're going to head for the main door." I

pointed down the hall to the double doors. "My partner, an officer in uniform, is checking the men's room. He won't hurt you. He's here to help." I waited until they nodded again before ushering them forward. The path between here and the door was clear, so I took up the rear guard position.

Rodriguez came out of the bathroom, and the group hesitated, but he went and held open the door for them. That was all the encouragement they needed to bolt for freedom. He ushered them the rest of the way out and got on his radio to ask for another officer to organize the mob and try to get a list of the missing.

While he relayed information, I checked the third bathroom and actually walked through the ladies room. Both were empty. I checked my phone while I waited by the door at the end of the hall.

Still no calls. Given how long it had been since Elron's abduction, I didn't know if that was good or bad news. I tucked it back in my pocket. That was a problem for after this mess.

"Officers will work on getting a list of the missing. I've been told all the exits but the one we came in through have been locked and are guarded by teachers." He sighed. "However, given the type of problems in here, it's you and me."

"No backup? Not even with a grizzly in the mix?"

"Too much unpredictable magic."

"Well that's just great." We'd be at this for ages. Gyms weren't small and easy to clear under the best conditions, never mind now.

"I'm sorry."

I sighed. "No, the distraction is good." I motioned at the door. "Shall we?"

He shoved open the door, which led to another empty

hallway with doors sprouting off. In the weight room, we found more students hiding. I escorted them out while Rodriguez finished checking that area. On my way back through, I noticed he'd placed a line of magic across the door that would turn from yellow to red if someone crossed it.

From there, we checked the surprisingly empty girls' locker room and put another line across that door. It wasn't as good as a containment spell, but it took less power. The boys' locker room was next. Rodriquez shoved open the door and stopped squarely in the way.

I peered around him. A bubbling river of green slime had busted through the wall of the gym and into the locker room, where it slowly oozed between the lockers and showers. That would've been enough, but a section of it had diverted to the lockers, and three boys held a terrified satyr's arms as the slime burbled around his waist. On the other side of the slime, a full-sized grizzly stood on its hind legs in a shower stall, the tile lip barely holding back the slimy river.

Since the bear looked terrified of the slime, that made the boys the priority. I shoved Rodriguez into the room and edged around the slime as I probed it. The magic had twisted it, amplifying the stickiness and feeding it to increase the size. Neither were good news for the satyr.

One of the boys spotted us. "It's taking Biko!"

"And we're going to get him out of there." Only I wasn't sure how. Spelling the slime was out of the question. I didn't need to give it any more capabilities than what it already had. That left spelling Biko. Risky, since the slime could twist other spells on contact.

Rodriguez pillaged a few lockers and used three pairs of pants to make a loop of rope. Rather than argue with the boys, he tied it under Biko's arms and tethered the other end to a bench leg that was bolted to the floor. That should give us a safety rope if the rescue went wrong.

On the other side of the room, the bear stretched out its neck and sniffed the slime. Its lip curled back, and it sneezed before hunching in the back corner of the shower.

"Do you have a plan?" Rodriguez asked.

I nodded.

"Then do it." He turned back to the boy. "Look at me, only me. No matter what happens, we are getting you out of here."

Taking a deep breath, I lifted my wand and pointed it at Biko. "*Nazid.*"

The spell spread through him, and he lifted off the floor. His friends yanked on him, and he slid halfway out of the slime. A victory rendered somewhat hollow by the complete lack of satyr fur on his lower half and the red, blistered skin. I averted my eyes.

A growl had me turning toward the bear. Slime spilled over the edge of the shower stall. The grizzly growled again as it peered at the tile wall next to him. Apparently it looked like a good exit to the bear, because before I could blink, the bear had its paws on top of the wall.

The magic shifted. Deciding the bear was the lesser threat, I looked back at the wrestling match between the boys and the slime. Biko had risen a good five feet in the air. Thankfully, he wasn't drifting any higher because of Rodriguez's quick thinking with the makeshift rope.

One last tentacle of slime held tight to Biko's hoof. He kicked, and it released him, taking the levitation spell with it. Biko screamed as he fell but managed to twist and land on his hooves. It had to be the part-goat that gave him that ability.

I lifted my wand, ready to undo the levitation spells, but it was too late. The magic shifted inside the slime, the taint twisting it. Between one heartbeat and the next, the slime went from a lazy river to beach-ball-sized blobs lifting off the floor. I dodged to the side as a blob floated toward me.

On the bright side, the hole the slime had punched through the wall was free of any blockage. Containment spell incoming.

"*Sowil*." Now nothing would be escaping into the gym to cause trouble, other than the slime that had already been on that side of the wall.

The bear roared.

I swung around, narrowly avoiding a blob of slime. If anyone had told me this morning I'd be staring at a magically-animated, stuffed grizzly bear perched atop a narrow wall dividing two shower stalls, I would've laughed. Only it wasn't funny. The slime the bear had been so carefully avoiding now drifted around it. Its glass eyes wide, the bear lunged off the stall, brushing against one of the blobs. It landed, now with a streak of bare skin.

My eyes met Rodriguez. "Time to go," I said.

I took one small step at a time, having to divide my attention between dodging slime balls and the bear. For once, luck seemed to be on my side: the bear was too busy leaning first one way and then another to avoid the slime to notice us.

After what felt like an eternity, I pulled open the door. "Quickly."

The first boy stepped through the door at the same moment the bear spotted the exit. I didn't even have time to get my wand up before the bear leapt and charged.

"Out!"

The boys lunged for the door. We lost precious moments as they struggled to all fit through the door at once. Rodriguez finally gave one of them a shove before going through the door too.

I bolted after them, having just enough time to cast another containment spell, this time on the locker room door. It swung shut in the bear's face and rattled as the bear tried to get through. None of this slowed the group down as we sprinted toward safety. Along the way, Biko had picked up a towel, and he held it in place as he ran.

A crash of wood had me twisting around. Pieces of the locker room door littered the hall. The bear had broken the object the spell was attached to, thereby destroying the containment spell too. Apparently having a healthy instinct for self-preservation even after death, it was running from the slime as fast as it could.

Which was a lot faster than any of us could move.

"*Sowil*." This time, I put the containment spell across the doorway, not on the door itself. That didn't fix the bear problem all but nipping at my heels, but it would stop the slime from getting all over the entire gym.

"Michelle, the bear!" Rodriguez yelled.

"I'm aware of the bear!" Which was only two bear-lengths behind me.

"Do something!"

"I'm open to suggestions." I put on a burst of speed, but a glance back told me I hadn't gained any ground.

"I don't know. Levitate it!"

"Because we need an angry flying bear?" Levitating Biko was what had caused the current mess. I wasn't going to risk using that spell again in this building.

Rodriguez reached the door at the end of the hall. "Do it!"

Another quick look back had me wincing. Not even two bear-lengths between us now. I went through every spell that might be able to help, but I didn't know how they would react when they touched the tainted magic that had awakened this oversized problem to begin with.

Desperate, I tried the same spell again. "*Sowil*." I fed more power into it than I had for the previous version.

It snapped into place around the bear, who put on the brakes but couldn't stop in time and tumbled into the front of the containment spell.

And just like that, the problem got weirder. Now we were being chased by a magical hamster ball with a grizzly tumbling around inside as the ball barreled toward us.

"Through the door!" I yelled. The opening was too narrow for the ball of grizzly.

I darted through after the boys and Rodriguez, tugging the door closed. The last thing I saw was the bear sliding around the bottom of the containment spell as it rolled into the door, forcing it shut. To be sure the bear wasn't coming through the door, even if it managed to escape its ball of a prison, I spelled the doorway, not just the door.

"Thank you," Rodriguez panted.

The boys nodded. "What he said."

I leaned against the wall. "Welcome."

Biko swayed, and two boys moved to support him.

"An ambulance will be outside. They'll take care of you." Rodriguez got the boys moving again.

I followed, casting one last look back. If the locker room was that bad, what was waiting for us at the science fair?

CHAPTER NINETEEN

Outside, the paramedics swooped in to take care of Biko. I relayed what I knew of the cause of his injuries while Rodriguez checked in with the officers in charge of accounting for everyone.

The paramedics were quicker than the officer, so I waited for Rodriguez in the atrium. Even with the spells I'd cast today, my magic was doing better. It pained me to admit Dr. Stiles had been right. Each time I ran out of power, my magic regenerated more quickly.

Rodriguez came in and let the door swing all the way shut before speaking. "Bad news. We have to go into the gym proper. Higher ups want a report on the supposed volcano, and a young dark elf is missing. Her parents last saw her at her sister's maglev booth."

"Please tell me maglev isn't what I think it is."

A light sparkle of humor crept back into Rodriguez's eyes. "A science project cooked up by a dark elf and her best friend who happens to be a dwarf? No. It doesn't have anything to do with using magnets for levitation and what two bright girls with different abilities can accomplish."

"And I'm sure it hasn't been affected by the tainted magic running around," I said dryly.

"On that count, I can cheerfully confirm they didn't use a bit of magic in the construction of their project."

"Thank the earth for small favors." I motioned to the door. "Shall we?"

I adjusted the containment spell so we could both pass. Rodriguez held the door open for me. A poster blocked my view of the room until I was inside. From here, I couldn't see a volcano because of all the booths, posters, and dividers, but the plume of smoke, cloud of ash, and rivers of lava snaking through the gym made it clear we were on the right track.

The volcano was far from the only item that had gotten too cozy with the twisted magic. Four super-sized beanstalks obscured the opposite corner of the gym. An actual full moon hung in the center of the gym. What that was for, I hadn't the foggiest idea, but there it was. Our old friend, the slime, floated through the air, which I'd expected, not that it made encountering it again any more fun.

A mechanical clicking drew my eyes to the ground, where spider bots crawled across the gym floor. They nimbly navigated over dropped purses, across fallen paper, and around one poor lost teddy bear. The bear broke my heart. I dusted it off and set it by the doors to the gym. Hopefully it would find its way back to its child.

"Did you happen to ask where the maglev table is?" I eyed Rodriguez.

He nodded but didn't look at me. "By the volcano."

"Of course. Where else would it be?" I muttered.

Without a word, Rodriguez headed into the maze of booths. I followed, dodging a few of the spider bots and hopping over a slender lava flow. Even when the magic died down, the damage to the building would take a while to fix. I didn't know of any gym floors that were naturally lava-proof.

We passed a booth with a whistling tea pot. I knelt down to unplug it, only to find it wasn't plugged in. I backed away, deciding that was one bit of science fair madness I could let run its course.

"I think the volcano is around the corner." Rodriguez pointed at a booth with a toppled-over display.

"Then the girl should be close." I waited for him to nod before raising my voice. "Hello? I'm with the police? We're here to help."

I followed Rodriguez around the corner.

"Stop!" A young voice shouted.

But it was too late. We both lifted off the ground. I spread out probes, but this wasn't exactly magic. In fact, I had a sinking suspicion we'd found the maglev technology. Though I wasn't sure why it was working on us. Humanoids like Rodriguez and myself weren't overly magnetic. Maybe that was what the tainted magic had twisted.

About four feet off the ground, we hit a current, magnetic rather than wind because I didn't feel much air movement other than what I generated. It swept us around a set of booths and within centimeters of a poster with a crumpled side.

That's when I spotted the volcano. It wasn't large, only mounded five or so feet above the gym floor. It looked just like a textbook drawing, with alternate patches of gray-black from previous lava flows and orange tones from lava currently cascading down its sides. Also like a real volcano, puffs of ash, steam, and smoke curled out of the vent to form an ash cloud hovering in the air.

A dark elf flailed desperately only a few feet from the

plume of smoke. She couldn't have been more than twelve. Her gray-brown skin was almost entirely covered by ash, which liberally decorated her jeans and t-shirt. The flailing wasn't helping her get away from the volcano, but it was keeping her out of the ash cloud. The same one the magnetic current was so helpfully carrying us toward.

"I told you to stop! How are you going to help me now?" she wailed.

"What's your name?" Rodriguez asked.

"Acadia."

"Acadia, we are going to get you out of here."

Oh, that was my part. The plan for escaping the magnetic flow that was taking us through a small, but active volcano.

The ash burned by eyes, and I blinked furiously as I carefully lowered the shield that blocked me from seeing magic. Surprisingly, the glow from the magic coating the room, while bright, wasn't overpowering. Even more surprising, a fair bit of the magic flowed through the magnetic field, illuminating it for me. It could've been a magical property I didn't know of or a trick of the tainted magic. Maybe later I'd have time to look it up.

A bright pulsing blob of magic obscured my vision. Before I could react, a blast of air pushed it away.

"You okay?" Rodriguez asked.

"Yup. Checking for an exit. Thanks."

"Anytime." He went back to talking to Acadia. "Do you like to read?"

While he tried to keep her calm, I traced the magnetic flow pushing us toward the volcano. Even though it looked like we were headed directly into the volcano, the magnetic flow actually turned only a foot past Acadia, descending parallel to the volcano before skating along the floor. That was the way out of this mess.

"Rodriguez, can you take care of any more blobs of slime?" I kept my voice low. If she didn't know the damage the slime could do, I didn't want to inform her.

He nodded. "I take it you have an exit plan. What do I need to know?"

"Follow my lead, and keep the slime away. I'll do the rest."

"Got it."

It was time I introduced myself. "Acadia, my name is Michelle, and my partner and I are going to get you out of here."

"From where I'm at, it doesn't look like that's likely."

If at any point I'd thought my life had reached the maximum amount of absurdity allowed for a single person, I'd been wrong. Swimming through a magnetic field dodging caustic slime and a rogue volcano while convincing a girl we really could help proved it. "We have a plan, and it'll work."

She lost a little ground and shrieked. From where she was, it had to feel like the volcano was about to swallow her. "I hope it's a good one."

"The best one I have."

Acadia muttered a few unflattering words. Given the circumstances, I didn't blame her. "When we get close, grab on to me and don't let go. I have to keep my right hand free, but I'll be holding on to you with my left. And no matter what, don't let go."

"Why do you need your right hand free? Are you going to shoot the bear? Someone tried that, and it didn't work." The words all came out in one long, breathless run.

I held up my wand. "I'm better with my right hand."

"Oh, cool! Do you know that movie, *The Witch vs. The Sorcerer*? The one with the witch who saves the world from a sorcerer?"

Rodriguez blasted a blob of slime out of our path.

On a whim, I summoned the soundtrack, a soaring electronic violin song. "Yup, and just like that witch, I'm getting you out of here."

"Cool!"

The magnetic current brought me close enough to grab her, and I wrapped my arm around her body. She clung to me. The music hit a high note, and we were falling.

Acadia screamed, drowning out the music.

"*Kannu Sowil!*" I held the shield between the volcano and the three of us, moving it as we moved to protect us from the lava beside, and then below, as well as debris falling from above.

Two blobs of slime appeared in our path, and Rodriguez shoved them out of the way.

Acadia stopped screaming, and we swooped down and leveled out just above the floor. The tempo of the music picked up.

I redirected the shield from under us to in front of us right before we bulldozed through three tables, sending posters and bits of science experiments flying.

We twisted around, heading for a stream of lava. I extended the shield under us in case the magnetic flow dropped us. The magnetic flow carried us away from the lava, and we dropped an inch closer to the ground. I released the shield.

Far from afraid, Acadia had her hands in the air, giggling as we leaned away from a booth.

The song ended just as we reached open floor and fell the eight inches down. I took the brunt of Acadia's fall, not that she even noticed hitting the ground.

Acadia all but bounced off me, grinning. "That was better than a roller coaster! Best ride ever!"

My backside ached, and my muscles protested as I stood. I couldn't help the small groan that escaped. "I'm glad you liked it. Now, would you like to get out of here?"

Acadia shoved her hair away from her face, leaving a smudge of ash on her cheek. "Yah. The last part was fun, but the rest was scary."

"That it was." I offered her my hand.

She peered around me at Rodriguez. "Could you both walk me out?"

Rodriguez got to his feet, moving as slowly as I had, and smiled at Acadia. "Of course."

With one of her hands in each of ours, we walked out of the gym. Of all the things her family expected, a tale of riding magnetic currents and dodging slime—and of course the volcano—wasn't one of them. Over her head, her parents looked at Rodriguez and me. I could see the thanks in their eyes and nodded.

Before either parent could get away from hearing all about Acadia's adventure, Rodriguez pulled me to the side. "I'm guessing you can't fix all the rotten spells in there."

"You would be correct." I was at half-power, which was great compared to where I'd been a few days ago, but that mess needed more than one witch.

"I block it off, and the school gets to call one of those pricey firms." He rubbed his temple. "No one is going to like that."

"Nope, but we have a different problem." My cheeks puffed out as I exhaled. "We didn't find the source. I'm betting cleaning supplies again, but…"

"It could be anything." Rodriguez grimaced. "Right. I'll have them lock up all the cleaning supplies and evacuate the campus until a firm can track down the source."

"A lot of the clans have a special rate for schools."

"I'll tell the administration." He waved over an officer.

"You have items to dispose of, and I can manage blocking off the building all on my own."

"You're sure?"

"I can block off a building, Michelle. And if I run out of magic, I'll have two rookies guard that door." The corner of his mouth turned up. "Lots of new officers will be on guard duty until this mess is taken care of."

"Got it."

Rodriguez turned to the officer waiting politely a few feet to the side. "Could you return Ms. Oaks to her car?"

The officer nodded.

A few more words a quick stop by Rodriguez's car for the bag of gear I hadn't used, and a quiet car ride later, I was back at my car. I stowed my stuff and sat heavily in the driver's seat. Leaning forward, I rested my head against the steering wheel.

What a whirlwind of a morning. Every time I thought we'd seen the last of the tainted magic, it came back again. Each time it returned, it distracted me from the important problems. Ethel's death, Elron's abduction, my future as the premier.

I couldn't think.

That's really where this went. I couldn't think about the cases as thoroughly as I should. I couldn't think about the accident and all its mysteries, or processing Ethel's death. I couldn't even pause long enough to think about Elron and how to get him back. All I'd done for days was run from one problem to another. Run. Run and never stop.

Run, because if I slowed down, I'd realize this had beaten me down. My magic was replenishing faster, but that was it. My soul couldn't take much more, and I couldn't even think about that because if I did, I'd collapse.

Collapsing wasn't an option, not until I rescued Elron.

My phone rang, and I groaned. "Please not another case."

I dug out my phone, eyes widening when I saw restricted flash across the screen where it usually listed the number. "Oaks Consulting. Michelle speaking."

"Announce you're stepping down and will not be premier by eight tonight, or we start hurting the elf." The voice switched from sounding like a young woman to that of an older woman with a heavy rasp before the tone changed to that of a gruff man. It shifted too smoothly to be different recordings spliced together, which meant a spell was altering the speaker's voice.

My heart pounded. "Proof of life, or I don't do anything." I didn't need the proof, but I wasn't going to let them think I'd do anything without knowing he was safe. Nor did I want to risk revealing the connection between our lives if this person didn't know.

"Speak." This voice was light and feminine, and it wasn't talking to me.

"Hello?" Elron's voice drifted across the line.

"The first week we met. You said you were curious about my clan scar. What did I say?" The mark on the back of my right shoulder identified my clan. Actually, clans. I was bound to my mother's Wapiti and my father's Docga. Along with those, it contained the mark of the Ieldra, a sign of a powerful witch destined to do great things. That part of my clan scar had been a lot more interesting before I'd realized great things meant scary and likely to kill you.

"You said curiosity might kill the elf." He kept going, his words tumbling over one another. "Don't do it. Don't listen to them!"

"That is enough proof." The voice was back, this time

rough and tired. "Step down by eight tonight, or we cut the elf."

The line went dead.

I stared at my phone even after the screen went dark. From that interaction, I couldn't tell if they knew about the connection or not. Initially, I'd thought they had because the death spell had affected me too. Now, it could go either way. All I'd learned from the phone call was Elron didn't want me to listen, and if I didn't do what they asked, they'd hurt him.

"Syed, you mistress of evil. What did I ever do to you!" I swore.

Think. I had to do what I'd barely done since all of this started. I needed to think.

It wasn't easy to focus though the haze, but I shoved everything aside so I could drive home safely. I got there without incident and skipped the lodge entirely, instead walking through the gardens. Eventually, the path carried me to the altar. I studied it before turning away and heading into the woods. I didn't stop until I found Ty hanging out by the A-frame building he called home. I sat on a bench, and he snuffled my hair.

At first I was too numb to do anything, even think. Inside me, a dam broke. Leaning against Ty's cheek, I cried.

When no more tears would come, I dried my face with the hem of my shirt. Behind the grief came fatigue. Today, I wasn't smart or clever or witty. All I had left in me was what I'd been doing for days. Dig in and push through.

If this was another police case, that would be enough, but it was my life, and Elron's life. There was a larger picture here, and right now, I couldn't see it.

"So, do I give them what they want, or do I try to be clever?" I asked.

Ty's breath ruffled my hair.

"I don't know how to fix this because I don't know how everything went wrong. Which events are linked and which aren't." I scratched under his chin. "Ethel's death, I guess. Which doesn't even make sense. I never took her for a liar, but ages ago, when she asked me to be the premier, she said I had time to get used to the idea. She knew when she would die, and it wasn't for a few years."

My breath caught. "Oh."

Ty huffed.

I started scratching him again. "Ethel didn't just know when she'd die. She knew how. She told me that. So, what changed?"

Ty cocked his head to the side so I could reach *the spot*.

"Nothing changed." I shifted my fingers to the side. "Yet everyone thinks she's dead."

Ty groaned and thumped his tail, shaking nearby trees.

"But she's not dead. Because this wasn't how or when. She would've told me." Brutal honesty had always been more Ethel's style than lies and deceit. "So, is she testing me? That doesn't seem like her."

Ty was too lost in the bliss of chin scratches to have answers.

"Or is she out there, hiding and plotting to deal with whoever tried to kill her? That would mean the bystander was right, and she escaped into the woods, likely after spelling a set of remains to foil the medical examiner." Now that sounded more like the Ethel I knew. "But that doesn't tell me what I should do. If she's out there plotting, why hasn't she contacted me?"

"Because she thinks I'm in on it. No, that doesn't feel right." I gave Ty's cheek a final pat, ignoring his nudge. "She knows me well enough to know I wouldn't betray her like this, plus all it gains me is a bunch of problems."

"She's alive." I counted off what I knew on my fingers. "She can't contact me for some reason. Someone wants me to give up being premier. Elron was abducted by the people who want me to step down. Magic has been running wild."

That's where I got stuck. Maybe someone had taken both Ethel and Elron because they had plans for a different premier. Not the easiest plan to pull off, and they didn't have any guarantee I would cooperate. Hardly foolproof. "What am I missing?"

Ty didn't have any answers.

I tried a different angle. "I don't want Elron to be harmed. I give the appearance of setting up another announcement. I go about my day as usual, take that stuff to be disposed of for Rodriguez. Then I… do what they ask. I tell the witch community I'm stepping down, which means my mom is also stepping aside. That keeps her from being a target, and at the same time, I tell them Ethel is alive, which is why I'm stepping down. How does that sound?" I looked up at Ty.

He wrinkled his nose.

"You're right, they could still hurt or even kill Elron, but why would they? I wouldn't be in line to be the premier, so I and Elron wouldn't be of value. Oh… that's the problem." I huffed. "No easy fixes there."

Ty bobbed his head.

"I know, but the overall plan is still sound. I schedule the press conference and then spend the rest of the day trying to find another out. It's the best I've got."

Ty tilted his head to the side before nodding.

"Thanks, Ty. Come down for a hug?" He lowered his head so I could wrap my arms around his nose. "You're the best."

I didn't tell him that no matter what I did, the people holding Elron could kill him. I didn't tell him this could be the last hug. Instead, I let it stretch on, wishing I could freeze time.

CHAPTER TWENTY

I thought scheduling a press conference would be hard. Turns out, when you're the next premier, a quick phone call to an assistant is all it takes. As an added bonus, Susanna didn't even press endlessly about the topic or whatnot. She agreed to set everything up for eight and warned me I had to be back here by six for hair and makeup.

I swung by my apartment long enough to grab a protein bar and an energy-boosting tea and hit the road. It wasn't exactly safe to be toting around tainted magic. One car accident and I could blow up a stretch of highway.

Any other day I would've been enjoying the fall breeze, leaves drifting down, and clear blue skies. All of which were lost on me today. I couldn't enjoy any of it because inside I felt empty.

Void.

Nothing.

No matter what I did, someone I loved could die. Likely Elron, taking me with him. No future wedding, no helping the witch community, none of our dreams coming true.

If everything went right, and Elron's captor kept their word, I might get him back after the press conference. That was assuming they wouldn't have another task for me, and then one after that.

That was assuming this wouldn't end in death.

Like Ethel.

My fingers tapped on the steering wheel. "I really could use some luck right now. That would be grand."

A single crow flew across the sky.

"Really? An omen of bad luck? I already know I have bad luck! How much worse could it get?" I took a right to head for Regional Disposal. "Never mind. I don't want to know."

I passed an old bungalow that had seen better days with a FOR SALE sign in the yard, and a tingle crept through my senses. Slowing, I scanned the area, but the fence at the edge of Regional Disposal's property appeared in good repair. Even the sedan in the oncoming lane kept to a reasonable speed for the road as it passed. As far as my eyes could see, the tingle was unwarranted.

The tingle persisted along the edge of my shields.

Unable to shake the sensation, I pulled onto the shoulder, flipped on my hazard lights, and silently swore.

I shouldn't look. I had enough problems. Not a one of which would be helped by poking my nose into a problem that wasn't currently mine.

Great logic. I ignored all of it, closed my eyes and released the shield blocking me from seeing magic. A deep breath, and I opened my eyes.

A riot of color vying for dominance washed across Regional Disposal, barely held in by the fence. The magic etched into the metal strained under the load, hardly able to hold it in. A fence post next to my car flared neon pink as the two magics collided.

Spots filled my eyes long after the flare of magic died. When I could focus again, I checked the fence. It was still holding, but weaker. "Narzel, you just had to, didn't you?"

Phone in hand, I got out of the car for a closer look. The way the magic inside the fence moved reminded me of…

No. Couldn't be. They'd destroyed the cleaning supplies from Happy Paws, right?

The magic pulsed, warring with itself inside the fence. Magical phantoms of dogs and cats sprung to life, battling forks, knives, and one jumbo-sized chef's knife. A fork sprang for a cat, who batted it out of the air and pounced before trotting off, tines thrashing as the cat carried it away. In retaliation, the chef's knife, easily the largest item on the battlefield, sliced through a cat and two dogs.

Before the knife could attack anyone else, a Roasted Beans coffee cup hopped onto the battlefield, leapt up, and came down on top of the knife, trapping it. Not to be outdone, a round ball of what I could only assume was ice cream rolled on to the magical battlefield, flattening everything in its path.

Either Regional Disposal's disposal efforts weren't doing the trick, or they weren't really disposing of magic items at all, but storing them. Now all these rogue magics —ones that should've run themselves out, not created phantoms to terrorize the magical landscape—were battling. Since they weren't dead, there had to be a source, but where? What would be powerful enough to keep magic of this scale operating for days?

I shook myself out of my daze and started dialing Rodriguez. The entire area would have to be quarantined. It was a big job, likely too much for me alone, but I could coordinate with a firm who specialized in problems, well, not like this, but close enough.

The first ring of the line was interrupted by a fire and pain spreading through my entire body. I fell to the ground shaking, tears leaking from my eyes, the phone forgotten.

A familiar looking woman with jaw-length blond hair pursed her lips as she considered me.

I didn't know what there was to consider. Pain still flared through my body, and given the stun gun in her hand, magic didn't have a damn thing to do with my current state.

"Oh, you're still awake." She knelt down beside me.

My eyes didn't want to focus on the swimming images of her face, but for a brief moment, they snapped into a cohesive whole.

I knew her.

She'd been on Isadora's side before the Trial by Magic. Marquette hadn't said much that day, but if she was involved, then maybe Isadora was behind this, and I'd been played.

"That won't do." Her wand tapped my forehead, and my world went dark.

Waking up hurt. I wanted to blame the stun gun, but frankly, the concrete floor under me bore more than a fraction of the responsibility. The cold metal cuffs around my wrists blocking my magic weren't helping. Even without opening my eyes, I knew the bracelet that allowed me to summon my wand was gone. Annoying, but not the largest problem.

Hoping to buy a little time before my captors realized I was awake, I kept my eyes shut. Before Marquette had zapped me, I'd been calling Rodriguez. The call had rung once, but I couldn't remember if he'd answered or not. If not, Susanna would realize I was missing in a few hours when I didn't show up for makeup.

Not that she'd have a clue where to find me. No tracking spell would penetrate the mess of magic around this place, which made it a pretty good place to hold someone if you knew a witch was looking for them.

That thought had my eyes open and me scrambling upright as best I could. Blinking, I noticed the relative lack of debris on the floor, which meant this area had been cleaned recently or didn't get much traffic. From the block walls and slit-window door, the most notable feature was the person chained to the opposite wall. In the dim light, I couldn't make out their features.

"Elron?" The tracking spell had failed. Maybe because he was here, and now we were here together. Which, now that I thought about it, didn't seem like much of an upgrade.

"So much for you saving me, not that being locked in here was a good start."

I'd recognize that sharp voice anywhere. "Ethel? You're alive? Right. The tracking spell failed the same way."

"I don't follow." She scooted closer, the dim lights revealing disheveled gray hair and a bright pink shirt.

"Have you seen Elron?"

"No."

"Oh." I sucked in a deep breath, reminding myself that Ethel didn't have to see Elron for him to be here. "Everyone thinks you're dead. So did I at first, but then I remembered you knew when you were—will—whatever, die and said you had time before then."

"If we live through this, I will be sure everyone knows I'm alive."

"If?"

Ethel sighed. "I've been told I should expect to have very few days left."

"But you told me you had years, and that was less than a year ago," I said. The electric shock hadn't done my reasoning abilities any good.

She shrugged. "How did you come to be here?"

It took a while to catch her up, partly because I had to untangle things as I went. Isadora's motives for all of this weren't clear to me, so I avoided blaming her until the very end. "I don't know why Marquette used the stun gun on me. Maybe magic near the edge of the property causes problems with what they have going on here. Anyway, she supported Isadora during the challenge. But I still can't figure out what Isadora gets out of this, and I really did think she was afraid."

"Marquette seems to be on day guard duty. She's been bringing my meals."

"And how did you come to be here?" I had questions too. A lot of them, since my brain power had gone to emergencies and spells, not critical thinking.

"I awakened here after the convention. In that time, I have seen three jailers, and Isadora hasn't been one of them."

"Do you remember getting in your car?" I had a bad feeling about the supposed accident.

"No."

I tapped my fingers on my thigh. "Everyone said you were in the car. The medical examiner was sure he had your body."

"As you can see, he was mistaken."

"Clearly, but that makes me wonder why everyone said you were in the car. And who's body is on his table." It was possible to alter a witch's memory. Changing the memory of seven witches was far from easy.

"The better question is how we leave this place."

"Unless they gave you the grand tour on the way in, all I know for sure was I parked along the fence line of Regional Disposal before Marquette stunned me." That came out bitter, which was fine. "Isadora won the challenge. I don't understand why she's doing this now."

"As I said, I haven't seen Isadora." Ethel shook her head. "I don't believe she is involved."

"Then wh…" The rest of the question died on my lips as the door rattled.

The lock clicked, and the door swung open. Light flooded the room. Susanna stepped inside, wand in hand. She stared at me, ignoring Ethel. "Why couldn't you follow simple directions?"

I blinked, but Susanna didn't go away or change shape. Of all the people I expected, she wasn't on the list.

"You'll have to be more specific," I said. "It's been a Narzel kissed week, and after that lovely jolt of electricity, I'm not thinking clearly." That reminded me to check my magic reserves. In one potentially lucky turn of events, I had most of the magic I could hold and was regenerating more.

Her foot tapped. "Stay home and announce your resignation like a good little witch."

I raised an eyebrow. "No one told me to stay home."

"It should have been clear."

"Then you needed to say it clearly." I really shouldn't bait her, not when in nullifying cuffs with Ethel and likely Elron as prisoners.

The corners of her mouth pinched together. "If you agree to do as I say, no fighting, no destined-to-fail escape attempts, I'll release you."

"And if I don't agree?" Some days I just couldn't keep my mouth shut. Today, looking at a woman who'd pretended to be on my side while abducting my friends, well, I was short a brain to mouth filter.

"Would you rather watch Elron or Ethel die?" Her lips curved up in a cruel smile. "Painfully."

She didn't know. Susanna didn't know my life was tied to Elron's, which was either the best news I'd gotten since waking up here, or the worst.

"I'll give you time to think." She turned and left.

Even after the key turned in the lock, I didn't speak for fear that Susanna or one of her co-conspirators were listening. On the bright side, she wouldn't be knowingly threatening my life while threatening Elron. On the horrible side, since she didn't know Elron's real value, Susanna could simply kill him to prove a point, and then we'd both be dead.

"Advisers and assistants can be valuable, but one should never be too free with information," Ethel said.

I'd been assuming she had told her entire inner circle. Silly me. "A lesson I'll remember."

We lapsed into silence as the minutes ticked by. I'd always prided myself on having a plan. No matter what went wrong or how a situation developed, I had a plan. Not today. I couldn't even figure out the best move.

Option One: agree with Susanna and hope I could rescue as many of us as possible before too much harm was done.

Or take Option Two: do not comply. Do not pass go. Maybe we all die.

Twice, I opened my mouth to ask Ethel what to do and thought better of it. Susanna was a competent witch and more than capable of listening in from a distance. Nothing we said was truly private.

"Susanna was behind the magic you've been chasing," Ethel volunteered.

"How do you know that?"

"Ever since you informed me illegal goods were still being discovered, I started an investigation. Susanna's first clan was disbanded for misusing their magic years ago. I hired her to keep a closer eye on her, though as you can see, that didn't go as planned." The chains clanked as Ethel motioned to the cell.

"It was a good distraction."

"Do what she asks Michelle," Ethel whispered.

I didn't answer my premier. Once I'd had to watch my mother and father being tortured. No matter how many times I replayed my actions that day, I always wished I'd intervened sooner. I didn't know if I could watch Susanna hurt Elron. I didn't know that he'd be safe if I complied.

Acting the part of the docile little witch didn't feel right either. I couldn't do it for long. Susanna had to know me well enough to know that, so she'd never release Elron. He'd be her prisoner until she no longer needed me, and then we'd both be dead.

"What does she want with you?" I asked.

Ethel hesitated. "I'm her contingency plan."

"And after telling everyone you're dead, just how is that going to work?"

Ethel didn't answer.

I leaned back against the wall. "I see."

She was the contingency if I didn't cooperate and Susanna killed me. My part in this mess would be rewritten. I would become the evil mastermind, the one who'd sacrifice anything to get power. Ethel would reappear, rescued by Susanna, only to resign or die publicly. That would clear the way for Susanna to step into Ethel's shoes. Once Susanna was premier, few would stand in her way, even if they disagreed with her decisions. Years of progress, gone.

The silence stretched on, with the block walls obscuring enough outside sound that it became the two of us in our own small world. At some point, I must've drifted off, not asleep but not truly awake either.

The door rattled, and I came back to myself with a jolt and shiver.

Susanna held the door open. Zach huffed his way into view, dragging someone along with him. The hall light caught on silver hair. Zach heaved Elron through the door.

He landed limply on the floor, skin sallow, a smear of dried blood across his cheek.

Elron was alive. For now, but they hadn't treated him as kindly as Ethel. It didn't take a clairvoyant to know our future depended on the next few minutes.

My gaze went from his prone form to Susanna. "What do you want?"

"You agree to do as I say, and the elf comes to no harm."

"That's a promise you've already broken."

Her eyes narrowed. "Most humanoids don't do well without food or water. I could remedy that, if only you'd do as told."

"You'll have to be very clear as to what you want."

Anything to buy time. Three captives and an open door. This was about as good as an escape opportunity got. Well, being out of the chains and nullifying cuffs would help, but baby steps.

Susanna shook her head. "I don't trust you, Michelle. I don't trust you'll hold up your side of our little bargain."

"Give him food and water, and I'll do what you ask."

"No." She pointed her wand at Elron. "*Algiz.*"

Invisible bindings pulled his arms against his body.

From the stiff position he ended up in, they seemed to reach from his knees to shoulders.

"*Nazid.*" Susanna levitated him off the ground, repositioning him so it almost looked as if he was kneeling next to her, head bowed. Through all the movement, Elron didn't stir.

She had to have another spell on him, perhaps a sleep spell. I hoped that was it. The other option was injury.

"All this hair. It won't do him any good here." The end of her wand flattened. She lifted a slender braid and brought her wand next to his scalp.

She sliced through his hair and into his skin. "It seems I need to work on my technique."

Blood ran down his temple, but he still didn't stir.

Susanna twisted another lock of hair around her fingers, pulling it taunt. The bladed tip of her wand scraped across his scalp. Blood oozed in its wake.

CHAPTER TWENTY-ONE

Wake up! I wanted to scream at him. *Fight back!*

Elron didn't react at all to that slice. Or the next one. If he'd been capable of waking up and fighting, he would've.

I bit my lip to keep from shouting at him. As bad as this was, it could be worse, and it would be if I antagonized Susanna. I couldn't do anything but watch as she carelessly cut another chunk of hair. She sliced into his scalp again, and again with the next cut.

"Stop, please, stop," I begged. "I'll do what you want."

She curled a strand of hair around her fingers. "You will learn I do not make empty threats."

I couldn't look away. I couldn't close my eyes. I watched every cut. I winced even though Elron couldn't. I cried. Not tears of pain, but of anger.

My hands shook as they tightened to fists. If Susanna thought this would teach me to be quiet and do as she said, she was wrong. I would be quiet, because I would watch. I needed one moment, a second where I could get the upper hand. That's all it would take.

"Last one." Her wand dripped blood as she let the last

strand of Elron's hair fall. It drifted down to the bloody pile of hair around him. His remaining hair, an uneven fuzz, held thick drops of blood, making his head look like one ragged wound.

Looking past Elron, I found Susanna watching me. Watching my tears.

"You'll do what I want, how I want, for as long as I want, or I'll find another way to hurt him." She rested the sharpened point of her wand against his throat.

"After the press release, he gets food, water, and medical care." My voice shook.

She tipped her head to the side. "That wasn't what I said."

I bowed my head, hiding the anger I couldn't keep out of my eyes. "Please. I'll do anything if you'll take care of him."

Ethel drew in a sharp breath.

"Fine." She lowered Elron back to the floor and turned her wand on me. "*Algiz.*"

Ropes pulled my arms in close, tightening until I could only take shallow breaths.

"Zach, undo her cuffs," Susanna ordered.

He stepped over Elron. His boots left bloody tracks marking the distance between Elron and me. Zach's fingers dug into my arm. He hauled me upright, but after all the time on the concrete floor, my legs had gone to sleep. Sharp pinpricks ran down them.

Zach fumbled with the lock as I swayed. He muttered a curse and steadied me with one hand as he removed the cuffs.

For a moment, I could access my magic, but I didn't know what to do. I hadn't cast complex spellwork without a wand since before the accident.

A heaviness settled over my mind, pushing away

thoughts of fighting. The pain in my legs battled for attention but fell beneath the blanket of the compulsion spell.

"Michelle, look at me," Susanna commanded.

My head moved, and my eyes went to her.

"Good." Her satisfied smile faltered when she noticed Elron. "Zach, lock him up. Michelle, follow me."

The spell told me to walk directly to her, but that would force me to step on Elron's hair, in his blood.

"Don't do it," Ethel whispered.

Susanna narrowed her eyes at Ethel.

In that fraction of a second, I pushed against the spell. My foot landed on the other side of his hair, but I couldn't miss the blood.

Susanna's attention snapped back to me, but she'd missed my little rebellion. She'd missed the real meaning of Ethel's words.

Don't waste effort on the small battle. Pick your moment. Fight to win.

With Elron's blood marking my passing. I joined Susanna in the hall.

She took the nullifying cuffs from Zach and tucked them through her belt.

I waited for her orders. Three other doors came off this hall, two on the same wall as the room that had been my prison and one at the end of the hall. The room I'd come from didn't have a sign, but the other two were labeled as storage and the bathroom. The door at the end of the hall would take me to the rest of the building.

That was where I could fight Susanna.

"Follow me."

Like a good little witch, I trailed after her.

"We can move the press conference here. I'd planned on you announcing your resignation, but I like this better." She stopped. "Open the door for me."

Dutifully, I moved around her. The door opened to a small office space with several desks. A strong air freshener warred with a sour odor I couldn't place. Marquette lounged in a chair.

If Isadora wasn't involved in all of this, she really needed better friends.

"Michelle, you will follow Marquette's orders as if they are mine." Susanna took a seat at the desk next to Marquette. "Get her ready for the conference. We're moving it here."

"Here?" Marquette leaned forward. "Are you sure that's wise, with, you know, going on?"

Susanna flicked her fingers dismissively. "They'll never know the broadcast came from here. And our newest asset should be able to take care of that other issue for us."

Through the haze of the compulsion spell, I didn't care about their problem. I didn't care about anything but my next orders. Under it, I waited. Once, I'd have risked two-against-one odds, but I wasn't that witch any more.

"Michelle, call Rodriguez. Tell him you found a magical problem at Regional Disposal and have sealed the border for the town's protection. You're working with a clan to come fix the issue. It isn't safe for him or his men to be here." Susanna pointed to a phone on the desk next to her.

I did as I was told and listened to the phone ring, her orders clear in my head.

"Officer Rodriguez."

"It's Michelle. I'm inside the gate at Regional Disposal and have sealed the area after finding magic similar to what we've been dealing with. I'm in contact with a clan to fix the issue, so the police aren't needed." The words filtered through the compulsion spell before reaching the part of me that could think. I didn't sound like myself.

"Is that so?" Rodriguez asked.

"I'm sorry for the confusion. It's a dynamic situation." The spell made me say exactly what Susanna would want me to say, not what I'd actually say.

"Why aren't you calling me on your phone?"

"It was damaged before I got the situation under control."

"Alright then," he said briskly. "I'll move everyone out and put up road blocks to ensure no one comes in contact with this area. We don't need another Roasted Beans situation."

"Thank you. I'll be in touch if the situation changes." I hung up and turned to Susanna. "Was that satisfactory?"

Her fingers tapped on the desk. "We will see."

Marquette toggled the screens on her computer until she found a video feed of the front gate. The police were getting in their cars and driving away. She switched to a different camera, watching until all of them had retreated down the road and out of sight.

Susanna turned to me and nodded. "You saved your elf more pain."

The compulsion didn't allow for a reaction, but it couldn't stop the spark of anger.

Soon. Soon I'd be in the right position to fight back.

"Get her camera ready. Zach and I will set up for filming. We can tape it now and show it later as if it's live." Susanna pushed away from the desk. "I'll write up questions we can ask, make it sound like press is there and interactive."

"She'll be ready soon." Marquette pushed away from her desk. "Follow me."

The compulsion had me on my feet and following Marquette. She led me back through the door Susanna and I had come through and ushered me into the bathroom. Before the door closed behind me, I saw Zach walk out of Ethel and Elron's room.

"Sit."

Either Susanna had planned to have me here at some point, or she'd been using this as her base of operations for a while because a small rack of suits sat in a corner next to a slender rolling set of drawers and two chairs.

Marquette took the seat across from me and rummaged in the drawers until she came out with cloths and a fistful of cosmetics. "Hold still."

I couldn't move while she scrubbed my face with a cloth and then slathered a lotion on me.

"I questioned Susanna when she had me buy clothing in your size. I questioned when she had me befriend Isadora, but Susanna is always right. With only a little encouragement, Isadora set in motion your downfall. Shame you interfered when we tried to set her up for Ethel's death, but Susanna said she had a better plan, and she was right." Marquette leaned back to inspect her work. "Let that soak in. After makeup, we'll do your hair and get you changed."

Her words flowed over me as I retreated to the part of me the compulsion couldn't touch. The two of us alone in a room seemed like a great opportunity, but it was too soon. I knew Rodriguez, and he wouldn't believe what I'd said on the phone. He was my back-up plan in case I failed, but that meant I had to buy him time to come back with a way through the gates. I couldn't gamble with Elron's and Ethel's lives.

Marquette did my makeup and hair, and she dressed me as one would a large doll. Eventually, she positioned me in front of the mirror on the back of the bathroom door. The woman in that mirror looked polished, the type of woman who'd wear a plum suit and decided the fate of her race. Only the eyes were empty. No spark, no passion, nothing but a shell.

I must've passed Marquette's inspection because she ushered me out of the room and into the conference room, where Susanna and Zach had set up a royal purple backdrop with the seal of the premier in the center. By tradition, only the premier or her representative could use this background. I hadn't used it before and wouldn't have until I was sworn into the office if the decision had been left up to me.

Susanna looked me over from head to toe. "Good. Stand behind the podium, but be careful not to lean on it."

From the front, it looked study and official, but when I rounded the side, I noticed the thin boards and equally fragile frame. For as nice as it looked, it had all the structure of a cheap prop. I took my place, complete with blank cards so it would look like I had something to refer to. But I knew how Susanna liked to organize her confrences. Letters took shape next to the camera.

"Questions and voice adjustments to use with them." Susanna handed a sheet to Zach and Marquette, keeping one for herself.

A man in Regional Disposal coveralls barged into the room. "I got it—"

"Stop." Susanna's order cut through his words.

He froze, mouth in mid-motion, body completely still.

That was a compulsion, just like the one she had on me. While she was distracted, I studied Marquette and Zach. They didn't jump to follow her orders the way I did, but there were different types of compulsions. Some were more mild. Even so, there would be signs. If I was a betting woman (not that my luck had ever given me a reason to gamble), I'd put money on them being true believers.

A shame, really. The more compulsions Susanna was holding, the less magic she'd have for other spells.

"You will knock before entering a room. You will not speak until spoken to." Susanna sighed. "What do you have to report?"

Even after the scolding, he didn't look the slightest bit upset. "I have the chemicals repackaged and set out for you to spell. What else do you want me to do?"

Susanna walked out of the conference room, returning a few minutes later with a small bag of white powder and a water bottle of fluid.

I tried to reach out a probe, but the compulsion wouldn't let me. Susanna hadn't told me to do magic, so I couldn't, but I could still feel a spell in the water. The powder she had dumped into the drink was the real problem. For humans, it could give them magical abilities for a time, but it was dangerous. Their bodies weren't designed for large energy transfers, and it could be unpredictable. When witches consumed the powder, it supercharged their magic for a time, but for us, the risk was even greater. For many, it was addictive, and a single dose was enough. Others couldn't manage that amount of power in their skin and burned themselves out.

"Take a sip, then take the potion to the rest of the employees. Each of them should take a sip. Defend against any intruders." Susanna handed him the bottle, sparks swirling through as the powder dissolved.

Damn. I should've staged my rebellion when I was in makeup.

He took a single swallow of the fluid before capping it, bowing, and retreating. "Yes, premier."

Susanna closed the door behind him before resuming our little farce. "Read the statement, then take questions as if this is real. Answers will appear in the same place as the statement."

The compulsion rolled over me again, shoving away the part of me that could function independent of her orders. My body did as told.

CHAPTER TWENTY-TWO

"Witches and warlocks, I come to you again in this troubled time to bring hope." Ugh. She'd even given me a terrible speech. "At the request of numerous clans, I will be taking over as Premier effective immediately. It has become clear to many of us that the path Premier Ethel laid out before her untimely demise isn't viable. An interim premier and a premier in training was an unprecedented solution that is unwieldy and impractical."

I had to give Susanna that point. Splitting power between Mom and me because of my age didn't work. It left the clans without a true leader. "Before we can move forward, we must honor the past. This week, we will hold memorials to honor Premier Ethel leading up to her funeral on Friday. The services will be televised on the Witch Network for those who can not be there in person."

The text literally told me to pause for effect. I followed the order, but it didn't feel like enough of a transition when I resumed the speech. "Next week, I will present myself before the ministers and be sworn in as premier. Moving forward does not mean forgetting those who came before and their contributions. Ethel will stay in my heart, and my time with her will guide me as I adjust to the responsibilities of the office."

With the compulsion still guiding my actions, I continued to the questions. They were as lame as the rest of the speech, but the three of them did a good job changing their voices. If they added in a little crowd noise, it would sound like a real press conference to the viewers.

As soon as the recording stopped, Susanna resumed giving orders. "Marquette, remove her makeup and put her back in her street clothes. Zach, get the recording ready for broadcast."

I followed Marquette back to the bathroom. The compulsion tried to glaze over my thoughts, but this time, I pushed back. It was me against one witch, and I had to put a stop to this before that interview aired. Once it was out there, nothing I or even Ethel did would undo the harm of that announcement.

The door closed behind me. I let Marquette remove my makeup, return my hair to a sensible ponytail, and order me to change clothes. While she hung up the dress, I made my move, throwing everything in me at the compulsion spell.

Once I'd been able to break these easily, but now, I fought to remove its hooks from my mind. It'd been attached long enough for them to sink in. Pain lanced through my mind as I dug enough of them out. They tried to stick, but I cut myself free. The last hook took the most effort, and some of my magic with it as it went.

I blinked and found myself free of the spell, standing exactly where I'd been before my rebellion. If Marquette had noticed, it didn't show as she put my dress back on the rack.

"*Mannaz.*" I pointed at her. The sleep spell took more

power than usual because I was wandless, but it worked.

Marquette slipped bonelessly to the floor, her head narrowly missing the toilet.

I couldn't remember if Susanna would've felt me dig out the compulsion spell. She might know, she might not. Or if the spell had snapped back, she could be out cold. Not likely given my luck, but a girl could hope.

I found a few pairs of stockings and used them to tie up Marquette. The bonds weren't elegant, but they should hold if she woke up before I got back up. Given how potent of a sleeping spell I used, I didn't expect her to wake up before morning, but with Elron's and Ethel's lives on the line, I wanted to be careful. I shoved her in the corner behind the clothing rack. If anyone came looking, they shouldn't see her from the door.

Marquette's wand had fallen to the floor when I moved her. I stared at it for a moment. This fight would be so much easier with a wand, but they could be fussy. My hand hovered over it. Susanna had enough control and power to hold compulsions on several people. I could use the focusing and amplification properties of a wand.

My fingers brushed the pine handle.

Electricity arced up my arm. My hand spasmed, and the wand fell back to the floor.

"Be that way." I nudged it under the clothing rack with the toe of my shoe.

My arm ached, and my fingers tingled. "Great. Just great." Now I would get to fight Susanna wandless and with sensory-deprived fingers.

I eased the bathroom door open enough to peer out. What I could see of the hall was empty, which I took as a good sign. If any shred of luck blessed me today, Susanna wouldn't know I'd shattered the spell, and Elron would be as safe as he could get while I dealt with her. My tingly fingers didn't want to work, so I shoved the door open left-handed.

The hallway was empty. I eased the door shut. Elron and Ethel were a few feet away. It wouldn't take long to check on them, but it wasn't the smart move either. Right now, Zach could still be working on the video, and Susanna might be alone. Since Zach wasn't exactly the brains of the operation, if I dealt with Susanna he might surrender.

With one regretful look back at the cell door, I turned away. With each step, I gathered my power, first forming a shield around myself to reflect spells, and layering a second one inside to absorb power and feed it back to me. Both spells took a chunk of magic, but they'd be worth it.

I shoved the door open with a sleep spell readied.

"Michelle, sit." Susanna didn't look up from the paper on her desk.

"*Mannaz!*" I flung the sleep spell at her.

She looked up at me, blinking slowly. "Unlike some foolish witches, I don't leave myself open to cowardly attacks."

The sleep spell oozed off a shield.

It didn't matter. I had other spells. "*Algiz.*"

The ropes tugged her arms off the desk. "*Obala fehu…*" The bindings muffled the rest of Susanna's spell.

Carpet surged around my feet, twisting around my legs and solidifying. Not the most worrisome attack since I wanted to be here. I stayed on the offensive. "*Isaz.*"

Ice encased Susanna.

I tried to take a deep breath, but it felt like I couldn't get any air. My eyes locked with Susanna's. That witch was still casting spells. I'd have to knock her out.

My lungs ached. I wouldn't be doing anything to her until I could breathe.

Stretching out probes in every direction, I found a boundary through which air didn't cross. It would take too long to unmake the spell. If I could reach it, I could break it. Focusing on my feet I softened the floor and put it back to where it belonged. "*Obala orzu fehu.*"

With my feet free, I formed my power into a blade. Kneeling, I shoved the magical blade through the spell and ripped it all the way up to the top of the sphere and back down to the other side. The spell collapsed.

I sucked in breath upon breath of air as I turned to face Susanna. Two spells ricocheted off my outer shield. I ignored them with a smile.

Water poured off Susanna. Rather than looking vulnerable, it drew attention to the hard set of her jaw and the anger in her eyes. "You still haven't learned, have you?" Her mouth continued to move, silently casting a spell.

My knees buckled, and once again, I was face down on the ground, struggling to move, struggling to breathe.

The crowd screamed, and the lights dimmed.

I was back at the convention, in the Trial by Magic, and didn't have enough magic to fight back.

Spells hit my shield, one after another. Sleep, bindings, another compulsion spell. With each strike, the shield eroded a little more, until it was as delicate as paper. Another hit and it would be gone.

If I could just get a breath, I could think. I could find a way out.

The crowd screamed louder.

Where is the audience? I forced my eyes open. The gray carpet was nothing like the mats from the Trial by Magic. *It's not real.*

This wasn't the trial. I wasn't in front of thousands of witches, and I wasn't facing Isadora.

But I had fought Isadora, and I knew how to counter

this spell. "*Nazid.*" The pull against my body lessened, but I stayed on the floor. I needed one good spell, one that could incapacitate Susanna or at least throw her off her game.

I shoved off the floor and flung my hand out toward her. "*Dagaz!*" I doubled the magic I'd usually use for the spell.

A fireball two feet in diameter barreled into Susanna. It sizzled as it hit her shield, burning through. The shield fell, and it shot forward.

Faster than my eyes could follow, it hit another spell, and came hurling back at me.

Not again.

It tore through the pathetic remains of my shield and I closed my eyes, knowing this would hurt.

Through my eyelids, I saw a bright yellow glow surround me before fiery hot magic poured back into me.

My eyes snapped open. I'd forgotten about the second shield, the one I didn't have during the challenge.

Susanna's mouth gaped.

I marched up to her and punched her, knocking her jaw shut.

Susanna's eyes rolled back in her head, and she slumped over.

"*Mannaz.*" The sleep spell should have been over kill but I didn't like taking chances.

I shook my hand, like that would reduce the ache. Retrieving the nullifying cuffs from the desk, I locked them around her wrists before pocketing the key.

A door squeaked.

I spun around.

Zach dropped the laptop he'd been holding in his haste to put his hands in the air. "Please don't hurt me."

"Back in the conference room."

He bobbed his head and scurried.

I scooped up the laptop as I followed him. "Sit."

Zach sat.

"Is the 'press conference' set to air tonight?"

His throat worked, but he couldn't manage a sound. Zach nodded.

"You're going to make sure it doesn't. In return, I'll tie you up and put you to sleep in a cozy spot next to Marquette. How does that sound?" I gave him my fiercest smile.

He bobbed his head and tugged the computer closer. "Good."

"Then we have a deal." I split my attention between watching him and the main part of the office. "How many of you are there?"

Zach's fingers paused. "Not sure. She only recruited me two weeks ago. Not many, I don't think."

"And how many people at Regional Disposal are on her side?" I leaned over to look at his screen. I wasn't a computer whiz, but as far as I could tell, he was doing exactly what I'd asked and deleting the video from the thingy that would play it.

"None, as far as I know. From what I heard, she only had a compulsion on the owner at first, but then others got suspicious, so she expanded. And fired people." Zach turned the screen so I could see it. "I took it down. It won't air."

"You're sure?"

"Y–yes." He nodded.

"I hope you're right, or instead of telling the police how helpful you've been, I'll make sure you come out of this sounding like you've played a very pivotal role." I locked eyes with him.

He lowered his gaze. "It's down. I promise."

"Good. Now, to the bathroom." I followed him, a sleep

spell ready, but he didn't cause any problems. He held the door open while I levitated Susanna into the bathroom and sat still as I tied him up. Since he cooperated, I let him use some of the clothing to form a pillow. "Any other helpful tidbits before you nap?"

"I think your wand and bracelet are in her purse. It's got some spells on it."

"Where is her purse? I don't have time to tear this place apart looking for it."

His brow wrinkled. "In a drawer at that desk she liked, I think."

"Thank you. Now, get comfortable." I touched a finger to his head. "*Mannaz*."

Zach's eyes drifted closed, and his body relaxed.

I shut the door. Even though my heart told me to go to Elron, I turned to the office. With other bad guys on the grounds, a magical barrier to take down, and a fiancé to heal, I needed my wand.

Susanna's purse was right where Zach had said. It took some finagling to break the spells on it. Even I didn't have three layers of spell protection on my stuff. Mostly because that meant recasting those spells every week or two, and I had better uses for my magic.

Once I got through the spells, my bracelet and wand were on top. I fitted the bracelet back over my wrist and tested it out. My wand summoned into my hand just as it should. The first bit of luck I'd had all day.

I eyed the phone before snatching it up and dialing Rodriguez's number. It rang and rang, before clicking over to his voice mail.

"Narzel's knees." I hung up the phone. Elron needed

medical attention, and as much as I wanted to be his witch with shining magic, my healing spells weren't the best. I had other police contacts I could call, but none of them would be able to get through the magical barrier or fight the employees high on magic.

I picked up the phone again and dialed 9-1-1. As quickly as I could, I relayed the pertinent medical information and location. When they said an ambulance was on the way, I thanked them and hung up.

The trip to the cell felt longer this time. I tried the door, but it wouldn't open. A quick tap of my wand. "*Purisaz*."

The knob turned, and I shoved the door open. My hand felt along the wall until I found the switch and light flooded the room.

My stomach clenched. With only the light from the hall, I hadn't been able to see just how much blood covered the floor or the silver strands of his hair turning brown as it dried. Zach had followed Susanna's orders and chained Elron where I'd been. From the way he lay with his arms at an awkward angle to attach to the chains, I doubted he'd awakened since I left. Under the blood, his skin was pale.

"Are you under your own control?" Ethel asked, still chained where she'd been when I left.

I took the key to the nullifying cuffs out of my pocket and set to work on her bonds. "Compulsions have never been terribly effective on me."

The corner of Ethel's mouth turned up, and her eyes brightened. "Susanna never did believe you were as talented as rumored."

"She can contemplate that when she wakes up on the bathroom floor wearing a pair of these." I forced the key to turn, and the cuffs released.

Ethel rubbed her wrists. "Thank you."

"My pleasure." The cuffs on her ankles were of the

mundane variety. A quick tap of my wand, and they released.

With Ethel free, I dodged around as much blood as I could to get to Elron. Up close, it was even worse. Blood coated the floor under his head. "I'm sorry. I'm so sorry. If not for me…"

I unchained him as carefully as I could and checked his pulse. To my inexperienced touch it felt, well, there. His chest rose and fell with what looked like normal enough breaths. "Thank the earth elves are tough." I lifted my wand to try a healing spell.

"Halt."

Ethel settled to the ground next to me. "For your many talents, healing has never been one."

"I have to." I sucked in an unsteady breath.

"No. You need to take down the barrier. I will watch over him until a true healer arrives." Ethel scooted around so she could watch the door too.

"You won't heal him?" I didn't take my eyes off him.

Ethel's lips flattened. "If he gets worse, I'll do everything I can to aid him."

I closed my eyes. "Because you might have to protect both of you."

"Yes."

My heart ached, but I knew what I had to do. Eyes open, and seared with the image of his tattered scalp, I leaned down and brushed a feather light kiss across his forehead. "I'll come back with help."

"Close the door behind you, and if you send anyone, tell them to announce themselves before they come in."

"Yes, premier." Closing the door behind me was one of the hardest things I'd ever done. The latch clicking sounded final.

Mother earth, don't let this be the end.

CHAPTER TWENTY-THREE

I walked out the office door before I remembered I could've checked the camera.

"You." A scruffy man in coveralls pointed at me. A fireball flew out of his finger.

Too late.

I dodged to the side, and it hit the building, scorching the paint.

He jumped back, started to look at his finger, but swore and hurriedly pointed it away.

"*Orzu*," I said.

He stepped onto the softened ground and started to sink. He flailed around, shouting and shooting fireballs in every direction. The more he struggled, the faster he sank. When he was chest deep, he plunged his hands toward the ground. They sank in like the rest of him, and he screamed.

"*Fehu*." The ground solidified. Now he wouldn't be casting any more fireballs, though the ones he'd already spread around were more than enough to attract the rest of the newly enhanced employees.

A shrill siren drowned out stuck-in-the-mud's screams.

That would be my fiancé's medical chariot, right on time. I had enough magic to take down the barrier or properly shield and defend myself. Like that was a choice.

I took off down the road. I had to get my hands on that fence to undo the spell. From here, several dumpsters were between me and the gate. Gravel slipped under my feet as I pushed myself faster. For the first time in hours, the tightness in my chest started to ease. One more spell stood between me and help.

Something smashed into me. My feet slid across the gravel, and I fell, a heavy weight on top of me. Air whooshed out of my lungs.

"Got her!"

I sucked in a breath. Dust coated my mouth. I lost precious seconds coughing.

My attacker flipped me over and grinned down at me. His bald head glistened with sweat. He wiped it away with his sleeve and grinned. "Boss'll give me a reward for catchin' you." He grabbed my left wrist.

It went numb. I couldn't feel his hand on my skin, wiggle my fingers, or bend my elbow.

"None of that magic." He touched my right hand.

My arm went numb all the way up to my elbow. Of all the abilities for one of these guys to get.

He hauled me over his shoulders in a fireman's carry, touching both of my ankles while he did it. "Can't have you going anywhere."

I could cast spells without a wand, or moving my hands, but if I did this, I might not have enough power left to fix the gate. Not seeing another option, I tried to relax. Supposedly falls hurt less that way. Closing my eyes, I focused on him, his shoulders, and used my favorite sleep spell. "*Mannaz.*"

His grip loosened, and he crumpled under me.

In the fraction of a second before I hit the ground, I tried to yank every limb in. I hit the ground shoulder first, without any arm or leg damage. The same couldn't be said for my head, which landed squarely on a sharp piece of gravel.

My vision graying over and the flood of adrenaline were blessings. By the time my vision cleared, my head throbbed, and my arms tingled.

Rolling over, I eyed the guy with the numbing power. He snored softly.

"Unbelievable." I muttered as I rolled on to my knees and forearms. A brisk crawl with gravel digging into my arms was my current top speed. "Narzel, you nasty old trickster, can't you find anyone else to pick on?"

After what felt like hours, mostly because daylight was fading fast, I made it all the way to the dumpsters. One more turn, and it would be a straight shot to the gate. "Note to self, crawling across gravel is even worse than it sounds."

A deafening crack interrupted my complaints. The parts of the fence I could see wiggled and sagged.

"No, Come back! Bad!"

I scrambled forward, ignoring the bloody rocks in my wake. All I had to do was make sure that ambulance came through the fence for Elron. They could run over another magically "improved" employee for all I cared.

The ground shook.

Narzel's nose. Of course someone who'd grown gigantic was chasing me. They were getting close too.

"Stop!"

Two big pink dinosaur feet stopped in front of me.

I knew those feet.

"I told you not to run off without me!"

And I knew that voice.

Canting my head to the side, I found myself nose-to-nose with a nose bigger than my body. "Ty? How'd you get here?"

Ty nudged me gently, his tail whipping through the air as it wagged.

"Hey! Watch that thing!" Rodriguez stepped out from behind the dumpster. "Oh. Never mind."

I wiggled around so I was sitting on my butt. The tingles in my arms and legs were getting worse. With the damage I'd done crawling across the gravel, I wasn't really looking forward to regaining feeling.

Ty snuffled me.

"Good boy." I leaned against his cheek and looked at Rodriguez.

"I got your message." He knelt down next to me and turned over my arms, wincing at the raw flesh.

"I know, but Elron's hurt. He's in a room with Ethel standing guard. Announce you're police and that I sent you before you go in." I held my arms close to my body. "He needs the help more than I do."

"Got it." Rodriguez spoke into the walkie-talkie at his shoulder.

Tears started to leak out of my eyes. "Oh, and there's two humans who were dosed with that magic powder along the road, and at least one more around here somewhere. Susanna and her two accomplices are on the floor of the ladies' bathroom. You'll need a few sets of nullifying cuffs."

An ambulance rolled past us.

I pressed a hand to the earth. "Thank you."

Rodriguez found and captured the third employee, who swore only the three of them were left. He got to enjoy a nice cozy seat in a police car with his two buddies.

A second team of paramedics tried to haul me away, but I refused to go anywhere without Elron. While I waited, I heard the full story from a nice medic who wrapped me in a blanket.

My first call to Rodriguez had gone through, and when I didn't answer, he'd driven by for a look and found my phone. He couldn't get through the gate, so he sent an officer by my house to see if anyone had heard from me while he checked out the magic. While the officer was at my house, Rodriguez had requested backup and magical assistance to get through the gate. The details got fuzzy, but apparently the officer at the lodge knew Ty's history and immunity to magic. They had loaded Ty on a flatbed and trucked him over here to bust down the fence.

When I got home, I owed Ty five new jumbo beach balls to play with.

Because I insisted, I ended up riding shotgun in Elron's ambulance. They didn't want me in the back with him, and I wasn't going to argue with people helping him.

At the hospital, the staff separated us. My nurses and doctor were ruthless. Fatigue, both magical and physical, was no match for the pain of having grit removed from arms and knees. I think they drugged me, because I woke up with my parents sitting next to my bed.

"Elron?"

Dad tugged on the cloth divider. Elron lay in the other bed, heavily bandaged. "He's going to be fine."

"The spell?"

"Removed," Mom said.

I swallowed. "His injuries?"

"I looked at his chart." Mom smiled. "From what I hear, he may not even have scars."

"Thank the earth." I exhaled shakily. "Can I have some water?"

Dad handed me a cup with one of those bendy straws.

Nothing like a bendy straw to let you know just how hurt you were. Fabulous. At least it was purple.

A few minutes later, Dr. Stiles came in, her hair in a tidy bun and her coat pristine white. "You are only here for observation. A few questions, and I think you'll be a free woman."

"And Elron?"

She frowned. "He's being kept asleep for a few more hours. He lost a lot of blood, and I want him to rest before we wake him."

"Sounds good." Especially since his color was closer to his normal hue.

Dr. Stiles was true to her work, and thirty minutes later, I was a free woman. Rather than my parents gathering around me, Dad got burgers for us, and we huddled around Elron's bed while we ate.

While I'd been asleep, they'd gotten most of the story from the police and Ethel. Susanna had used magic, including a compulsion spell on a poor medical examiner, to fake Ethel's death. She'd also caused the accident and flooded the area with tainted magic to distract me. That part hadn't worked as well as she'd hoped. Ethel had spent the entire time since the crash at Regional Disposal. Susanna had taken Elron to get leverage over me because she wanted to control the premier if she couldn't be the premier.

The police would be doing paperwork for weeks tying together all of Susanna's crimes. Zach was busy telling anyone who'd sit down everything he knew. Word travels quickly when a dinosaur gets trucked through town. Isadora had already paid a visit to the lodge. She felt bad about for challenging me.

Frankly I was glad I hadn't been there for that conversation.

At two in the afternoon, Dr. Stiles woke Elron.

His body tensed, his hand curling to summon his sword.

"Hey, it's me. You're safe, in a hospital." I edged a little closer.

Elron's eyes opened and went right to me. "Michelle." His hand relaxed, and he reached for me.

I pressed his palm to my cheek. "You're going to be okay. We're both okay."

CHAPTER TWENTY-FOUR

Three weeks later, I smiled at the camera—and tried to scratch my leg through the itchy wool skirt.

Mom's eyes narrowed.

I gave up on being comfortable.

"Everyone involved with this conspiracy has been brought to justice. Today, those words feel hollow. Justice cannot bring back the dead. It can not hug a child, kiss a spouse, call a parent, or comfort a friend. Know I mourn with you." Ethel paused to let that sink in.

Her tone went from somber to purposeful. "Given the events that transpired while I was presumed dead, I have adjusted the path forward. I will step down in two years. Michelle Oaks is my chosen successor and will take my place at that time. Until then, we will work to ensure a smooth transition." Ethel stepped back from the podium.

I took her place and looked into the camera. "It is with relief that I hand the duties of the premier back to Ethel until it is my time to take the office. If you still doubt me, join me at the Spring Convention and get to know me. If you think me young, you are correct. However, we've seen age alone does not gift one with good sense and the ability to lead. In our history, two premiers have taken the mantle at a younger age than I will. One of those is Premier Ethel. Over the next two years, I will do everything I can to learn from her, follow in her path, and benefit from her wisdom so I may best serve you."

Ethel took the podium again.

I stood to the side and tried to smile, but not too much. Or something like that. The directions had been confusing, but standing here? That wasn't confusing at all. Under the lights, next to Ethel, focused on what I could do in the future, this was where I should be.

More precisely, it was one of the places I should be. Two hours later, back at the lodge, I found a note taped to my door.

Meet me in the garden.

I dumped my bags and fancy suit inside the door and headed outside. The cool air carried with it hints of wood smoke. I followed the scent around the corner of the building.

Elron dangled a skewered marshmallow in the flames. The silver in his hair caught the yellow and red light, making the buzz cut all but glow a soft orange.

Dr. Stiles had been true to her word. His scalp had healed with only two scars I could find. His mind, well, it was a good thing Susanna was behind bars. He was rather fond of old school justice. Not that I blamed him in this instance. The justice system even agreed, and she was scheduled for execution next week.

I'd asked if he had nightmares. He said he'd lived through worse and would be fine.

I didn't tell him I dreamed of being back there, unable to stop his pain. I didn't tell him in those dreams, Susanna leaned down until her breath heated my skin and whispered, "I know."

The marshmallow went up in flames. Elron yanked it out of the fire, blowing frantically.

"I hope you like them charred."

A curl of smoke drifted into the air. Elron nimbly topped the cracker and chocolate combo, sandwiching it with another cracker. "How else would one get the chocolate to melt?"

"Oh, that's how you do it?" I sauntered closer.

"Indeed." He held out the s'more.

I leaned down and took a bite. Warm melty chocolate and a hint of fire. "You know, you might be right."

Elron tugged me down beside him and handed me the rest of the s'more. "How did it go?"

"Good, I think." I munched on the gooey goodness. "Witches can't live on s'mores alone, no matter how good they are."

"That is why I got you hot dogs." He pointed to a container on the log over.

"You don't like meat."

He slung a leg over the log and pulled me against his chest, his cheek against my temple. "Tonight, I want to cook hot dogs on a stick with my fiancée, kiss her silly, and plan a wedding. Unless she objects?"

I twisted around so I could get lost in his blue eyes. "I most certainly do not object."

"Good." He grinned. "Can I take your last name when we marry?"

"I'd be proud to be married to Elron Oaks." I tugged him down for a kiss.

"Wedding planning will wait." His eyes sparkled. "We can start with the kisses."

I had to say, he did kiss me silly.

ABOUT THE AUTHOR

N.E. Conneely lives in northern Georgia with her husband, her dog, and a mountain of books. They sweat through the summer and freeze through the winter, and life as they know it comes to an end when so much as a single snowflake falls out of the sky.

For fun, N.E. plays with her dog, reads, knits, crochets, paints, and does tie-dyeing and origami. She makes a great pizza and is currently negotiating with her husband about sea monkeys and growing a vegetable garden.

Please visit neconneely.com to find information on her current projects.

www.neconneely.com
author@neconneely.com

CPSIA information can be obtained
at www.ICGtesting.com
Printed in the USA
LVHW091117260120
644815LV00002B/539